THE WHEEL OF JUSTICE

MILTON HIRSCH

This is a work of fiction.
Names, characters, places, and incidents are either the product of the author's imagination, or are used fictitiously.
Any resemblance to actual persons, living or dead; or to business, establishments, events, or locales; is entirely coincidental.

ALSO BY MILTON HIRSCH

THE SHADOW OF JUSTICE

LAREDO SLIDER

CONTENTS

ACKNOWLEDGEMENTS

Many thanks to Margaret Meeks, Tom Meeks, and Brian Spector, without whom this book would never have seen the light of day.

CHAPTER ONE

PROLOGUE

I am looking at an autopsy protocol. Two of them, actually: One for a man named Herman Bilstein, and one for a woman named Boots Weber. As far as the police could tell, Mr. Bilstein and Ms. Weber never knew each other in life. But their dead bodies had been found together, hers almost piled on top of his, in a courthouse stairwell.

An autopsy protocol is the report prepared by the medical examiner after he has concluded his examination of a dead body. The protocol lists every major organ system in the human body. Next to those organ systems that were involved in the cause of death, the medical examiner will scribble an explanation: bullet wounds to the chest, for example, would be noted in the sections for the cardiovascular and pulmonary systems. Next to those organ systems unrelated to the cause of death, the medical examiner will simply write, "unremarkable." Years ago when I was a prosecutor I handled a case in which two gangs of drug dealers shot each other to pieces in the parking lot of a Miami shopping mall. A younger colleague, fresh out of law school and new to the criminal law, read one of the autopsy protocols in the case and noted that next to "genitalia" the medical examiner had written "unremarkable." The kid looked genuinely miffed. "The guy's dead, for Christ sakes," he said. "They don't have to go writing things like that."

The punchline to an autopsy protocol is the section headed, "cause of death." As to both Herman Bilstein and Boots Weber the cause of death is given as blunt force trauma to the head.

The protocols helpfully include sketches of a human head, showing exactly how and where the skulls had been cracked and the brains bashed in. In the case of Mr. Bilstein there were abrasions on the arm and face, indicating perhaps that he had fallen or slid down half a flight of stairs. But there was "no exudation of amber serum," according to the protocol, which indicated that Mr. Bilstein did his falling or sliding after he was pummeled to death, not before. At the bottom of the protocol appears the signature of Dr. Stephenson Riggs, Chief Medical Examiner, Miami-Dade County. None of this tells me anything I didn't know already, or anything I particularly want to know.

These are old autopsy protocols, the pages worn and yellowing. They describe events that occurred ... my God, can it be 20 years ago? I had put them away in the bottom of a filing

cabinet, put them away because I wanted to forget what was written in them. And now, so many years later, I've taken them out because ... because I've given up trying to forget.

I realize now that I'm telling this to you out of order. An autopsy protocol is, in some sense, the place where the story of a murder ends, but in no sense the place where the story of a murder begins. It's just that I'm not sure how far back I have to go to put this story in order.

That Friday, I suppose. I can think of other times and places to begin, but ... yes, that Friday.

That Friday.

CHAPTER TWO

FRIDAY

The Albatross was easy to find. Jack had said it was about half a block off Duval Street. "Close enough for the tourists to find it and close enough for the locals to know to stay away from it," he had said. It wasn't much more than a ten-minute walk from the hotel. In Key West nothing is much more than a ten-minute walk from anything else.

Above the door was a large wooden carving of what could have been a bird. I suppose it was an albatross. The sign said, "The Albatross," and underneath it, in smaller print, the word, "bar."

They were open for lunch but doing no business. A heavy-set waitress picked up a menu and asked me with no particular enthusiasm, "Just one?".

Lunch wasn't what I had come for. "Is this where Jack Sheridan works?"

She put the menu down again. “It is when he works.”

“Is he working today?”

She shrugged a little bit. “He’s supposed to.”

“What time will he be here?”

“Five o’clock, if he comes on time. You a friend of his?”

• • •

I was in Key West attending a judicial conference, a meeting of judges from around the state. As I always do I had asked Miriam to come with me. I reminded her that many, perhaps most, of the judges bring their spouses and make a little vacation of it. As she usually does she had turned me down. She reminded me that one judge in her life was her limit.

During the morning I had attended two sessions on developments in the law of civil procedure – the law that regulates personal injury suits, contract claims, commercial disputes, that sort of thing. My entire judicial career to that point had been spent in the criminal court, the Richard E. Gerstein Justice Building, the ugly runt of Miami’s litter of state and federal courthouses, and my knowledge of civil practice was rusty at best. Now I needed to get up to speed, and quickly. On Monday I would be rotating into civil court, swapping places with Judge Floyd Kroh Jr., who would take over my courtroom in the criminal courthouse. I knew the criminal justice system, and I knew the people who came to court to try to make it work. In civil court I would be the new kid on the block. I would be called upon to make rulings for and against lawyers who would believe – and justifiably so – that they knew more about the civil justice system than I knew, perhaps more than I would ever know. I had paid close attention during the morning’s lectures, and I had taken careful notes.

In the afternoon, however, I was stuck attending a meeting of the *ad hoc* committee on something-or-other, to which Administrative Judge Kay Surrey had appointed me. I sat in the back of the room and built a paperclip chain. I was facing a paperclip supply crisis when the door to the conference room opened a crack and Floyd Kroh stuck his head in. He caught my eye, crooked his index finger at me, then pointed outside. I left the room quietly.

Floyd was about my age, but still in his first term on the bench. His father, Floyd Kroh Sr., had been a legendary figure on the Miami legal scene. Floyd Sr. was born in some small town in upstate Florida and had moved to Miami to practice law after a stint in the military. He had been blessed with everything nature can offer a man: a genius IQ, debonair good looks, charm in abundance. He founded a law firm that is now one of Miami's largest and still bears his name on its letterhead. He had served a term as president of the Florida Bar, and a term as president of the American Bar Association. His specialty was land-use law, which meant that his was the guiding hand behind most of South Florida's expensive shopping malls, office towers, and condo developments. He could do the complex legal work necessary for such projects, and he could romance the city or county commission into granting the zoning variances needed to make the projects thrive.

Floyd Jr. is living proof that there's still a lot we don't know about genetics. He has inherited all of Daddy's looks and charm and almost none of his brains. He went into the law because he was Floyd Kroh Sr.'s son, and he went into his father's firm because he was Floyd Kroh Sr.'s son. When Floyd Kroh Sr. died, one of the members of the firm's management committee took Junior aside and told him that he would have the firm's full backing in his application for a judgeship. Junior had been unaware up to that point that he was applying for a judgeship, but he got the message. With the firm's influence and his father's name, Floyd Kroh became Miami's next circuit judge.

In truth Floyd is not a bad judge. He is unfailingly polite to the lawyers, witnesses, and jurors who come before him, because lawyers, witnesses, and jurors are also voters and Floyd understands that his career options are re-election or unemployment. He is an inherently affable man whose courtesy is appreciated by one and all, so his prospects for re-election are good. He makes no pretense of legal scholarship and most of his rulings are based on what strikes him as fair at the time, but that approach works more often than not; and when it doesn't, it creates no problem that the court of appeal can't fix. In any event Floyd always puts off ruling until the last possible moment, because ruling means ruling *against* one side or the other, and the losing party might not have time to forget before the next election.

I was grateful to Floyd for calling me out of the committee meeting from Hell and I told him so. We exchanged a few pleasantries in the hallway and he suggested that we go to the hotel's outdoor coffeeshop to chat. I was as eager to talk to him as he was to talk to me, and for the same reason: I needed to know what landmines not to step on when I took over his courtroom in the civil division on Monday, just as he needed to know what to expect when he took over my courtroom in the criminal division.

I suppose that anyone who saw Floyd and me wander out to the coffeeshop would have noted the study in contrast that we presented. Floyd is several inches taller than average, and I am several inches shorter. His hair was a reddish brown, slightly wavy, receding in front, and he combs it straight back. Mine was – I hadn't yet passed 40 back then – still very dark, very full, very curly. I had no gray. Not yet.

Floyd is pale and freckled, and a few minutes in the Key West sun had left his nose and cheekbones red. His jaw is large, strong, and builds toward a chin that is dimpled – a feature noticeable in photos of his father. I, too, am pale, but somehow I never burn in the Florida sun. My features are regular, which is to say that I have no strong jaw, no noticeable dimpled chin. I wish I had.

There are no natural beaches in Key West. A couple of the larger hotels have imported sand and built small artificial beaches, but the hotel at which we were staying was not one of them. The coffeeshop was on a terrace at land's end, with nothing beyond the tables but a few dock slips for small boats. All the tables offered spectacular views of the ocean; we chose the one positioned to offer a little shade from the afternoon sun.

"Miriam come down with you this trip?", asked Floyd. Floyd has no memory for statutes or case law, but it was just like him to remember the name of my wife, whom he couldn't possibly have met more than a couple of times.

"No ... no she's not much for this sort of thing. How about, um," ah, what was his wife's name, she was such a pretty girl, "your family? Everyone come down with you?" I could quote my way chapter and verse through the Florida Statutes Annotated but I could not at that moment think of his wife's name. I looked out across the ocean, as if something of sudden importance had caught my attention. Floyd, either unaware of my shortcomings or too gracious to draw attention to them, carried on the conversation.

"Oh sure. Ellie and both of the kids. They're out shopping. By now I must own half the straw hats, coconuts, and conch shells on Key West." He laughed a little, and I laughed a little.

A young man who didn't look old enough to serve drinks wandered over and asked to take our order. Floyd subjected him to a searching cross-examination to make sure that a pina colada could be made with double rum and would come with a pineapple wedge and a little umbrella. I ordered an iced tea. When the kid had gone Floyd leaned forward and said with a very earnest expression, "Clark, I'll tell you frankly that I'm worried as hell about swapping divisions on Monday."

So was I. What I didn't know about civil litigation could, and did, fill volumes. I didn't look forward to the prospect of being the least informed person in my own courtroom. "Me, too."

"I keep thinking about last year, when Del Howard and Judith Waller traded places," Floyd went on gravely. Judith had been a judge in criminal court for as long as I could remember, and Del had spent at least half a dozen years in civil. They had rotated places, just as Floyd and I were about to do. So far as I was aware each had made the adjustment with no more than the usual lumps and bumps. "Judith had that wonderful collection of Confederacy memorabilia that she had inherited from her mother's side of the family. By the time the Administrative Office of the Court moved her chambers suite down to the civil courthouse, and Del's chambers suite out to the Gerstein Building, half of her collection was lost or destroyed. And Del says he's still missing two chairs and an end table." Floyd leaned toward me with a look of what, for him, must have been the most intense concentration. "You know, my dad had one of the finest collections of pipes and ashtrays ...."

Floyd's narrative was cut off by the arrival of our drinks. I couldn't imagine what it was that Floyd was telling me, or was about to tell me, that was too confidential for the waiter to overhear, but while my iced tea and his pina colada were being served Floyd said not a word. When the waiter had gone Floyd took the straw out of his glass and placed it on the napkin alongside his drink. He took a sip and chewed some ice chips thoughtfully. "My father had one of the finest collections of pipes in the world: Stokkebyes, Von Ercks, Meerschaums, Ser Jacopos. He had a corncob pipe he claimed to have gotten from Douglas MacArthur." Floyd smiled and jiggled his drink a little. "You know, I'll bet I've met a couple hundred fellows who claim to have gotten their corncob pipes from Douglas MacArthur. MacArthur must have been so busy handing out corncob pipes, I don't know how he found time to land at Inchon." Floyd smiled again and chuckled. I smiled back, mostly because I didn't know what else to do. "And there are the ashtrays, dozens of them. Three Laliques. Another one by a French artist named Travies that's worth I know not how much. He had one from Maxim's in Paris that he claimed he got from Catherine Deneuve." Floyd took another sip of his drink and gave me a wink, to suggest that maybe an ashtray wasn't all Daddy got from Catherine Deneuve. "It's not just the money value. When I was a little boy I'd visit my dad in his office and he'd let me play with his pipes. He'd be smoking one, and he'd let me pick another one out of the cabinet and pretend to smoke along with him. He never let anyone else near those pipes, but he and I would sit there, me pretending to smoke and to look at the legal documents on his desk. Those pipes and ashtrays represent some of my favorite memories of my father, Clark." Floyd paused in such a way as to suggest that he expected me to say something.

To say what? I looked at my watch. "Floyd, it's almost three o'clock on Friday afternoon. By now the Administrative Office of the Court probably has all your office furnishings moved into what used to be my chambers in the criminal courthouse, and all my office furnishings" – I thought of three rickety chairs, a badly worn desk, and a nameplate that reminded me that I was The Honorable Clark N. Addison – "moved to your old chambers in the civil courthouse. If you're concerned you can call your secretary before she leaves for the weekend. When you get back to Miami on Sunday you can even stop by the courthouse and check. But right now ... well, right now Floyd, I'd be very grateful if you'd go over your pending cases with me, so that I can know what to expect when I take over your courtroom on Monday."

Floyd was nodding thoughtfully, as if I'd said something very profound. After giving the matter due consideration, he pulled out his cell phone and called his secretary, who -- so far as I could follow the conversation -- assured him that the moving process was underway and going along just swimmingly. I drank some iced tea and thought that if he was that concerned about Daddy's pipes and ashtrays, why didn't he just box them up and move them himself?

Floyd put away his cell phone and stared into the middle distance, still nodding as if he were agreeing with something that someone, somewhere, had said. I tried again. "Floyd, there's some courthouse scuttlebutt about an emergency hearing you set for Monday morning and that I'm going to inherit. Can you tell me ...."

Floyd turned at the sound of his name. Emerging onto the terrace from the hotel was a woman whom I recognized as Ellie Kroh, and two very young children. Ellie was a picture from a Florida postcard: the blonde hair, the suntan, the long legs. She wore a straw hat, a T-shirt that said something about the "Conch Republic," a seashell necklace, jean shorts, and sandals. The children at her side bore their father's stamp: redheaded, freckled, sunburned.

"Floyd," Ellie called again, still smiling and waving. The boy smiled and waved too, but the little girl pressed her faced into her mother's side, eyes closed, looking tired or sick or both. Floyd and I stood as they approached, and Floyd did the Ellie-you-remember-Clark, Clark-you-remember-Ellie drill. Of course. Of course. Nice to see you again.

"Floyd, feel Brooke's forehead," Ellie said, directing him toward his daughter. Floyd touched the child's forehead, cheek, neck. Then he picked her up and put her in his lap, meantime looking up at Ellie and nodding, yes, she's feverish.

"Poor little Brookie, are you feeling puny?" The child, by way of answer, curled up tight as a fist in her daddy's lap, closed her eyes, and nuzzled her head against him. Floyd picked her up against his shoulder and stood again. "Let's go up to the room," he told Ellie. He took a step or two, then remembered me and turned. "Clark, she's not well. I'm going to take her up to the room."

"Of course, Floyd. Poor thing. But ... look, when you have a minute, just a minute, if we could talk about Monday's docket ...."

"Absolutely. Sure." He had started to walk away, but he took a step back toward me and spoke in the low voice men use to impart urgency to their speech. "Clark, promise me you'll look carefully to see if anything is left behind. It would be so easy for the Administrative Office people to overlook an ashtray or a pipe, now that we can't smoke in the building anyway. And sometimes they leave things on handtrucks in the hallway ...." He was walking away again now, the little girl in his arms, his wife and son by his side. In two and a half days I would, for the first time in my legal career, enter a courtroom unprepared. And all he wanted to talk about was Daddy's pipes and ashtrays.

• • •

I went up to my room, closed the blinds so as not to be distracted by the ocean view, and turned on a couple of lights. I took a paperback copy of the Florida Rules of Civil Procedure out of my briefcase, along with a yellow legal pad and a couple of pens, and spread out as best I could at the tiny desk provided by the Key Conch Hotel. (The Key Conch has been, for some years now, part of one of the major hotel chains – Hilton, Sheraton, something like that – but scrupulously keeps up the pretense of being a quiet little bungalow to which a man could flee for a life, or a weekend, of primitive beachcombing, except that there are no beaches.) I had always been a good student. I made notes, and I copied them over, and then I copied them over again.

It was a few minutes after 5:00 when I looked at my watch. I went into the bathroom and rinsed my face with cold water. Then I went back into the bedroom, sat on the edge of the bed, and started to call home. Before the call went through I hung up. Miriam had never liked Jack. I would call her later.

• • •

I walked back to the Albatross slowly. The sidewalks in Key West are uneven in places, buckled by the enormous roots of royal poincianas and other exotic flowering trees, trees that seem too large for the tiny front yards along which the sidewalks run. So I drifted back to the Albatross, watching the slow progress of my steps along the uneven pavement.

The interior of the Albatross is done in dark wood, heavily lacquered, and the walls are hung with memorabilia that is supposed to be nautical in theme: rusty anchors, hurricane lanterns, paintings of old ships. To the left of the entrance the bar runs the length of the place, and the balance of the room is given over to small tables. On the wall behind the bar are shelves of liquor, and above the shelves is a large plaque. The plaque features a painting of an albatross, as amateurish as the sculptured bird above the exterior door, and below the painting these words:

And a good south wind sprung up behind;
The Albatross did follow,
And every day, for food or play,
Came to the mariners' hollo!

In mist or cloud, on mast or shroud,
It perched for vespers nine;
Whiles all the night, through fog-smoke white,
Glimmered the white moon-shine.

"God save thee, ancient Mariner!
From the fiends that plague thee thus! –
Why look'st thou so?" – "With my cross-bow
I shot the Albatross."

There was something else behind the bar. It gave every appearance of being a man, tall, skinny as dental floss, topped off with sandy brown hair. It wore an open-neck shirt and an apron of some kind, and it appeared to be tending bar. I walked over and sat on a bar stool. The skinny thing behind the bar looked at me and smiled a smile I well-remembered, and it spoke. "Hello, Clark." *Clahk*, it drawled, in proper Southern.

So I said, "Hello, Jack."

About five hours earlier the lunchtime waitress had asked me if I was a friend of his, "his" being John Wentworth Sheridan IV, Blackjack Sheridan, Jack Sheridan. That was a question that would take some answering. Three years earlier it would have been the easiest question in the world. Three years earlier I would have told her that Jack and I had started our careers together as prosecutors in the Miami-Dade County State Attorney's Office. I would have told her about the famous cases we handled together, and the successes we achieved. I would have told her how even after Jack left the State Attorney's Office to become one of the most famous criminal lawyers in a city famous for its criminal lawyers, and I became a judge in that city's criminal courts, we remained the best of friends. Am I a friend of his?, I would have asked; why, we're like brothers. That's what I would have told her.

But she hadn't asked if I was a friend of his once upon a time. She wanted to know if I was his friend now. That, as I say, was a question that would take some answering. Fortunately, at that particular moment no one was asking it. So I asked a question of my own. "How are you, Jack?"

Four hours drive north, back in Miami, 5:00 would have been the beginning of happy hour and the bars would be starting to fill up. Happy hour, of course, is an institution for people who are employed and get off work at 5:00 p.m. In Key West few people are employed and those who are don't finish work at 5:00 p.m., they start work about then. The Albatross was all but empty.

So Jack reached under the bar – not on the shelves behind him, but under the bar – and produced a bottle. He cradled it gently, to underscore its precious quality and great value. "A. H. Hirsch Bourbon, 20 years old. The finest whiskey of any kind ever" – *evah* – "made on the North American continent. The distillery was in Pennsylvania, but it's been closed for years. They aren't making any more of it. When it's gone, it will be gone forever." *Fau-evah*. I had, on many occasions, seen Jack offer exhibits in evidence during trials. He had done so with the same reverence, the same sense of crucial, critical importance, with which he now exhibited this bottle of bourbon. He set a shot glass on the bar, poured about two fingers neat, and offered it to me as if it contained a Faberge egg.

What followed was more remarkable still. He put the cap back on the bourbon and returned it to its secret cache beneath the bar. Then he took a water glass, filled it with club soda, dropped in two lime wedges, touched his glass to mine, and drank. Blackjack Sheridan drank club soda. I made a mental note to check tomorrow's paper to see if Hell had frozen over. "I'm fine, Clark," he said. "I'm really just fine."

"Where've you been?"

"Here and there. Mostly here."

Two, almost three years earlier, Jack had fixed a trial. He hadn't fixed it to win, he could win his cases without any fixing. He had fixed it to lose. He had sold out his client, fixed the trial so that his client would be convicted of a crime he never committed. And he had done it in my courtroom, done it in a case in which I was the judge.

I was the one who discovered what my best friend had done. I was the one who demanded that my best friend make it right.

So Jack got the verdict set aside, which was what I wanted. And then Jack disappeared, which was something I hadn't wanted. He disappeared like a teardrop in the ocean. No one seemed to know where he went, or with whom, or for how long. I checked with the Florida Bar records department in Tallahassee and his bar dues were paid up, but his license status was marked, "voluntarily suspended." A lot of months turned into a couple of years and I concluded that if Jack were still living, he was living someplace from which he would not return.

"Not practicing?" Law, I meant.

"Not practicing." He knew what I meant.

I took a sip of the bourbon. I'm not much of a drinker, but clearly this was very special stuff. "Miss it?" Practicing law, I meant.

Jack placed his forearms on the bar and hunched forward, studying the bubbles in his club soda. "I don't, Clark. Honest to God, I don't." He shifted his weight a little bit. "You know who a criminal defense lawyer is supposed to be, don't you, Clark?" It wasn't really a question. "He's supposed to be Paul Revere."

"Paul Revere?"

Jack stood up straight and began to declaim:

"So through the night rode Paul Revere;

And so through the night went his cry of alarm

To every Middlesex village and farm –

A cry of defiance, and not of fear,
A voice in the darkness, a knock at the door,
And a word that shall echo for evermore!
For, borne on the night-wind of the Past,
Through all our history, to the last,
In the hour of darkness and peril and need,
The people will waken and listen to hear
The hurrying hoof-beats of that steed,
And the midnight message of Paul Revere."

Jack sipped his club soda. "That was how it was supposed to work. You were supposed to go to court believing that somehow, in the hour of darkness and peril and need, you could get the jury to awaken and listen and care and acquit. When you stopped believing that you became an alcoholic, or worse, a civil lawyer."

"You won your fair share of cases. More than your fair share," I said.

"My share wasn't fair. Nobody's was." He finished his club soda and chewed on a lime wedge.

I tried to make a joke of it. "Anyway, you were an alcoholic before you became a famous big-shot criminal defense lawyer."

He made a better joke of it. "I was never an alcoholic. I was a drunk. Alcoholics go to meetings." He smiled, that jury-winning, jury-wowing, witness-disarming, bright-eyed, clear-teeth, taught-skinned smile. I smiled back. You had to. "And hell, winning cases had less to do with being a good lawyer than you think."

I felt one of Jack's stories coming on. It wouldn't be the first time I had played the straight man for Jack, so I said, "What did it have to do with?"

He leaned forward on the bar again, adopting a conspiratorial look. "Now Clark, I know you were always the smartest little boy in class. Who do you suppose was the greatest philosopher of the 20th century?"

It obviously didn't matter what my answer was, but just to have something to say I said, "Sartre?"

"Never heard of him." Jack shook his head. "No, the greatest philosopher of the 20th century was Rico Carty."

"Never heard of him." Well, I hadn't.

Jack took a slow breath to organize his thoughts. I had seen him do so at the outset of closing arguments in criminal trials. I was to be a jury of one. "Along about ... oh, thirty years or so ago, Rico Carty played outfield for the Atlanta Braves. He was a good but not a great ballplayer. He was not universally liked by his teammates, so this is not the lecture about good sportsmanship and team spirit. But one summer" – one *summah* – "it might have been 1970, thereabouts, Rico Carty took a .400 batting average into the month of July." Jack paused, as he would have in closing argument, to emphasize how remarkable that was.

"The sporting world was agog. No player since the great, the immortal Ted Williams in 1941 had succeeded in maintaining a .400 batting average for a full season. Sports reporters from coast to coast and beyond our shores dogged Carty's tracks. They watched him hit. They watched him shower. They watched him dress. They watched him eat. If they could have, they would have watched him sleep.

"And there were the questions; the constant, unending, mindless questions that sportswriters pose. 'Are you faster, quicker, stronger? Are you eating differently? Are you sleeping differently? Did you change your grip on the bat you hit with? Did you change your grip on the fork you eat your pie with?' And so on and on and on.

"One day Carty got out of the shower in the locker room and there was the swarm of locusts, with microphones and cameras and notepads in hands. The mindless, endless questions started again. Now, Rico Carty was not a well-spoken man. He was what we call in Miami, 'bi-moronic,' which is to say he could barely express himself in English *or* Spanish. But in that moment, Rico Carty had a vision as profound" – Jack paused, to underscore the profundity of it --- "as Paul's on the road to Damascus. 'I not faster! I not quicker! I not stronger!' he said, with a depth of feeling that caused the pack of reporters to take a couple of steps backward. '*I just lucky!*'"

Jack topped off his club soda and tossed in a couple more lime wedges. "In due course Rico Carty's batting average fell below .400, never to return. No batter, from 1941 to this very day, has ever reached the lofty heights scaled by the great Ted Williams." Jack paused for a sip of soda, more for effect, I think, than out of thirst. "But Ted Williams didn't win the Most Valuable Player award in 1941. You see, in that year of all years, Joe DiMaggio hit safely in 56 consecutive games – something no one has done since, and no one had ever done before. DiMaggio got the MVP award.

"Ted Williams just wasn't lucky." Jack smiled a little, looked down at his drink, shifted his weight. I half expected him to say, "Ladies and Gentlemen of the jury, find Rico Carty not guilty and send him home to his family." But he didn't. He didn't say anything. The story was good enough, I suppose, but Jack hadn't really told me anything.

I didn't say anything either for a minute or two. Then I asked, "So what are you doing with yourself these days?"

He gestured expansively at the establishment around us. "The place is owned by a widow-woman, Chancie Frank. This being Key West, she's just tickled to have a bartender who's used to practicing law instead of running from it. I work three or four nights a week, five p.m. till whatever in the wee small hours. I don't drink anymore" – he held up the club soda, in case I'd missed it – "and I come to work more often than I decide not to."

"Still have the boat?"

"The Blackjack? Oh, hell yes. Docked right up the street from here. I live on it."

"Seems like a nice life." It seemed like a nice thing to say.

Now Jack leaned forward again, peeking left and right as if there might actually be someone somewhere listening in on us. "You know, Clark, most of the local talent is queer" – Key West was famous for its large, very much out-of-the-closet gay community – "but we get a lot of European tourists here. Pretty blond-haired, blue-eyed ladies from England, Germany, places like that. The American tourists from up north don't always make it farther south than Mickey Mouse" – Orlando's theme parks – "but we get the Europeans. Those girls take a fine interest in a lawyer-turned-bartender with his own boat and many a tale to tell. I tell them about the soap opera star who came to my office fearing that she was the target of a grand jury investigation. I tell them how she gave me a $250,000 cash fee, a blow job, and a pair of her panties, and then fled the jurisdiction, never to be seen again."

"Which soap opera star was that?"

"Oh, it depends. Sometimes I make up a good Latin-sounding name and claim she was the star of some *telenovela*, you know, some South American soap opera. I'll tell you, that story goes over big with those European girls. And they're not bashful, either. They're on vacation, they came for a good time, and they don't have time to spare."

I liked Jack's girlie story even less than I liked his baseball story. We were shadow-boxing, and we both knew it. For lack of anything else to do I drained my drink, and Jack reached down for the bottle. I started to cover my drink with my hand, to indicate I didn't want another one, but the truth was I did want another one and I let Jack pour it.

So a few minutes went by, nobody saying anything and me looking down at my drink, and then I looked up and asked, very quietly, "Jack, why did you call?"

He started a smile, but it wasn't the good one he used for juries and he let it go. "Oh, I saw a little something in the local newspaper, the Key West Citizen or whatever they call it, about how this important judicial conference would be held here at one of the big hotels, and I thought, 'I'll just call my old buddy Clark Addison and see if he's coming'."

He stopped, but looked like he'd say more if more were needed. More was needed, but not more of the same. "Miriam thought you were dead, because nobody ever heard from you," I said. "Two, almost three years went by and nobody ever heard from you. Nobody. Not even your old buddy Clark Addison."

The shadow-boxing was over. Jack dropped his gaze, and his voice. "I wasn't too sure my old buddy would want to hear from me." He looked up at me again. "I'm a little problem for you, aren't I, Clark? What you would probably call a 'moral dilemma'."

Now it was my turn to look away. Jack had a point, a point that had troubled me since the day he had disappeared. Jack had committed a crime, maybe a couple of crimes, serious crimes. I and I alone had realized what he had done. I had caught him with his hand in the cookie jar and I had made him put the cookie back. But a crime once committed can't be un-committed, not even by putting the cookie back. I was a witness to crime – the *sole* witness to crime – and I was a judge. Yet I had told no one and done nothing.

There is no law making it a crime not to report a crime. I had done some research and came across a case from 1999 in which the Florida Supreme Court had publicly reprimanded a judge who impeded a criminal investigation, warned off witnesses, lied to the cops, but that was very different. I told Jack the day I had confronted him with what he had done: If anyone asks me what I know, I'll tell them; if no one asks, there'll be nothing to tell. So far, no one had asked.

I tried to smile. "That's you all right – Blackjack Sheridan, Moral Dilemma." I drank some bourbon. "This is good stuff."

"Top it off for you?

"No, I'm fine."

A few long seconds went by. Jack chewed a lime wedge, but that didn't break the silence. Then he said, "Somebody famous wrote something about how it's better to rat out your country than your best friend. Who was that?"

"'If I had to choose between betraying my country and betraying my friend, I hope I should have the guts to betray my country'." E. M. Forster. In an essay called, *What I Believe*"

That got me the good Blackjack smile. "You looked it up."

"No I didn't. I just came across it on the way to looking up something else." Of course I had looked it up. Of course Jack knew I had looked it up, no matter what I told him. Good, duteous, diligent little Clark, he was probably thinking, of course he looked it up. Good, duteous, studious little Clark, who instead of confronting a moral dilemma would take refuge behind words in a book. That's what Jack was probably thinking.

And Jack was right. As long as he was gone, disappeared, as good as dead, I could let myself avoid confronting the moral dilemma he represented. I could take refuge in law books, in which it was written that it is not a crime to fail to report a crime. I could take refuge in Forster, who in turn relied upon Dante; Dante placed Brutus and Cassius in the lowest circle of Hell because they had chosen to betray their friend Julius Caesar rather than their country. Every day that Jack was gone, disappeared, as good as dead, it was easier than the day before to do nothing.

But now Jack was back, sort of. He wasn't in Miami, and he wasn't practicing law, but he wasn't dead or gone either.

A couple of tourists – they looked like tourists, they had Key West T-shirts on – drifted in and sat at the end of the bar. That gave Jack something to do for a couple of minutes, which was fine with me. By the time he got back from serving them we had both thought of other things to talk about.

"So how long you figure to be in town?" he asked.

"I'll drive back Sunday morning. Maybe late tomorrow, if I don't feel like staying for the reception tomorrow night."

"Any interesting cases going on at the building?" By which, of course, he meant the Gerstein Building, the criminal court.

"As a matter of fact, on Monday I start a rotation downtown in the civil courthouse."

Even the new, laid-back, Key West version of Jack Sheridan had a wide-eyed reaction to that one. "You, Clark?" I nodded. "Now, what did Que Sera Sera have to offer to get you to go down to the civil division? Chocolate chip cookies?" Kay Surrey, who exercised her authority as administrative judge for the criminal division by virtue of her looking and acting like Mrs. Santa Claus, was a legend for her baking prowess. Entering her chambers was a challenge to anyone's resistance to cookies, brownies, and pie.

"There's an opening on the federal bench. I figured ..."

"That you'd have a better resume if you had both criminal and civil experience?" I nodded again. Jack shook his head a little. "Ambitious little Clark ...."

Ambitious little Clark. Did tall, strapping men get called "ambitious, tall, strapping, Clark" every time they sought advancement? I had been ambitious little Clark in high school, in law school, at the Office of the State Attorney. I had learned long ago to say nothing when friends, and those who were anything but friends, muttered "ambitious little Clark." That's me, ambitious little Clark. First in my class in law school, and one of the youngest lawyers ever made a circuit judge in Miami-Dade County history. Ambitious little Clark.

"When will they decide on the federal judgeship?" Jack asked.

"No time soon. You know how these things are."

Jack's turn to nod a little. He knew how these things were. "What's the old saying? 'The wheels of justice drive slowly ....'"

"The wheel of justice grinds slowly, but it grinds exceedingly fine." The reference was not to the wheels of a car or cart, but to a mill wheel. Slowly but surely, rolling around and around again, it ground grain into flour. Judges and lawyers had used that saying almost as long as there had been judges and lawyers, almost as long as there had been mills and millstones.

"Well, hell," said Jack, holding his club soda up as if to make a toast. "Good luck."

He took a drink of his club soda, and I took a drink of my bourbon. I slid off the bar stool. I knew better than to try to pay for my drinks. "So ..." I said.

"So ..." said Jack.

"Maybe we'll see you back in Miami?"

"Maybe," said Jack. "You never know. A lot of folks don't believe me when I tell them that someday twin sisters or maybe triplets from Sweden will wander in here arguing like hell about which one is better in bed and ask me to referee, but you never know."

"Seriously. You'll come back to Miami? At least to visit?"

Jack smiled the good smile, the one he used to keep for juries and willing women. "Some day. Some day. You know what they say, Clark. The wheel of justice grinds slowly."

"That's what they say," I told him. "They say that." Then I walked away. I got almost as far as the door when I heard him.

"Hey Clark?" I turned. "Give my regards to Miriam, will you?"

At that I had to smile. Miriam had never approved of Jack and made no secret of her disapproval. But she would want to know what had become of him after all this time, where he had been and what he had done and what he was doing. I would tell her that he was working a sort of a steady job and had even given up drinking. I was looking forward to telling her that. "You know," I said, "I believe I will." And I left.

• • •

I had scarcely known the late Judge Thomas Needham. I have a vague recollection of having been introduced to him at a bar association function of some kind, or perhaps at a couple of bar association functions. He had been a federal judge long before I became a state judge, and in the ordinary course of things our paths would seldom cross. According to my secretary Carmen and other reliable sources of gossip, Tom Needham was a quiet-living man who had never married or fathered children. The only life-forms with whom he shared his existence were the occupants of a goldfish bowl, and of course his colleagues and staff at the United States district court. The only interest that absorbed his leisure time was golf. He belonged to several of Miami's best golf clubs and spent all his spare time on the links. Several weeks earlier, on a particularly beautiful Miami afternoon, his heart gave out in mid-fairway. Those who knew him said that it was how he had always wanted to die.

A few days later I stopped by Que Sera Sera's chambers, declined the offer of oatmeal butterscotch cookies, and asked Kay if she had any interest in applying for Judge Needham's now-open seat on the federal bench. She smiled and told me she'd been expecting me. "My term will be up in three years and four months, not that I'm counting," she said. "After that I qualify for senior status. I'll visit the grandchildren, then move to Sanibel, pick up sea shells by the seashore, and try out a new pecan pie recipe I've been holding on to. If I feel the urge to judge, I can preside in Naples or Ft. Myers as much or little as I please and still get paid the same. I wouldn't trade any of that for ten federal judgeships. Sure you won't have a cookie?" I wouldn't have a cookie. "But you knew all that Clark. You're just being nice. You really came here to ask for my support for your application for Tom Needham's seat."

"Will I get it?" And that's when Kay and I brokered our deal: I'd agree to transfer down to the civil courthouse and take over Floyd Kroh's division, and she'd do what she could to push my candidacy for the federal judgeship. Then she put two cookies in a napkin and told me to take them back to my chambers for my secretary. "They're the same ones I made last Christmas," she said. "Carmen likes them."

• • •

When I got back to the hotel the desk clerk had a note for me from Floyd. Brooke and Trey (a nickname for Floyd's son, Floyd Kroh III) were both sick, and he had taken the family back to Miami. He was sorry to cut our conversation short, he knew we had a lot to talk about. There was a postscript reminding me about his father's pipe and ashtray collection. I handed the note back to the desk clerk and asked her if she could throw it in the waste paper basket for me. Then I went up to my room to call home and to study the rules of civil procedure.

When the phone answered on the third or fourth ring I expected to hear Alicia's voice. Our twins, Marc and Alicia, were very young back then. So far as I could recall no one had beaten Alicia to a ringing telephone in our house for about a year.

"Hello?" It was Miriam.

"Hi there. Where's Alicia?"

"Spending the night at a girlfriend's house. Before she left she reminded me what to do if the phone rang, just in case I'd forgotten."

"That was very thoughtful of her." I asked about the other kids. Marc was on the computer. Joel, our eldest, had gone out with his friends. "He said to remind you, if you called, that you promised to take him driving this weekend." Ah yes. Joel has his driver's learner's permit, and wants to be taken driving as often as possible. This, apparently, is a father's job.

"Sunday. Tell him Sunday. I've got a long drive back from Key West tomorrow, and there'll be less traffic Sunday. What are you up to?"

"Bagel and I are watching one of those TV shows you don't like." Bagel is our dog. He is a very old, surly dog, supposed to be a beagle. My own theory is that he is a cross between a beagle and a compost heap, and I have told him so on a couple of occasions but never when Miriam could hear me. Miriam is very fond of Bagel. "What about you?" I was about to answer when Miriam went on, "You're studying." It wasn't really a question.

"Yes."

"Have you eaten?"

"Yes."

"I didn't mean in your lifetime, Clark. I meant dinner, today. Have you eaten dinner today?"

"Ah, I'm about to. I just wanted to call you before I went out for dinner."

That didn't fool either of us, but apparently Miriam didn't feel like arguing; so she asked, "Are you excited about Monday?"

Was I excited about Monday? I was anxious about Monday. I was nervous, concerned, preoccupied about Monday. I was frustrated that Floyd Kroh hadn't told me anything I needed to know, and more frustrated because the illness of his children made it impossible for me to complain about his not having told me. So I said, "I'm looking forward to Monday." That didn't fool either of us.

CHAPTER THREE
MONDAY

The civil courthouse is downtown on Flagler Street, Miami's north-south dividing line. It is, by Miami standards, a very old building. For many years its twenty-some stories made it the tallest building in Florida, but that was long ago. Its top is done in a pyramid-like structure, which appears to serve no purpose but to provide a perch for the turkey vultures that flock south for the winter. These are large black and gray birds, graceful in flight but ungainly and ugly at rest. The notion that vultures and lawyers congregate at the same building has provided amusement for generations of Miamians.

I made a point of arriving early, but I knew that Carmen would have already arrived. Like me, she had always worked at the Gerstein Building, and for weeks now she had been apprehensive about the move downtown. She had probably spent part of Saturday driving back and forth from her home in West Miami to the civil courthouse, just to be sure she knew the route and how much time to allow. Most days Carmen is past caring about her appearance, but on this occasion she wore a dress, a blue dress, and she was carefully made up. She was sitting at what would be her desk in what would be her secretarial area in what would be my chambers suite, and when I said good morning to her she looked up at me with an expression of desperate determination.

The good news was that there was furniture. In fact there was furniture everywhere. There was furniture for me and there was furniture for Carmen. There was furniture in the hallways, some of it piled up on hand-trucks, some of it just piled up. None of the furniture in my chambers was anything I had seen before – it certainly wasn't mine, and I had a guess that it wasn't Floyd Kroh's – but it seemed good enough as courthouse furniture went. I saw no pipes or ashtrays anywhere.

Carmen's look of desperate determination had nothing to do with the furniture. As far as Carmen was concerned, one desk was like another, one chair like another, one filing cabinet like another. In the years that I had been a criminal court judge, Carmen had managed the flow of paper – the countless motions, pleadings, opinions, documents, that wind their way into and out of a judge's chambers – with Prussian discipline. Floyd's chambers – my new chambers – were a scrap heap of legal paperwork. Files were piled on empty chairs, on all available desk space, on the floor. There was nothing to suggest what order the files were in, or even that they were in any order at all. It was Carmen's idea of a Kafkaesque nightmare.

"There's a reporter from the *Herald* sitting in the courtroom. He wants to know if you're willing to give a statement of any kind regarding the emergency hearing on the Holtzman Museum case."

"Do you have any idea what ...." I never got to the far end of that question. I didn't need to. Carmen gave me a look that said, more eloquently than words, that it would be days before she would know what, when, or where, and that I had no business asking. "Tell him it would be inappropriate for me to comment on a matter pending before me. See if you can encourage him to go away."

While Carmen went to deal with the press, I wandered down a small corridor into my private office. It was more than adequately furnished – desk, chairs, sofa. None of these things were the ones I had at the Gerstein Building, but they were as nice if not nicer than the ones I had at the Gerstein Building. The little desk ornament telling me that I was The Honorable Clark N. Addison had disappeared, but I was sure that I could remember anyway. The photos of my wife and children I had taken home with me last week; now I took them out of my briefcase and arranged them on my new desk, facing me. The room was small and spare, the walls done in a neutral beige and the floors in a dull and neutral brown, but in that respect, they were much like my old judicial chambers, and probably like every judicial chambers in every state courthouse in Florida. Behind my desk was a bank of windows, and although the view was of the top level of a parking garage it was at least an outdoor view. So far, civil court posed no insoluble problems.

I was checking the desk drawer for pens and pencils when Carmen came charging in. "The guy from the *Herald* wants to know if the emergency hearing is still set for 11:00. He says if it is he'll come back then."

"Tell him ... tell him that it's still set for ... when is it set for?"

"He says 11:00."

"Right."

Carmen turned to go but the telephone rang. Rather than run out to her desk she picked up the one on mine. "Chambers of Judge Clark N. Addison. ... One moment please, I'll see if he's in yet." She put the phone on hold. "Someone from the *New York Times* wants to know if you're willing to answer a few quick questions about the Holtzman Museum case."

"I'm not in yet." Carmen passed the news along, then pretended to take down the caller's name and phone number. After she hung up, I asked, "Did you see a bailiff assigned to our courtroom?"

"Uh-huh."

"Go find him, send him down to the clerk of the court, and see if they have a Holtzman Museum file. Then let's you and me check around here to see if we can find one."

Carmen, who picked the wrong day to wear heels, headed back for the courtroom as fast as circumstances permitted. She had just moved out of earshot when the phone on my desk began ringing again. By about the third ring I glanced at my wristwatch. It was well after 9:00 a.m, and I was supposed to be on duty, so I picked up the receiver and said hello.

"Clark, is that you? Have they got you answering your own phones?"

"Kay. Yes, well, actually it's surprisingly hectic, and ...."

"Then I won't keep you. I just called to wish you all the best in your new assignment."

"You're too kind. If you had a cookie to offer me, I'd take it."

"I have something better to offer." Kay's voice became lower, conspiratorial. "There's no point in your doing a tour of duty in civil court if you don't get what you want out of it. I made some calls. Don't schedule anything for Wednesday morning. You're going over to federal court. One of the judges will introduce you around, spend some time with you. Of course it's no guarantee that you'll get nominated for the open federal judgeship, but it can't hurt."

She had gone out of her way to help me, using up a favor or two. “This is very good of you, Kay. Which of the federal judges is going to be my Dutch uncle for the day?”

“Bob Aguilar. You know him, don’t you? Didn’t you go to school with him?”

“Uh. Yes. Kay, actually, it doesn’t make sense for me to visit federal court this week. Perhaps in a few weeks, when I’ve got my bearings, but not now.”

“Clark, you said you wanted to apply for the open federal judgeship. It’s a highly competitive, highly politicized process. I have made several phone calls for you. I have burned several favors for you. A very politically connected federal judge is willing to set aside part of his Wednesday morning to give you some guidance. I suggest that you show up.”

There was no way around it. “Kay, I’m very grateful, really. Of course I’ll show up. Thank you. Thank you for your help.”

She told me that I was welcome, and we hung up. I had told the truth when I said that I was grateful. It wasn’t that I didn’t appreciate Kay’s help. I just didn’t particularly want to have anything to do with Bob Aguilar.

I had known Bob since law school. I remember him as a handsome, personable kid. I was ambitious, but his ambition dwarfed mine. Our ambitions found different outlets. I was bookish, introverted, aware that my only route to success would be by getting the best grades, becoming editor in chief of the law review. Bob was the big man on campus. Women worshiped at his feet, and he knew that his ambition could be advanced by his choice of wife. He married a plain-looking girl, not nearly as attractive as the ones he had dated; she was the daughter of a big-firm partner and the niece of a state senator. Her trousseau was access to the highest levels of legal and political influence. With Bob’s looks and charm, access was all he needed.

Bob was the rarest of Miami fauna, a *Cubano arrepentido*. It is a Miami-Cuban slang term, very derogatory. Literally, it means a repentant Cuban; but its sense is a turncoat, an Uncle Tom, one who wishes to pass as non-Cuban. Why any Cuban would want to pass as a non-Cuban in Miami is a mystery to me. Cubans are the dominant ethnic group in politics, business, law. But Bob wanted to work both sides of the street. When it benefitted him, he was Roberto Aguilar, son of a prominent Cuban family that had lost everything to Castro's communist revolution and arrived penniless in Miami. When it benefitted him, he was Bob, all-American Bob, *Cubano arrepentido*. Working both angles had gotten him a federal judgeship just a few months ago. I resented his success and the method by which he had achieved it. Now I would have to go to him, hat in hand, and seek his support and guidance.

It was not something I wanted to think about, and fortunately for me that Monday morning I had other things to think about. Carmen was back in her office, tearing the place apart looking for any file marked "Holtzman Museum." I telephoned Floyd Kroh's chambers – my old chambers – at the Gerstein Building, was told that Floyd was on the bench, and left urgent word for him to call me at his next break. Then I tried to help Carmen. During the course of our search through files we were interrupted by a telephone call from the *Washington Post*, another from *Le Monde*, and two others from European papers the names of which Carmen did not even bother to pass along to me before telling them that I was unavailable to comment on the Holtzman Museum case.

The bailiff returned from his mission to the clerk's office and reported to Carmen. I didn't hear what he said, but it earned him a passionate cursing in Cuban Spanish. Carmen then came to share the news with me. "The bailiff says that the person he spoke to in the clerk's office told him that the Holtzman Museum case is assigned to Judge Kroh." She rolled her eyes. "I told him to go back to the clerk's office, explain that Judge Addison has taken over Judge Kroh's division, and *find out if they've got a god damn file for the Holtzman Museum case*." Carmen took a deep breath and was about to switch into Spanish – not for my benefit; my attempts at Spanish are a source of laughter to Spanish-speakers – but simply to get a few things off her chest. Just then the phone rang again. "Chambers of Judge Clark N. Addison. ... Yes, yes he's right here." She covered the receiver. "It's Judge Kroh returning your call."

I took the phone. "Floyd, look, I need ...."

"Yes, I can imagine. It's a disaster." The man seemed genuinely concerned.

I looked at my watch. There was still time to acquire at least a very basic familiarity with the case before the hearing began if I could just lay my hands on the file. "Let's don't say disaster yet, Floyd. Can you tell me where to find the file?"

Concern became confusion. "File? What file?"

"The Holtzman Museum file. Apparently, you scheduled some emergency hearing for this morning at 11:00 in a case in which one of the parties is the Holtzman Museum. I need to see the pleadings. Where's the file?"

For a moment there was no response. When he spoke it was with real anguish. "Clark, I have nothing. None of my furniture, my father's collection, nothing. I've had my secretary on the phone with the Administrative Office of the Court all morning, but we get nothing but double-talk. Are my things there with you? Are they anywhere in the civil courthouse?"

I took a deep breath. Screaming at Floyd about his furniture fetish, telling him that I didn't give a hoot about his father's pipes and ashtrays, wouldn't get me what I needed. I tried a different tack. "We're looking for your things now, Floyd. Incidentally, have you noticed the clock on the back wall in your courtroom?"

"Clock? Uh ... I glanced at it, I suppose. Why do you ask?"

"Well, it means rather a lot to me. It's an Elgin, made by the old Elgin Watch Company of Elgin, Illinois. My home town, you know, I was born there. Would you mind terribly having it sent down here? It means a lot to me."

If nothing else I had gotten Floyd to focus, so far as he was able to do so. "Of course, Clark, I perfectly understand. I'm sure they can find me another clock for the courtroom. I'll have it sent to you right away. Unless you'd rather come pick it up yourself? I mean, what with all that's happened, I don't know if I'd trust ...."

That was a direction I didn't want to go. "That will be fine, thanks, Floyd. And we'll track your things down ASAP. Now Floyd, please, think very carefully. Where might I find a file or files for a case involving the Holtzman Museum?"

He made a sort of a humming noise, which might have meant that he was thinking. "The Holtzman Museum over on Miami Beach?"

That was the only Holtzman Museum I had ever heard of, but what I wanted to know was where the pleading file was, not where the Museum was. "I suppose so, Floyd. You must have seen the pleadings recently. Can you think where you put the file?"

More humming. "I ... hmm ... I don't recall. I'll take a look to see if it's here somewhere."

"There? There with you? Why would ...."

"Oh, it's a hell of a thing, Clark. They were supposed to transport my furnishings and they've lost them. Of course they were supposed to leave all the files there for you, but they've brought some of them here. Which one did you say you were looking for?"

The Holtzman Museum file, damn it.... "A file in which one of the parties is the Holtzman Museum."

"Right. We'll look around for it. Meantime, I'll make arrangements for your clock." He paused. "We should talk again at the end of the day, Clark, if they haven't delivered my office suite by then."

I managed to get off the phone. At the other end of my chambers the bailiff had returned and was getting a second helping of Carmen's bilingual wrath. I didn't have to ask if he had found the file.

• • •

There are judges who will tell you that what matters most is to take the bench on time, wearing a crisply-pressed robe and bearing an air of command. A knowledge of the case and of its facts, say such judges, is of little help; it may even be an impediment, because an ignorant mind is an impartial mind, and an impartial judge is a good and fair judge. I have never been one of those judges. Although I make a point of getting to court on time, I have never paid much attention to the pleats in my robe. Lawyers who appeared before me in the Gerstein Building, however, knew darn well that they better come to court prepared, because I would.

I have two judicial robes. I spent a moment deciding which one looked cleaner, newer, more crisply pressed, and put that one on. I wasn't sure how I'd fake the air of authority.

I was in fifth grade when my family moved down to Miami Beach from Elgin, Illinois. During the spring of that school year our class had a field trip to the Holtzman Museum of Judaica. Once upon a time there had been a Mr. Holtzman, who had made an enormous fortune developing and operating hotels. He had built himself a mansion on a large piece of property several blocks away from the seashore – there was a superstition in those days that "humors" blowing in from the ocean at night were bad for the health, so oceanfront property was only second best – and directed in his will that it house a museum for his collection of Judaica. He either had no family or was estranged from it – a fifth grader had no attention for that portion of the tour-guide's lecture – and had left virtually all of his money in trust to maintain the museum and expand its collections. I suppose I had returned to visit the museum half a dozen times over the years, and for a short while Miriam insisted that we pay the small annual fee that would entitle us to call ourselves "subscribing members". Like many Miamians I had a general awareness that the Holtzman was considered one of the finest museums of its kind in the world, public or private, and that its collections were the object of admiration and study. Beyond that I knew nothing of the museum or of the hearing over which I was about to preside. I had difficulty imagining what kind of litigation a museum could get itself into. Had a visitor slipped in the cafeteria and filed suit for personal injuries?

My chambers and my courtroom were, of course, next to each other on the same corridor. I could, if I wanted to, exit my chambers into the public hallway, make a left, and enter the courtroom through the same entrance used by the public. But a judge does not enter through the same doorway as the public. He is provided a private door connecting his chambers to the courtroom, through which he and he alone appears. At 10:59 I entered my new courtroom and took the bench. The bailiff who had been the object of Carmen's execration for his failed efforts to track down the missing file possessed, it turned out, a booming bass voice. His cry of, "All rise" put me in mind of an old-time railroad engineer announcing, "All a-board" and added – I hoped – an element of authority to my entrance.

The courtroom was larger than the one I had had at the criminal courthouse, but its appearance was more or less the same. The woodwork – the bench, the jury rail, the bar of the court – was dark and ornate. The wall that ran on my left-hand side from the front of the courtroom to the back was mostly windows, and although they gave no particular view they gave a good deal of light. The portions of the wall that were not wood-paneled were a sort of an off-white, looking like stucco but not stucco. The high ceiling was more of the same, with four dark wood timbers at intervals in the plaster. The gallery – the public seating area – was large, and it was filled. Several rows were occupied by reporters, cellphones or notepads at the ready. Some few of them I recognized; most I did not, which probably meant that they were from out of town. I had no idea who the balance of the visitors were, but they were a noisy crowd, seemingly very excited about what was to take place. What, I wondered, could possibly be exciting about a slip-and-fall?

The bailiff bellowed for order, and got it. I took advantage of the sudden silence. "Counsel please approach the bench."

I had noticed to my surprise when I entered the courtroom that I actually recognized a couple of the lawyers involved in the case. I know few civil litigators, but I know Raul Santos. Raul was the head of the litigation department at Williams, Santos, and Banks. Raul is – or was, in the old days – a fishing buddy of Jack Sheridan, and the Williams, Santos firm used to refer any criminal cases that came its way to Jack. Through Jack I had met Raul on half a dozen or more occasions. He is a charming man and, as Jack used to like to say, money isn't wasted on Raul. His tastes are expensive but always elegant and understated; he cultivates an old-money image. He is a small man, very physically fit – tennis champ most years at Grove Isle Club, if I recall correctly – with a full head of prematurely silver-gray hair, combed very precisely into place. His clients are always very rich people, and very rich people like having Raul as their lawyer.

Four lawyers trooped after him to the bench, Mother Goose and her goslings. Civil law firms bill by the hour, so it would never do to send the senior partner to court alone. Raul would do the talking, and my guess was that his words would cost someone seven hundred and fifty dollars an hour; but he would be assisted by a junior partner, a senior associate, a junior associate, and a law clerk or paralegal, the hourly billing rate declining from one to the next. An hour's-worth of court time would easily cost the client a couple of thousand dollars or more.

Approaching from the other counsel table was a lawyer whom I did not know personally, but whom I knew well by reputation. It was impossible to live in Miami, to read the newspapers, to watch the television news, without knowing of Zachary Taylor Davis. I had seen photos of him, dressed in what I took to be traditional African garb, being sworn in for yet another term as president of the Miami Chapter of NAACP. I had seen televised press conferences on the steps of the federal courthouse in which he explained with furious righteousness why he had just filed a class action suit against hotels or restaurants or municipalities. He was perpetually being appointed to gubernatorial commissions, blue-ribbon panels, and whatnot. He had served a term or two in the state legislature some years back.

He was a man of above-average height, very fleshy, fashionably dressed. His hair and beard were close-cropped; the hair was dark, but the beard had begun to turn gray at the chin.

It took only seconds for the attorneys to walk to the bench, but it was more than enough time for me to realize that this was not a slip-and-fall case. Raul Santos and Zachary Taylor Davis did not come to court because someone had fallen down in a museum cafeteria.

"Counsel, please state your appearances for the record."

Raul spoke first. "Good morning, Your Honor. Raul Santos of Williams, Santos, and Banks on behalf of plaintiff, the Holtzman Museum of Judaica. Also appearing with me are my colleagues ...." Raul identified the other attorneys from his firm. I nodded at each in turn.

"Good morning, Your Honor. Zachary Taylor Davis on behalf of defendant Dr. Bernard Gumbiner. I am joined by my junior partner, Aimee Arrants." Standing at Davis's side was a woman who could not have been more than a few years out of law school. She said good morning in a voice that had in it the slight hint of a Caribbean accent.

"Counsel, as you know I'm new to this case. I've had some difficulty with the court files. It would be a convenience if you could supply me with duplicate copies of the principal pleadings." The most junior of the Williams, Santos lawyers raced the few steps back to counsel table and returned with a thick document which passed up the chain of seniority, finally to Raul, who gave it to me. It bore the caption, "Complaint for Injunctive and Declaratory Relief." Ms. Arrants produced a document entitled, "Defendant Dr. Bernard Gumbiner's Answer to Complaint for Injunctive and Declaratory Relief, and Motion to Compel Arbitration." Both sides' pleadings would require careful study, study that I could not provide now. But I had at least learned, without embarrassing myself unduly, who the litigants and lawyers were. That would have to do for the present. "Are both sides ready to proceed?" They were. "Mr. Santos, this is your application. Please call your first witness."

Raul stepped to the lectern while the other lawyers returned to their seats. He opened a manila folder, glanced at its contents briefly, and announced, "On behalf of the Holtzman Museum of Judaica, I call Morris Arnovitz." The witness who came forward looked ... well, he looked like me: short, slightly built, pale complected with very dark, very wavy hair. He wore a navy sport coat that looked new and a brown knit tie that looked old. He took the oath and Raul began his examination. "Please state your name."

"Morris Arnovitz." Ar- NOV-itz, he said, with the accent on the middle syllable.

"How are you employed, Mr. Arnovitz?

"I am a curator at the Holtzman Museum of Judaica." He spoke in a soft, firm voice, very formally.

Raul moved the witness rapidly through his academic and professional history: the universities he had attended, the degrees he had earned, his training at various museums and other artistic institutions, how he came to be a curator at the Holtzman. Then

Raul slowed the pace to focus on what really mattered. "Mr. Arnovitz, within your general expertise, do you have a particular area of specialty?"

"Yes. Art of the Holocaust."

"In fact, you are the author of a book entitled just that – Art of the Holocaust – are you not?"

"I am."

"And in the context of art of the Holocaust, do you recognize the name Ernst Adler?"

"Yes."

"Would it be fair to say, Mr. Arnovitz, that you are the leading scholar and biographer of Ernst Adler?"

Arnovitz pursed his lips for a moment, caught between the competing demands of modesty and accuracy. "I have published several scholarly articles on Adler's life and work. I ... I have been described by colleagues whose judgment I respect as being the principal authority on Adler."

Raul gestured in my direction. "Mr. Arnovitz, please tell the Court who Ernst Adler was." Raul deliberately took a couple of steps back from the lectern. He was taking himself out of the picture, focusing all attention on the witness.

The witness shifted in his seat to face me. "Ernst Adler was born sometime in the first decade of the 20th century. We don't have an exact birthdate for him. He was born in Vienna, to a Jewish family that was well-to-do and determined to assimilate into Austrian society. He and his sisters had a strict and thorough education in the home from early childhood. That education included the study of art." Arnovitz paused for breath or for thought or for both. "Beyond that we know little of Adler's childhood.

"We next see him in Paris and Barcelona during the 1920's. His family had wanted him to go into the family business, to pursue and expand their financial and mercantile interests, but he has broken with his family. He is attempting, with very little success, to make his way as an artist. He is seen in the company of many of the great artists of the day – Picasso, Miro – but unlike them he has not developed a style of his own. He has affairs with many women. He is, for example, one of the many lovers taken by Tamara de Lempicka. He marries once, briefly. A daughter is born to the marriage." Arnovitz gestured toward Dr. Gumbiner, seated between Zachary Taylor Davis and Aimee Arrants. "It is my understanding that Adler's daughter was Dr. Gumbiner's mother.

"Sometime in the late 1930's he returns to Vienna, apparently in an attempt to reconcile with his family, or to assist them in some fashion. He will never be free to travel again. He is arrested and sent to Weeghman." Raul took a step toward the lectern and was about to pose a question, but the witness anticipated it. "Weeghman is actually the name of a very small farming village on the German-Austrian border. But the name is used to refer to the concentration camp built and operated just outside of the village.

"The inmates of Weeghman are an extraordinary lot: Jewish artists, scholars, intellectuals, many but by no means all from Vienna. Like all Nazi concentration camps, Weeghman is a place of unimaginable privations. Yet within its barbed-wire enclosures, an artistic miracle occurs: Ernst Adler finds his own artistic voice, his own style. He works with paint, with pens and pencils, with pieces of charcoal. He works on scraps of cloth, on canvasses torn from mattress linings, on pieces of paper, on pieces of wood. Surrounded by starvation, torture, and death, he produces a luminous *oevre*." It appeared to me that for a split-second Raul considered interrupting the witness to make him explain the word "*oevre*." Arnovitz had given his testimony in a soft, almost monotonous voice. His manner of speech was too formal for most purposes, and his description of long-ago events in the present tense seemed to me a theatrical affectation. But he spoke so earnestly, with such conviction, that the courtroom had become hushed and attentive; so much so that the very occasional scribbling of one of the newspaper reporters in the front row was clearly audible. Raul did not want to break the spell. He said nothing.

Arnovitz went on. "After Weeghman is liberated by the allies, word of Adler's remarkable body of work spreads like an electric current through the European artistic community. But the Nazis have left a devastated continent in their wake. It is impossible to get accurate information, to separate fact from fiction. Adler himself dies at or shortly after the end of the war. Curators and collectors struggle to locate, to reconstruct, to preserve his work, only half believing that work to be anything more than a myth.

"To this day there has never been a thorough cataloguing of Adler's body of work. We know that the overwhelming majority of what has survived is in the possession of Dr. Gumbiner who, presumably, received it from his mother. Dr. Gumbiner's private collection is, of course, just that – his private collection. He has never exhibited it publicly." Arnovitz looked at Raul, then at Gumbiner, then back at Raul. "I ... I did not mean to sound critical in any way. I perfectly understand Dr. Gumbiner's feelings about the collection."

Raul nodded approvingly at his witness. "Did there come a time, Mr. Arnovitz, when Dr. Gumbiner approached the Holtzman Museum regarding his collection of Adler's works?"

"Yes."

"When was that?"

"Last year."

"Please tell Judge Addison about that."

Arnovitz cleared his throat quietly. "Dr. Gumbiner's legal representatives contacted the museum and indicated that he might be interested in loaning us his Adler collection."

"What was the reaction of the museum's leadership?"

"We were ... we were tremendously excited. This would have been a watershed event in the history of the Holtzman, and in the history of art of the Holocaust."

"What happened next?"

"We entered into negotiations." Arnovitz turned to me. "The loaning for display of a valuable art collection is a common enough event in the art world, but it is contractually complex." He dropped his gaze for a moment and repeated himself. "Contractually complex." He looked at me again. "Many of the terms are standard, of course, but every situation is different. Mr. Santos's firm represented us in the negotiations."

"Were you also involved in those negotiations, Mr. Arnovitz?" asked Raul.

"Yes."

Raul approached the witness and placed a hefty document before him. "Do you recognize Exhibit A, Mr. Arnovitz?"

"Yes. This is the contract, the written contract that was worked out between the Holtzman Museum and Dr. Gumbiner."

"Now Mr. Arnovitz, I want to direct your attention to numbered paragraph 43 of the contract, and its various subparagraphs. Please take a moment to turn to that portion of the contract." The witness began to leaf through the documents before him. One of Raul's young colleagues silently handed me a copy and I paged through it furiously, hoping for minutes or even seconds to scan the material about which Raul would be asking. Paragraph 43 – including subparagraphs (a) through (r) – extended over several pages. It was written in elaborate lawyer-speak, but as far as I could tell on a quick reading, it provided that the Holtzman Museum, upon receipt of the Adler collection, would be permitted and even obliged to conduct certain examinations of Adler's works.

Arnovitz looked up, to indicate that he had found the passages to which Raul was referring. Raul resumed his examination. "Sir, based upon your considerable experience, is this sort of provision customary in a contract of this kind – a contract pursuant to which a museum will be accepting the loan of a valuable art collection?"

"Absolutely customary," Arnovitz answered. "I would say that this language, or similar language, almost invariably appears in such contracts."

"Why?" Arnovitz shifted in his seat slightly and started to answer, but Raul wanted to make sure that the answer was directed to the proper audience. "Please tell Judge Addison why you say that."

Arnovitz turned to face me. "Any museum, and certainly a world-renown museum such as the Holtzman, is responsible for the artistic integrity of its exhibits. When a new collection is received, even if only on loan, the museum routinely, customarily conducts examinations of the work or works." Clearly Arnovitz had been carefully prepared by Raul's junior lawyers. His answers came readily, in well-rehearsed form.

"And would this be particularly true in the case of the Adler collection?"

"Yes." Arnovitz explained without waiting to be asked. "You must remember that the Adler collection has never been examined, authenticated, catalogued by any expert – never even seen by any expert. There are serious art critics and scholars who have questioned what they refer to as the myth of Adler's work in Weeghman and of the Adler collection – questioned its very existence. For years it has been, in some sense" – here, unusually for him, Arnovitz was obliged to pause to choose his words – "in some sense the Holy Grail of the 20th century art world." I saw one of the reporters in the front row of the gallery make notes. Somewhere, tomorrow, a newspaper column would be headed "Court Hears Argument Over 'Holy Grail of Art World'."

"What sort of examinations would the Adler collection be subjected to by the Holtzman Museum?"

"Two kinds. First, a general visual examination by experts."

Raul interrupted. "You would be one such expert?"

"Yes, as would other Holtzman curators. In addition, we would bring in colleagues from New York, Europe, Israel, who may be familiar with Adler and his work. We would examine Dr. Gumbiner's collection for form, for content, for consistency with what is known of Adler's *oevre*." Arnovitz was big on *oevre*.

Raul nodded. "You said there would be a second kind of examination. Of what would that consist?"

"Scientific examination," explained the witness. "Minute samples of the paints, or the ink, or the surface on which the paintings or drawings were done, would be subjected to various kinds of scientific analysis. This analysis enables us, in some instances, to confirm that the works come from the time and the place we believe them to have come from."

"Would you perform these analyses?" asked Raul.

"Myself? No. My area of expertise is art, not chemistry. We have scientific laboratories with which we have worked in the past, and to which we would refer this sort of analysis."

Raul moved slightly, paused slightly, signaling that he was moving to another area of inquiry. "Did the Holtzman prepare to receive the Adler collection?"

"Yes. We actually arranged to set aside an entire wing for the Adler collection. We informed the art world, and the general public, that it would be on display." The witness turned to me, intent on getting his message across. "This was to have been one of the defining events in the history of the Holtzman. It would perhaps not be too much to describe it as one of the defining moments in the history of fine art in this country."

"And what happened?"

"Dr. Gumbiner refused to deliver the Adler collection. He continues to refuse to deliver the Adler collection. He objects to the examination provisions of the contract, although he signed the contract." I thought perhaps that Arnovitz's last remark would draw some kind of objection from Zachary Davis, but he sat quietly and impassively at counsel table.

"What does the Holtzman Museum want, Mr. Arnovitz?"

"We want Dr. Gumbiner to honor his agreement with us. We want him to deliver the Adler collection, we want to conduct our examination of the Adler collection, and we want to display the Adler collection."

"Is there any particular reason that the Holtzman Museum felt obliged to file this lawsuit at this time?" Raul drew out the last three words, placing emphasis upon them.

"Yes. The end of this year will mark the anniversary of the liberation of Weeghman. A series of celebratory events are planned, some of them in Europe, some here. The culminating event was to be the unveiling of the Adler collection at the Holtzman. In anticipation of that event, plans and commitments have been made ... plans and commitments of all kinds. I don't mean just by us at the Holtzman, I mean by political, charitable, and historical organizations on three continents. We have conveyed the importance of this date, of this event, of these plans, to Dr. Gumbiner." Arnovitz's speech remained very cogent, very organized, but he was struggling to control an obvious sense of frustration. "This particular anniversary of the liberation of Weeghman will not come again. There will be other anniversaries, of course, but those who have a living memory of the Holocaust are passing from the scene. We've got to, we've absolutely got to begin to make the Adler collection ready for display. Now. Without more delay."

Raul closed the manila folder on the lectern before him, as if to signal that his examination was ending. "One final matter, Mr. Arnovitz: You indicated that no expert has ever conducted a thorough examination of the Adler collection. That being the case, is it possible to know what the collection is worth?"

"In dollar terms?" The witness seemed slightly put off by the question.

"Yes. Forgive my asking, but can you assign an approximate dollar value to the Adler collection?"

For the first time since he had taken the stand, the witness seemed pressed for the right answer. "If, as I hope and believe, the collection is ... is as I ... well, as I hope and believe it is ...." A pause. "Millions, dozens of millions, perhaps ... perhaps hundreds of millions of dollars."

"Would 25 million dollars be too high a number?"

"No, Mr. Santos, it would probably not be too high a number. Of course so many factors go into ...."

Raul cut him off. "Fifty million?"

The witness looked away for a moment. Raul did nothing to hurry his answer. "I ... I can't say that it would necessarily be too high. I really ... I really just can't say at all."

The visitors' gallery, quiet to this point, was quiet no longer; and the bailiff felt moved to call for silence in court. Raul asked if he could confer briefly with his cocounsel before concluding his examination of the witness. I knew perfectly well that he had nothing to ask his colleagues, and that they had nothing to tell him. But Raul was in no hurry to hand his witness over for cross-examination. Better to let the last few answers hover in the courtroom for a few extra minutes.

When he had gotten what there was to be gotten out of this dramatic pause, Raul turned to me and announced simply, "Nothing further at this time, Your Honor."

I turned to Zachary Davis. "Cross examine?"

Davis rose and, with a great deal of dignity, said quietly. "If the Court please." He walked to the lectern with no notes of any kind, nodded at the witness, and said, "Good morning, Mr. Arnovitz."

"Good morning."

"My name is Zachary Taylor Davis. So far as I am aware, we have never actually met. Is that your recollection as well?"

"Yes."

"Mr. Arnovitz, you are familiar with a work of art known either as 'La Gioconda' or the 'Mona Lisa'?"

"Of course."

"It is one of the most recognized paintings in the western world?"

"Certainly. I would say so."

"It hangs in the Louvre Museum in Paris?"

"Yes."

"If the Louvre offered to loan the Mona Lisa for display at the Holtzman, you wouldn't insist that the Mona Lisa be subjected to artistic or chemical analysis first, would you?"

Davis had accurately assessed the witness's sense of self. Morris Arnovitz would take great pains to avoid looking like a fool, and saying that the Mona Lisa would have to be subjected to testing and analysis could only make him look foolish. "No. I would not."

"If Hadassah Hospital in Jerusalem offered to loan for display at the Holtzman the famous Chagall Windows, you wouldn't insist on evaluating them first, would you?"

"I don't know if the Chagall Windows can be moved ...."

Davis parried the answer, pressed his question. "Assume that they can be moved. Would the Holtzman decline to show the Chagall Windows, among the most magnificent specimens of Judaic art in the world, unless and until they were chemically analyzed and artistically evaluated?"

"No. No."

Davis's hands remained always tightly gripping the sides of the podium, in the same way that some clergymen gripped the pulpit. He gestured not with his hands but with his body, moving his considerable bulk left or right, forward or back, for emphasis and to accompany the lilt of his voice. But the hands did not move. "In your experience, sir, no museum would require a formal examination before gratefully accepting the loan of such a splendid, well-known work of art, would it?"

"Probably not. Of course I can't speak for all museums."

"You speak for the Holtzman. You are aware that the Holtzman has, from time to time in its history, accepted the loan for display of valuable art objects without insisting on the analysis or testing of those art objects?"

"Yes, when the object was well-known."

"The need for testing will depend on a number of factors, such as how well-known the art objects are?"

"Yes."

"In some cases testing might be important, in other cases less so."

"Yes, but in this case ...."

"Yes, Mr. Arnovitz, in this case you have taken the position that testing is necessary?"

"It is necessary."

"You are aware that Dr. Gumbiner has taken the position" – Davis gestured with body weight, head, and eyes, to the pages of the exhibit before the witness – "that testing is not necessary?"

"He's wrong."

"So that as matters stand now, the need for testing is in dispute between you and Dr. Gumbiner?"

"Yes."

"Now let's talk, sir, about these chemical tests you have in mind. You indicated that you yourself will not be performing them?"

"That's correct."

"Because you are not scientifically trained and qualified to perform them?"

"No, I'm not."

"You are aware that chemical testing has the potential to damage the work of art being tested?"

"Not if it's done properly."

"Whenever something is done by a human being, Mr. Arnovitz, there is the potential for error or mistake, isn't there?"

Arnovitz wanted to fight. "The lab people we call in to perform this testing are extremely experienced and expert. They won't make mistakes."

Davis wasn't fighting, but he was firm. "They are experienced, and expert ... and human. They are human, aren't they, Mr. Arnovitz?"

Arnovitz looked annoyed. "Yes, Mr. Davis, of course they're human."

"And human beings -- even experienced, expert human beings -- are imperfect?"

"Yes."

"And imperfect human beings are capable of error?"

"Yes."

"And if error occurs in the chemical testing of the Adler collection, it could damage the works of art being tested?"

"If error occurs, which it won't."

Davis bore down on the lectern. "So the answer to my question is: Yes, if error occurs it could damage one or more of the beautiful works that make up the Adler collection. That is the answer -- the truthful answer -- to my question?"

"Yes." Arnovitz had nowhere else to go.

"Depending on the nature of the damage, it could be permanent and irreparable?"

"I don't know. I suppose it could, although I've never heard of such a thing happening."

"So the danger associated with chemical testing is something else that remains in dispute between you and Dr. Gumbiner?"

"Yes."

The two junior-most lawyers at Raul's table were taking notes furiously. Raul watched intently but so far had nothing to object to.

Davis's eyes never left the witness. "Incidentally, Mr. Arnovitz, the chemical testing you are describing is typically done to determine the age of a work of art?"

"That's one common purpose. It isn't necessarily the only one."

"If, for example, a painting was alleged to have been done in Europe four or five hundred years ago, it would likely contain the pigment white lead in it somewhere?

"That's very possible."

"White lead is manufactured from ores which contain uranium and elements to which uranium decays?"

"That's my understanding."

"One of these elements is Radium 226?"

"I believe so."

"Radium 226 has a half-life of 1600 years, and decays to an isotope of lead with a half-life of 22 years?"

"I really don't know, Mr. Davis. As I said, I'm not a scientist. If you tell me these things are so, of course I accept them."

"But someone who is a scientist and knew these things, and understood the principle of radioactive equilibrium, could, by a series of mathematical calculations, determine if a painting were really four or five hundred years old, correct?"

"I believe so."

"Of course the Adler collection is alleged to be only about 60 some-odd years old?"

"That's right."

"Sixty-plus years is too short a period for this method of analysis by radioactive half-life to be useful, isn't it?"

"I don't know."

"You don't know. But you continue to insist that the Adler collection be subjected to scientific analysis before being displayed by the Holtzman?"

"Yes. And I believe that there are other, more discriminating tests available."

"Can you name any of these other tests?"

"I don't know all their names."

"Can you name *any* test that you can confidently tell us will be accurate in dating the Adler collection?"

Arnovitz took a slow breath to dispel his frustration before answering. "No."

"Yet you continue to insist that there is some point in subjecting the Adler collection to scientific testing?"

"Yes, I certainly do."

"That's something else that is a matter of dispute between you and Dr. Gumbiner, isn't it?"

"Apparently."

"So if I follow you, Mr. Arnovitz, there are at least three important disputes between the Holtzman and Dr. Gumbiner: whether there is any need at all for testing of the Adler collection, whether scientific testing could damage the Adler collection, and whether scientific testing could actually tell us anything about the authenticity of the Adler collection. Am I correct?"

"If you want to put it that way."

"As a result of these disputes Dr. Gumbiner has not provided, and the Holtzman has not accepted, the Adler collection, correct?"

"He hasn't provided the collection. We're ready, willing, and able to accept it under the contract terms."

"The contract terms," Davis repeated. "Yes. Mr. Arnovitz, please turn to numbered paragraph nine of the contract itself."

I tore through the pages to get to paragraph nine ahead of the witness. It was headed, "ARBITRATION" and, like most of the provisions of the contract, included several subparagraphs. Davis waited patiently, hands gripping the lectern, while the witness found his place. "Would you please read the introductory sentence of that paragraph, Mr. Arnovitz?"

Arnovitz read without looking up. "Any controversy or claim arising out of or relating to this contract, or the breach thereof, shall, in the first instance, be addressed to arbitration as more fully set forth below."

Davis continued. "I realize that you aren't a lawyer yourself, Mr. Arnovitz, but I believe that you had some involvement in the negotiations culminating in that contract, is that correct?"

"Yes."

"You understand what arbitration is?"

"Yes, I know what arbitration is," Arnovitz replied. "When people enter into complex contracts, they anticipate that problems may arise. Arbitration is a way of resolving those problems without resorting to the expense and formality of a lawsuit."

I silently gave Mr. Arnovitz an "A" for his answer. I was glad Zachary Davis hadn't asked me the same question.

"Dr. Gumbiner made the Holtzman aware that he was prepared to submit the disputes between you to arbitration, didn't he?"

"Yes."

Davis pressed the point. “He informed the Holtzman repeatedly, and in writing, that he was prepared to submit the disputes to arbitration?”

“Yes.”

“Just as the contract provides?”

The question seemed inoffensive, but Arnovitz – who had for the most part remained expressionless during his testimony – had apparently reached his limit. “What Dr. Gumbiner proposes is absurd! The idea of resolving these disputes by this kind of ... by ... these aren’t the kind of questions that can be resolved other than by ... it’s absurd! It’s ridiculous and ... absurd!”

Davis, probably pleased with the witness’s reaction and hoping for more of the same, raised his voice and leaned into his next question. “So the Holtzman has brought suit to restrain and enjoin Dr. Gumbiner from submitting this matter to arbitration?”

“Yes.”

“To restrain and enjoin Dr. Gumbiner from doing *precisely what the contract calls for*?”

The witness, agitated, drew breath to begin his answer, but Raul stood quickly, spoke calmly. “Your Honor, I object. What the contract calls for is a question of law for this Court, not a question of fact for this witness.”

I looked right at Davis. “Sustained. Anything further, Mr. Davis?”

“Nothing further, thank you.” His hands left the lectern, and Zachary Taylor Davis returned to his seat.

I looked at the wall at the back of the courtroom but there was no Elgin clock there, so I looked at my wristwatch. The witness had been on the stand for some time and it was not too early for the lunch recess. Raul, however, moved rapidly to the lectern, making it clear that he wanted to proceed with redirect examination now. "You have redirect, Mr. Santos?"

"Yes, Your Honor."

I made a point of looking at my wristwatch again. "How long do you expect to be?"

"It will be a brief redirect, Your Honor."

In the history of courtrooms, no lawyer had ever been candid enough to say, "It will be a long, drawn-out, boring redirect, Judge. You'll probably zone out half way through it." I don't know why I bothered to ask. But I had asked, and I had gotten the stock answer, and now I was stuck with it.

"All right, Mr. Santos. Please proceed."

Raul nodded respectfully in my direction, then turned to the witness. "Mr. Arnovitz, Mr. Davis asked you about the arbitration provision of the contract between the Holtzman and Dr. Gumbiner. Please turn to that provision again." The witness did so, as did I. "Does the contract indicate who or what the arbitrator is to be? I particularly direct your attention to subparagraph G."

"Yes." Arnovitz looked up. "The arbitrator is to be the *bes din* of Miami Beach."

"Do you know what a *bes din* is, Mr. Arnovitz?"

"As I understand it, it is a rabbinic court. A panel of rabbis."

"Mr. Arnovitz, based on your many years of training and experience in the art world, would you say that there are few or many people qualified to conduct an artistic assessment of the Adler collection."

"There are few."

"You are one such person?"

"Yes. I am." The witness had long since triumphed over modesty.

"Do you personally know the others?"

"Many of them, yes, I do."

"Are any of them members of the *bes din*, the rabbinic court, of Miami Beach?"

"No, they are not."

"And based on your many years of training and experience in the art world, sir, would you say that there are few or many chemists, scientists, qualified to conduct a chemical assessment of the Adler collection?"

"There are few."

"Do you know, or at least know of, most of the principal scientists in this highly-specialized field?"

"Yes I do."

"Are any of them, to your knowledge, members of the *bes din*, the rabbinic court, of Miami Beach?"

"They are not."

Raul asked for, and I granted, a moment to confer with his cocounsel. This time it may have been for more than show. I stared fixedly at my shirt cuff, not because there was anything of interest about it, but because I didn't want anyone to see my facial expression. I was thinking that I had been in civil court for less than two hours. I was thinking that I had spent those couple of hours presiding over a case in which South Florida's most prestigious museum and a physician bickered about the temporary resting place of an art collection that might or might not be worth $50 or $100 million; a case in which the physician wanted the bickering resolved by a court composed of Orthodox rabbis. I was thinking that life in criminal court – even with its murders, drug deals, robberies – had a clarity to it that I was starting to miss.

Raul's whispered conference with his colleagues was over. "Nothing further, Your Honor."

Zachary Taylor Davis, moving with surprising quickness for a heavy man, was on his feet asking for recross-examination. Had we been in criminal court I would have denied his request and moved on. But I was unsure of myself in this, my first civil case; and I hesitated. A judge who hesitates is lost. A judge, I was told long ago, does not sometimes decide, always correctly; he always decides, sometimes correctly. In the instant in which I had failed to decide, Davis had placed his death-grip on the lectern, his eyes on the witness, and begun his questioning. "Mr. Arnovitz, you tell us that you know the leading authorities in the art world who can evaluate the Adler collection. Is Judge Addison among them?"

Arnovitz had the decency to attempt a smile in my direction as he answered, "No."

"But those experts can come before Judge Addison and testify about what they know – just as you're doing now?"

"Yes."

"You also know the names of many of the chemists capable of performing scientific evaluations of the Adler collection?"

"Yes."

"Judge Addison is not one of those scientists, is he?"

"No, he isn't."

"But those scientists can testify in court before Judge Addison, can't they?"

"Yes."

"Do you know of any reason why all those art experts, and all those scientists, couldn't testify before the rabbinic court mentioned in paragraph nine of the contract?"

"I don't know how rabbinic courts function, Mr. Davis."

Davis leaned into his question. "So you don't know of any reason that experts *couldn't* testify before the rabbinic court, do you?"

Arnovitz gave up. "No."

Without stating that his recross was over – it obviously was – Davis headed back to his seat. I immediately announced that we would recess for lunch till 1:45.

I went to my chambers to hide. I didn't particularly want to be cooped up in chambers, but I was afraid to go anywhere else. The hallways would be crammed with furniture and reporters, and although I didn't want to bump into the furniture, I absolutely could not take the chance of bumping into the reporters.

Carmen followed me into my private office, carrying a pile of files. When I was seated at my desk she asked, "This hearing isn't going to be over today, is it?" I shook my head, no. "Because you have," she jiggled the stack of files in her arms, "you know, lots of other hearings we need to set." I gestured for her to put the files down on my desk. I would get around to looking at them. "You want me to get you some lunch?"

"No thanks. Not hungry."

"You're never hungry. You should eat something."

I was rifling drawers in my desk, looking for something. "No thanks, really."

"I have a *colada*. You want a *cafecito*?" She had Cuban coffee, espresso but with sugar, to be shared in thimble-sized cups. It would be thick, strong, syrupy, sweet. It couldn't possibly be good for anyone.

I was still inventorying the contents of my desk drawers. I looked up at her. "Yes, thanks." She pointed at the files she had placed on my desk. On top of the pile was a brand-new box of paper clips. My search was over.

Apart from its therapeutic value, the building of a paper clip chain develops manual dexterity and other important skills. Most people don't know that you can build a paper-clip chain two or even three clips wide. When I retire from the bench I intend to run for president of the American Society of Paper-Clip Chain Builders. I'm hoping that their national headquarters are on the seashore somewhere in the Florida Keys. Maybe Key West, not too far from the Key Conch Hotel.

In the length of time it took me to make an important contribution to the history of paper-clip chain building the din in the hallway died down. Even reporters must eat lunch, and they certainly couldn't do it in the corridor outside my courtroom, so I decided it was safe for me to take a walk as long as I didn't stray too far.

When I opened the outer door of my chambers suite the first thing I noticed was that the supply of furniture in the hallway had multiplied. The courtroom was to the left, so I took a right and strolled, not that there was much of anywhere to go. Halfway down the corridor, on the right-hand wall, I noticed a moving dolly stacked with a desk, several chairs, and what appeared to be two small display cabinets filled with pipes. The pipes had at some point been carefully arranged in the cabinets, but the cabinets had been stacked upside-down on the dolly and the pipes had fallen every which-way. On several other hand-trucks I saw, tossed one on top of another, odds and ends of Floyd's daddy's ashtray collection. Some of them were actually quite striking-looking.

Beyond the last pile of furniture was a small corridor running to the right, only a few feet in length. It led to a doorway, and past the doorway to the stairwell that served lawyers too impatient to wait for the ancient elevators that crept from floor to floor. There being nowhere else for me to go and nothing else for me to see, I returned to chambers.

Carmen was on the phone. "No, wait, he just walked back in," she said to whoever was on the other end of the line. Then to me, "It's for you. Miriam."

Miriam and I have been together almost our entire lives. We were neighbors from the time my family moved to Miami Beach. We went to the prom together. I asked her to marry me the night I graduated college, although we and everyone around us had long known that it was only a question of when we would get engaged, not if. I have never had any other girlfriend, and I have never wanted one.

I have no reason to believe that Miriam wants another husband, although I am probably not the easiest person in the world to live with. One of the reasons I am not the easiest person in the world to live with has to do with telephone calls during the work day. When I started my career as a prosecutor in the Miami-Dade State Attorney's Office long ago, I told Miriam that she was not to call me at work unless it was an emergency, and that nothing is an emergency unless blood is flowing. From time to time Miriam tells me that she read in a magazine at the beauty parlor that it is important for married couples to communicate during the day, however briefly, to assure one another of their affection. I then assure her of my affection and renew my request for no non-emergency phone calls at work. For the most part Miriam complies, however grudgingly. So there was at least the prospect of a blood-flowing emergency when Carmen said that Miriam was on the phone.

I took the call standing by my desk. "Hello."

"Clark, it's Uncle Billy."

"What about him?" It was clear from Miriam's voice that she had not called for us to assure one another of our affection.

"He's had a heart attack."

I sat down at my desk. "When?"

"I don't know, exactly. This morning, I think early. It's ..." -- she sounded almost apologetic -- "it's a mild heart attack."

"Where is he?"

"Mt. Sinai. They said he can have brief visits, but that he probably won't be able to talk." For just a moment neither could I. Miriam went on, "Do you want me to meet you there after you leave court?"

Mt. Sinai Hospital is on Miami Beach. Miriam and I live in the south suburbs of the City of Miami. In afternoon rush hour traffic it would take an hour for her to get to Mt. Sinai. "No, I'll go. Have you told the kids?"

"They're not home yet." Of course they weren't, they were at school, it was a stupid question. "Should I tell them?"

"Yes. They're entitled to know. Start dinner without me." I paused for a moment. "Thank you for calling, Miriam. I love you."

"Love you too."

"No, wait, don't hang up. I didn't mean 'I love you,' like, 'I'm hanging up now.' I meant, I love you."

A few seconds passed before she spoke. "We've been awfully lucky, haven't we, Clark?"

"That's ... that's what I meant."

"I love you, Clark. Give my love to Uncle Billy. Get home when you get home." And we hung up together.

• • •

When I took the bench just before 1:45 the courtroom was, if possible, more packed that it had been for the morning session.

There was a low din of whispers, moving bodies, shuffling papers, but rather than call upon the bailiff to restore order I turned to Raul Santos and asked, "Is the prosecu ..." damn it, there is no prosecution, this is civil court, "the plaintiff ready to call its next witness?"

Raul stood, and the buzzing of the visitors' gallery abated slightly. "Our next witness is Herman Bilstein." As he spoke the name, Raul gestured toward a man seated in the first row of the gallery. The man was age itself: shrunken and bald, as wrinkled as a Shar-Pei puppy. He clutched a walker.

"And besides Mr. Bilstein, how many more witnesses do you expect to call in your case in chief, Mr. Santos?" I wanted some idea how long this hearing would go on, and I didn't want it going on forever.

"In addition to Mr. Bilstein one other, Your Honor."

I turned to Zachary Davis. "Mr. Davis, do you also have your witnesses present?"

Raul sat, and Davis stood. "May it please the Court, we intend to call but one witness: Rabbi Chaim Stein."

Excited whispers, the movement of bodies; it was unnecessary for Davis to gesture toward Rabbi Stein. Every head, every gaze in the courtroom turned as if drawn by a kind of gravity to a large man seated in the very back row. He was dressed in the traditional garb of the very orthodox: black hat, long black coat. But I was struck, as I looked at him, with the absurd, the almost blasphemous, thought that if wore a red costume and cap, he would make an excellent Santa Claus. He was a large man, and heavy. His face was pale, and his skin remarkably smooth for a man who must be well into his 80's. His full beard was as white ... well, just like Santa's, as white as snow. And from one end of the courtroom to the other I could see clearly that his eyes were a blue as bright as cobalt.

The men seated around him – about half his age, most of them, I suppose – made up his entourage. Like him, they wore the black hat and coat. Each had very dark hair, long curly-que sideburns, a dark and unkempt black beard. Each was thin, sallow, dark-eyed. Each seemed somehow uncomfortable, anxious, unwillingly present.

But not Rabbi Stein. He sat still and relaxed in his place, and although he was not smiling I couldn't shake the impression that he was about to smile, or even to laugh.

Of course it is not necessary to be Jewish, or to live in Miami, to have heard of Rabbi Chaim Stein. When the Dalai Lama was last in the United States he altered his itinerary to pay a visit to Rabbi Stein. They were closeted together for two or three hours, after which the Tibetan holy man told the press that Rabbi Stein was a blessed spirit, or something like that. Without ever leaving his modest home on Miami Beach, Stein has, over the decades, become a legend in religious circles, gentile as well as Jewish. His followers make extraordinary claims about his scholarship and his sanctity, and although most of us in the secular world discount those claims considerably, there is a mythology that has grown up around Rabbi Chaim Stein.

Zachary Taylor Davis was still standing, and he spoke again. "Rabbi Stein is the presiding judge of the *bes din* on Miami Beach, Your Honor." Davis was speaking slowly, articulating his words carefully, using his deep voice to maximum advantage. He would be calling a living legend to the witness stand, and he intended to make the most of it. "And as it happens, Rabbi Stein is also a survivor of Weeghman." Another wave of sound and motion rippled through the visitors' gallery; again the murmuring, the soft but furious tapping of reporters' fingers on cellphones or the scratching of pens on notepads, the shifting of weight and limbs.

I nodded at Davis, turned to Raul. "Mr. Santos, proceed with your witness."

But Zachary Davis was still standing. “Your Honor, before the witness is called, may we have a proffer of his testimony?” Davis was asking me to make Raul tell us what it is the witness would testify to.

“Why is that necessary, Mr. Davis?”

“Because I believe that I can demonstrate to the Court that this witness’s testimony should be excluded.”

This was a wrinkle I had not, could not have, anticipated. So I decided to break one of my own rules. “Counsel, let’s take a 15-minute recess and discuss this in chambers.” I addressed the audience in the visitors’ gallery. “Ladies and gentlemen, we are all eager to see this case move forward to a prompt and just conclusion. We will resolve this case by close of business today. At present, however, the best way for us to proceed is to take a short recess so that I can sort out certain technical matters with the lawyers in my chambers.” I stood, and the bailiff bellowed All Rise over the growing swell of sound in the gallery.

Some judges favor what are called “chambers conferences.” I do not. A judge’s chambers is a private place. A courtroom is a public place. The business that a judge does is the public’s business, and should be done in a public courtroom. Four centuries ago Sir Edward Coke, still perhaps the greatest figure in the history of the English law, made the same point when he complained that “judges are judges of courts and not of chambers.” When judges and lawyers huddle behind closed doors justice may be done, but it is not seen to be done. I could count on the fingers of one hand the number of chambers conferences I had permitted in all the years I sat in criminal court.

But I was not in criminal court, and Zachary Davis had thrown me a pitch I wasn’t ready for. So in front of reporters from around the country and around the world, in front of a packed visitors’ gallery humming like a tuning fork with anticipation, I had left the bench no more than ten or 15 minutes after taking the bench. I had broken my rule and squirreled the lawyers off into chambers with me, to get up to who knew what kind of mischief. It was a lousy way to start the afternoon.

I didn't take my robe off, and I didn't even ask the lawyers if they wanted coffee. "Mr. Santos, can you briefly proffer the testimony of your witness?"

Raul made the best of a bad situation. "Certainly, Your Honor. Mr. Bilstein is a citizen of Israel, where he has resided since shortly after the close of the Second World War. He is originally from Austria, but during the war he was interned in Weeghman. He knew Ernst Adler. He can testify as an eye witness to the conditions in which Adler lived and worked, and to events at and after the time of the liberation of the concentration camp. He will testify that there were others in the camp who painted or drew, or who attempted to do so; and that the chaotic circumstances at and after the liberation of the camp were such that it would have been next to impossible for Adler's work to have been isolated and properly preserved. His testimony evidences our concern that some of what is included in Dr. Gumbiner's collection may not be Ernst Adler's work."

Raul was seated in one of the two chairs opposite my desk. There was a sofa along the wall, but the other lawyers from the Williams, Santos firm, rather than avail themselves of it, had chosen simply to stand behind Raul. The other chair was occupied not by Zachary Davis, but by his partner Aimee Arrants; Davis stood behind her. When Raul finished his proffer I asked Davis for the basis upon which he sought to exclude the witness's testimony, but it was Ms. Arrants who spoke.

"Your Honor, the Holtzman Museum has brought suit for equitable and declaratory relief claiming that Dr. Gumbiner is in breach of contract for failing to produce the Adler collection for examination and, subsequently, for display. If the Holtzman's suit raises a question of law, that question is for the Court; the contract is clear on its face and it is Your Honor's duty to construe it. If the Holtzman's lawsuit raises a dispute of fact, then by operation of the contract itself that dispute must be referred to the arbitrating body for resolution in the first instance.

"It appears from Mr. Santos's proffer that the witness Bilstein will be called to establish a dispute of fact. That is, he will be called to testify that the Adler collection may -- or may not -- be inauthentic in part. But this is not the forum for such testimony. Given the existence of a dispute of fact – something that the plaintiff's desire to elicit Mr. Bilstein's testimony virtually concedes – the forum for the resolution of that dispute is the arbitrating body. If and when the *bes din* convenes to hear this matter, Mr. Bilstein may testify before it.

"In other words, Your Honor, Mr. Bilstein's testimony before *this* Court at *this* time is wholly irrelevant, and serves only to illustrate the force of our position: that the Holtzman is entitled either to no relief at all, or at most to have this matter referred to arbitration as provided by the contract."

Aimee Arrants had spoken without notes. She had spoken with great force, in a very formal and organized style. I would have bet that she had worked her speech out and memorized it. She sat very still while she spoke, her posture as correct as her syntax, and she maintained eye contact with me throughout. When she stopped speaking it was clear that she was finished, not just out of breath or out of thoughts; and for a moment no one spoke at all.

Then Raul began again. "Judge, Mr. Bilstein has traveled here at great expense and inconvenience. The Court may have observed that he is ... I believe about 83 or 84 years of age, and in extremely poor health. He disobeyed doctor's orders to come here. He is very eager to testify. His testimony need not be lengthy, but I respectfully urge the Court to hear him. It would be wrong to turn him away, Your Honor."

I knew what was wrong with Raul's argument, and so did Ms. Arrants. "Your Honor, we have nothing but respect for the determination that Mr. Bilstein has shown in coming here to testify, and nothing but sympathy for the difficulties he has endured and continues to endure. But a witness's irrelevant testimony is not made relevant because the Court and counsel feel sorry for that witness."

She was right, of course. Perfectly right. Raul's argument was no argument at all. I probably should have excluded Mr. Bilstein's testimony as irrelevant. But then again, what harm was done by affording this desiccated old man a few minutes of the Court's time, a chance to make a record of his suffering before he passed beyond suffering? I was eager to move this hearing to a conclusion, but I could spare 20 or 30 minutes for Herman Bilstein along the way. There was no jury. I sat alone in judgment. I could receive Bilstein's testimony and then discount it, and neither Dr. Gumbiner nor his lawyers would be the worse for my having done so.

I looked at Ms. Arrants. "Your argument has a certain force to it, but I am going to deny your application to exclude this witness." I turned to Raul. "But please, Mr. Santos, let's keep the witness's testimony within the narrowest bounds of relevance. If the testimony becomes protracted I will reconsider my ruling." I stood and walked back to the courtroom, leaving the lawyers to follow.

The bailiff had, apparently, drifted off during the recess and there was no one to cry All Rise as I entered. Nobody in the visitors' gallery was seated; people stood in the aisles, moved about as much as the crush of bodies permitted, wandered into and out of the courtroom.

I banged the gavel a few times – in civil court they actually let you have gavels – and shouted, "Mr. Santos, please call your next witness." Raul, who does not like to raise his voice, was obliged to do so to announce that he called Herman Bilstein. But Bilstein, like the bailiff and some of the audience, had wandered off during the recess, no doubt in search of breathing room and a more comfortable place to sit. Raul whispered urgently to his two junior-most colleagues, who then elbowed their way out of the courtroom in search of Bilstein.

"Your Honor, my apologies. Mr. Bilstein must be out in the hallway. We'll have him here in just a moment."

I pounded the gavel a few more times. Where was that bailiff? "Ladies and gentlemen, kindly be seated and come to order. We cannot proceed until the courtroom is completely quiet." With no particular enthusiasm people shuffled to their seats and lowered their voices. "Ladies and gentlemen, I will not hesitate to clear the courtroom of anyone who cannot maintain absolute quiet during these proceedings." Another drop in the decibel levels, although absolute quiet was still a long way away. The bailiff appeared, stood to one side of the bench, and, by way of explanation for his tardiness, held an imaginary cigarette between the forefinger and middle finger of his right hand and rapidly moved the hand toward and away from his pursed lips: the universal sign for "I was taking a smoke break". I beckoned him. "Mr. ...." It was high time I knew his name. I looked at his name tag, which read "Bud Teachout." "Mr. Teachout, please see what you can do to restore order and quiet." He waded into the visitors' gallery, casting baleful glances at mumblers and whisperers.

A courtroom version of quiet – something very far from the absolute version, but good enough – finally settled upon us, and visitors had moved out of the aisles and into their seats, when Raul's two colleagues came bursting back into the courtroom. They whispered to Raul, who then stood and said very urgently, "Your Honor, may all counsel approach the bench?"

Unusually for Raul, he wasn't even waiting for an answer; he, and his colleagues, were moving toward me already. Zachary Davis and Aimee Arrants, not wanting to be left out of whatever was happening, joined them.

"Your Honor," said Raul, attempting to keep his voice to a controlled whisper, "please come with us at once."

This was preposterous. Lawyers do not approach the bench and invite judges to leave, to go with them, whether later or "at once." I looked at Raul, at Raul the unflappable, at Raul the courtly and composed, and saw something .... I picked up the gavel, brought it down with a loud, angry frustration, announced that "the Court will be in brief recess," and got up and left. I followed Raul and his colleagues out the front door of the courtroom, to the right down the corridor, past my chambers entrance into the stairwell.

A walker lay on the stairwell landing. Half a floor below, on another landing where the stairwell turned, lay Herman Bilstein. He was not moving. He was not breathing. He would never do either again.

In death he was not alone. A woman lay on her side, her upper body atop his, her legs on the stairs that led down from the landing. She was a black woman, heavy-set, younger than middle aged. I had a good view of her head, of where her skull had been bashed. I had the feeling that I recognized her, that I had seen her before; but many people say they get that feeling from the dead. Perhaps in death our differences are somehow diminished, our similarities enhanced.

I recall that after some time Raul started speaking. He was explaining that one of the junior attorneys whom he had dispatched to locate Bilstein – a young lawyer whom he had earlier introduced to me as Woodrow English; Raul gestured toward the young man to his left – had found the body. Mr. English, prior to law school, had served in the military and had received paramedic training. English had discovered Mr. Bilstein, and the woman. He had not moved the bodies, but he had confirmed that both were dead.

I nodded. Yes. Quite right. Bilstein was dead. He had survived Weeghman, and war, and the ravages of time. He had defied his doctors and flown halfway around the globe to give voice to what had happened a lifetime ago. He had outlived history itself, and he had died within minutes of making his last testament.

I looked at Woodrow English. He was so young, so very young and fit and alive. His white cotton dress shirt bloused and billowed out over his belt, because his waist was too trim to enable all the fabric to be tucked into his trousers. His face was unlined and unwrinkled, and his hair grew thick and full. Woodrow English's young manhood had been given to the service of his country, and to the service of the law. Herman Bilstein had had a young manhood, I suppose, but it was taken by Weeghman and was lost forever. It seemed almost cruel for Herman Bilstein's corpse to have been discovered, and pronounced a corpse, by Woodrow English. It seemed unfair. But then Herman Bilstein was past caring about unfairness.

"Mr. English," I said, "kindly go to my chambers and ask my secretary, Mrs. Escobar, to join us." And he left.

I wandered out of the stairwell and into the corridor. I leaned against a hand-truck half-filled with furniture. I glanced at it and noticed that it contained, among other odds and ends, half-a-dozen assorted ashtrays which were no doubt part of Floyd's daddy's collection. That, strangely, struck me as funny. It struck me as hysterical, really. I might even have started to laugh – I hope not – but at that moment Carmen and Woodrow English walked out of chambers. They marched very quickly down the corridor, past me and into the stairwell. I leaned against the wall, I think I closed my eyes. In a few moments Carmen had returned.

Her voice was very still and steady, and she looked at me very fixedly. She informed me that she had called building security, and that they were sending people who would preserve the scene until the police arrived. She had also called 911. Police and crime-scene personnel would be here promptly, and there was nothing for me to do. My presence, anyone's presence, would simply be in the way. I was to dismiss further proceedings in this matter till tomorrow, which would help get everyone out of here and out of the way. She would start coffee, and I should come into chambers and have a cup. If we had still been in the Gerstein Building she probably would have sent to Que Sera Sera's chambers for cookies.

For just a second, I said nothing. Then I asked, "Do you know who the woman is?"

Of course she knew. "Bootsie Weber." She paused, waiting for me to remember. Then she added, "Judge Waller's secretary." And she pointed up, because Judith Waller's chambers and courtroom were one floor above mine.

I took a deep breath and headed toward the courtroom. Once inside I walked straight to the bench, had a seat, and pounded two or three times. It occurred to me that I had done more gavel-pounding in a morning in civil court than I had done in a term and a half as a judge in criminal court, but that brilliant insight and a first-class postage stamp would do no more than get a letter mailed. "This matter is recessed until 10:00 tomorrow morning."

• • •

I have seen dead men. Of course I have seen dead men.

When I was a prosecutor in the State Attorney's Office I saw my share of dead men. From one homicide scene to another the activities of the cops, the crime scene techs, the medical examiners, remained pretty much the same; but the creative ways Miamians found to get themselves killed were unendingly original. I saw my share of dead men, and of dead women and children too.

If I saw my father dead, then he was the first dead man I ever saw. Strange as it seems, however, I cannot quite recall whether I saw him in death or not. I was very young when he died, and the adults in my world were eager to keep from me the fact – what they considered the shameful fact – of his suicide. Perhaps I saw him. I really don't remember.

For no particular reason I was seized with a desire to know more about Herman Bilstein, who had traveled around the world to my courtroom and then died on the stairwell landing just down the hall from my courtroom. I asked Carmen to see if Raul Santos was still in the corridor; and then, considering that it would never do to be seen speaking in chambers with only one side's lawyer in a case pending before me, I asked her to find both Raul and Zachary Davis. In a few minutes Carmen had them seated in the chairs opposite my desk, and was plying us with Cuban coffee.

We were all beyond small talk. A few minutes passed in silence. Then I asked Raul, "So ... how did you find Mr. Bilstein in the first place?"

"When Judge Kroh set this matter for an emergency hearing I had one of my young associates do an internet search. It's just amazing what these young lawyers can dig up on the internet." Apparently, Herman Bilstein was one of the amazing things that some young lawyer had dug up on the internet. "I believe Mr. Bilstein belonged to an organization of Holocaust survivors, and that the organization maintains a website. They send observers to political and legal events that commemorate or relate to the Holocaust. If I recall correctly, Mr. Bilstein had volunteered to be an observer at trials in Germany some years ago. In any event, when we contacted him and explained the circumstances he seemed eager to testify. We sent him a plane ticket, informed the airlines about his age and health, and ... well, that was it. He arrived yesterday morning, and one of my colleagues spent most of yesterday preparing him to testify."

"He spoke English?"

"Passably. Well enough."

I still didn't know much about Herman Bilstein, and it appeared that Raul Santos didn't really know much about him either.

It was then that Zachary Davis spoke. "Was he a man of faith?" he asked. Raul said he didn't know.

Was he a man of faith? The back row of my courtroom had been filled with religious men. They proclaimed their religion in their wardrobes, in their hairstyle, in their smallest mannerisms. Their lives were about nothing so much as about their relationships with God.

But Zachary Taylor Davis had not asked whether Herman Bilstein was a religious man, an Orthodox, observant man. He had asked if Herman Bilstein was a man of faith, a man possessed of a belief he would not abandon and upon which he was willing to act. The law is not about religion, but it is surely about faith. I have seen lawyers, young lawyers, come into the profession brimming with faith, possessed of the belief that justice would be done and would be seen to be done. But time and the realities of the justice system wear hard upon such a faith. Lawyers, older lawyers – and judges too – may find that they continue to observe the rites of a votary, but that they have ceased to worship in their hearts.

Was Herman Bilstein a man of faith? He had survived Weeghman and war. A lifetime later, as he teetered on the edge of the grave, he set out upon a journey that would prove to be fatal, propelled by a belief in ... what? What was it he so desperately needed to say or to do that justified the risk he took?

Those were my musings. I don't know what Raul or Zachary Davis were thinking, but no one was talking. People sometimes speak of an embarrassed silence, but the silence in which we sat was not embarrassing. It was just silence.

The silence was dispelled by the appearance in my doorway of a balding man with a gray mustache. He was an older man, not overweight but clearly no athlete. His clothing had the odds-and-ends look of the absent-minded professor. He was smiling, because he was glad to see me. And I was very glad to see him.

"Clark!"

"Hello, Doc. What ...." And I stopped. I had been about to ask a stupid question, such a very stupid question. What brings the chief medical examiner of Miami-Dade County to see a dead man? "Come in." I made introductions: Raul Santos, Zachary Taylor Davis, meet Dr. Stephenson Riggs.

Stephenson Riggs had been chief medical examiner for many years. He was nationally reputed as one of the pre-eminent figures in his field; *Time* magazine, or some such publication, had once referred to him as "the dean of the morgue." Jack Sheridan had expressed the same sentiment when he said to me, "Clark, Doc Riggs knows more about dead bodies than you did when you were single and dating."

Dr. Riggs took a seat on my couch – the only available real estate – and tugged rhythmically at his mustache. It was his nervous habit, as mine was making paper-clip chains. His mustache was steel-gray, very thick and carelessly overgrown. He answered the question I had almost asked. "You know perfectly well, Clark, that anytime someone dies who wasn't under medical care, it's the policy of our office to have one of the medical examiners show up at the scene." He paused, still tugging on his mustache. "How long have you been here in the high-rent district?"

"Civil court? I started today."

"Jesus. Some welcome you get."

I gestured toward Raul. "The male decedent was to be Mr. Santos's witness. He may be able to provide you with some information about him."

Riggs nodded. I thought he was going to say something, but when he didn't Raul spoke up. "We have Mr. Bilstein's personal information – address, telephone, that sort of thing – but almost nothing relating to his medical history. In any event, I suppose that when a man his age slips on the stairs there's not much for the medical examiner's office to do." Raul wanted no part of whatever sort of paperwork Dr. Riggs was obliged to fill out.

It wasn't really a question, but Riggs – who held some kind of associate professorship at the University of Miami Medical School and loved to teach – chose to answer it. "We'll perform an autopsy, as we would in any such case. The death, if not of natural causes, must be classified ...?" It was Dr. Riggs' teaching method of choice; he would begin a sentence, then turn to a student with an expression that made it clear that it was the student's responsibility to finish the sentence. When I was an assistant state attorney I had prosecuted perhaps half-a-dozen homicides in which Dr. Riggs had been my witness. Since I became a criminal court judge I had had him before me as a witness another dozen times or so. There were no medical students in my small office – just two civil lawyers, Dr. Riggs, and me. It was clear from his face that I was the student who was expected to finish the sentence.

"... as either a homicide, a suicide, or an accidental death." That got me a small smile and nod of approval.

Dr. Riggs was now in full teaching mode. He actually stood to address the little student body arrayed before him. "If a moving human head strikes a fixed object, as with a fall, then the resulting cerebral contusions will be more severe on the point of the brain that is ...?" He was looking at me, eyebrows arched to form question marks.

"... opposite from the site of impact."

Another nod of his head. "Such a contusion is described as ...?"

"Contrecoup."

"If, however, a stationary human head is struck by a moving object, as with a blow from a weapon, the cerebral damage will be more severe ...?"

"Beneath the area of impact."

More nodding. "Which we term ...?"

"Coup."

Dr. Riggs sat, pleased with my recitation. "You were always a quick study, Clark. If you hadn't decided to waste your talents on the bench we might even have made a pathologist out of you." A man doesn't get a compliment like that every day.

Zachary Taylor Davis and Raul Santos were both struggling, manfully but unsuccessfully, to look interested. The Chief Medical Examiner of Miami-Dade County and a sitting circuit judge before whom they had a pending case were engaged in a discussion of autopsies, and it would never do for them to look bored or disaffected. Bored they may not have been, but disaffected they surely were. A frail old man, believing that he had lived long enough to bear witness to injustices that only a dwindling few still remembered, had stepped into a stairwell for a moment of solitude and found that he had lived not quite long enough. It was a death that evoked in Zachary Davis and Raul Santos feelings ironic, tragic, fey. But to Dr. Stephenson Riggs, dean of the morgue, Herman Bilstein was simply an item of inventory.

Raul's feelings came to the surface. "Doctor, a man of very advanced age and very declining health traveled through half-a-dozen time zones to participate in an event that must have been a source of tremendous anxiety for him. I should never have let him come. I suppose it would have been surprising if he *hadn't* died. What autopsy findings do you expect? Why is an autopsy necessary?"

Riggs tugged his mustache and looked at Raul without expression. "I expect to find that a man who was old and sick and overtaxed fell down and died. And an autopsy is necessary, counsel, because the law says it is."

Raul, being Raul, apologized; but he did so coldly. Raul had asked nothing about Bootsie Weber. I suppose that was understandable; Herman Bilstein was to have been Raul's witness, and Raul may have felt a certain responsibility for his death. Perhaps it would make Raul a little less uncomfortable to believe that Bilstein -- given his age and health -- might just as well have fallen down half a flight of stairs at his home in Israel. But Bootsie Weber was dead too; and it was too much to ask of coincidence to suppose that she and Herman Bilstein had chosen the same stairwell and the same time to fall down and die. Our little coffee klatch had become awkward and unpleasant, and I wanted it over. "Gentlemen," I said, standing up, "I have business to be about, and I know that each of you does as well. I won't keep you any longer. This has been a difficult day for all of us." I walked all three men out of chambers, shook their hands, wished them well. As they departed I noticed that the hand-truck holding Floyd Kroh's personal effects had been moved. The hallway was, at last, empty.

There was the day's consolation. Judge Floyd Kroh Jr. had finally gotten his pipes and ashtrays.

• • •

Carmen waited a few minutes after my visitors had left and then brought coffee. It was American coffee, not espresso, but very strong and dark. She brought it in a mug, took a long sip from it before she put it on my desk, then she sat down.

Judith Waller had been a judge in criminal court when I was a prosecutor. She had worked very hard to become a judge, and was fairly well along in her career before she finally got promoted to the bench.

There are all kinds of reasons that lawyers want to become judges. Some lawyers are simply overwhelmed by the pressure of practicing law for a living and crave the regularity, the steady rhythm, of life on the bench. For some, of course, there is the prestige, the status. Even a lowly county judge gets to wear a robe and be addressed as "Your Honor." Lawyers will laugh at your jokes, and a man in a uniform will order a room full of people to rise when you enter. You'd be surprised how much some judges get out of that.

Judith had become a judge because the practice of law had lost meaning for her. That, too, is a common phenomenon. Law school, even with all its drudgery, has moments of pure inspiration. The highlights of hundreds of years of Anglo-American legal history are packed into six semesters, and the students leave believing that they will go forth and do good. What follows may be a couple of decades spent hunched over deliberately unintelligible documents, or listening to clients who are in trouble because they deserve to be. Judith had reached that point in her career at which she felt that she had never added her grain of sand to the edifice of the law, and that her only chance to do so was by becoming a judge. So, after much lobbying and struggling, she managed to become a judge. As hours spent on the bench turned into days, and months into years, she found no more meaning in the endless cantata of plea colloquies and sentencing hearings than she had found as a practicing lawyer.

At some point I think that Judith gave up. I don't mean that she stopped coming to work. She worked about the same hours as the rest of us. But she was just connecting the dots.

Lawyers actually liked appearing before her. Nothing upset her, because she really didn't care. If a lawyer or a litigant decided to pull down his pants, jump on the jury rail, and squawk like a chicken, her reaction would probably be nothing more strenuous than to mumble, "Let's move along, counsel." (Judith is a congenital mumbler, and the problem has gotten worse over the years. I know for a fact that lawyers refer to her behind her back as "Judge Mumbles" or "Judge Mutters.")

I hadn't seen Judith with any regularity since she transferred to civil court a couple of years ago. From what I heard, she took an even less enthusiastic interest in her civil cases than she had taken in her criminal cases. She spent most weeks counting down the days and hours from Monday to Friday, and most weekends on the boat that she and her husband own. During the summer, when it stays light very late, she sometimes found ways to adjourn court early so she could get out on the boat in the late afternoon.

Boots Weber was Judith's secretary, had been for some years now. She was well paired with Judith, because Bootsie was the most relentlessly cheerful, up-beat individual anyone had ever met or heard of. She was a black woman, born – if I recall correctly – in Jamaica, or perhaps in Miami to Jamaican parents. She was in her mid-thirties, maybe a little older. And she was, I felt sure, the reason that Carmen was sitting quietly in my office, staring down at my desk.

"Had you spoken to her recently?"

Carmen shook her head slightly, more an expression of frustration than an answer. "I was meaning to. We've been so busy with this Holtzman Museum case I haven't had a chance to talk to anybody."

"Any idea what she was doing in the stairwell?"

She shook her head again. This time it was an answer.

For a moment I said nothing. Then I asked, "That wasn't her real name, was it? Boots, Bootsie?" I didn't really care about her name, but I had a sense that Carmen wanted to be drawn out, wanted to find a place to begin talking.

"Boots. It was a family thing. She had a grandfather or great-grandfather or someone who was in the British army in the old days, and somehow her name got to be Boots. I don't know the whole story."

I tried again. "She wasn't married, was she?"

She shook her head. "Lots of brothers and sisters, they're all very close, but no husband. I think she was always waiting for some rich lawyer to come along and marry her. She was a sweetie-pie, but, you know ... *gordita*." Chubby. In a nice way. This was awkward for Carmen to say, because she herself is ... well, *gordita*.

"But everyone liked her. She was always smiling and laughing. She was enthusiastic about everything. Nothing made her sad, or anyway not for long. Energy, she had so much energy. That's how I remember her, going a mile a minute." She sighed and stood up. "That's how I remember her."

Carmen had delivered her eulogy. She had said it, not because I needed to hear it, but because she needed to say it. And having nothing else she needed to say, she went back to her desk.

• • •

Carmen, who normally leaves work at five o'clock, didn't get out till quarter to six. Her hair and make-up were in a sorry state, and when she got home she'd probably need the jaws of life to remove her high-heeled shoes, but she had succeeded in imposing her notions of order on our chambers and everything in it. I stayed till one minute after six. I had received stacks of memoranda and documents from both law offices. I stuffed everything into my trial bag as best I could – duplicate copies of pleadings and documents the originals of which were no doubt in a court file that would be found somewhere, someday – and in a few minutes I was on the Julia Tuttle Causeway heading east, with the sun setting behind me. The causeway arches across Biscayne Bay, linking the City of Miami to Miami Beach. Its steep incline blocks the sight of the clustered spires of Miami Beach's condos and office towers. Until you crest the highest elevation of the causeway and start to descend again there is a view only of sky above and sea all around, an extramundane solitude.

My cellphone rang. It was Kay, who of course had heard about what happened. I didn't ask her how she had heard, or what version she had heard. She asked if I was all right and I told her I was. She asked if I was headed home and I explained that I was headed to the hospital to visit a family member who'd had a heart attack. My God, she said, what a day you've had; and she asked if there was anything she could do. I told her that was very kind of her, that I'd be fine, I appreciated her call. She understood without being told that I didn't feel very chatty. Love to Miriam, she said.

My grandfather or great-grandfather – the family history has always been sketchy on this point – immigrated from somewhere in Eastern Europe, aiming for Chicago. He overshot by the width of the state of Illinois, settling in Elgin. Somewhere along the way he passed by, or through, a little town called Addison, and took that as a portent. The family name was Americanized from Adelstein to Addison, and so it remains. I was born in Elgin, but have lived in Miami since childhood.

I never quite figured out where Uncle Billy first came into the picture. I know that he is not truly my uncle. As far as I can tell he and my father were friends in Illinois and later reconnected in Miami. When my father died Uncle Billy became the closest thing to a father figure in my life. My first job was working after school as a stock boy in his clothing shop. It was a good job.

That Monday I found him in the cardiac care unit at Mt. Sinai Hospital. He had fallen into a light sleep and his breathing, I was relieved to see, was rhythmic and not strained. He was wearing one of those ridiculous hospital gowns, and an oxygen tube was affixed below his nose. This skin of his face and arms was chalky and pallid.

I sat in the one chair that was available, pulled out some of the files -- should I have left them in the car? -- that the attorneys had delivered to my chambers, and began to leaf through them. As a strictly legal matter the case was less complicated and frightening than I had first supposed. At issue was something as indefinable as the concept of artistic beauty and as concrete as one hundred million dollars. Whether the individual works that make up the Adler collection are good or beautiful according to someone's notion of goodness or beauty is a consideration, but a secondary consideration. If a given piece was done by Adler while he was at Weeghman, it is authentic. And if it is authentic, it is valuable. If a given piece was done by the prisoner next to Adler; or by a camp guard who beat the prisoner next to Adler; or by the man who delivered bread to the camp guards; or by the wife of the man who delivered bread to the camp guards; then it is not authentic. And if it is not authentic, it is not valuable however good or beautiful it might be. *Holtzman Museum v. Gumbiner* was not about whether the Adler collection possessed artistic beauty, or even whether such a thing as artistic beauty exists. It was about contractual rights to determine the authenticity of some things which, if authentic, were worth millions of dollars; and which, if not authentic, were worth nothing. One of the legal memoranda submitted by the Williams, Santos firm included a quotation from Picasso:

> *And for a painter fame means selling, making money, making a fortune, growing wealthy. So today, as you know, I am famous and I am rich. But when I am quite alone I have not the courage to think of myself as an artist in the ancient, splendid sense of the word. Giotto and Titian, Rembrandt and Goya, were true painters; I am only a public entertainer who has understood his times and to the utmost of his powers has exploited the silliness, the vanity, and the stupidity of his contemporaries. Mine is a bitter confession, more painful than it may seem; but it has the merit of being sincere.*

I know little about art, but reading those words I wondered how different a lawyer's or judge's role is from the one Picasso claimed to be playing. I am a judge, respected and re-elected. But more often than not I have not the courage to think of myself as a judge "in the ancient, splendid sense of the word," a judge who adds a grain of sand or more to the edifice of justice. More often than not, are our courts places of public entertainment rather than public justice? Do I occupy the bench and wear the robe only as a consequence of the silliness, the vanity, and the stupidity of my contemporaries?

It was, at least initially, a dismaying thought. Then again, if I was no worse off than Picasso, I wasn't so bad off, was I?

Billy took a deep breath, smacked his lips a few times, stirred. He turned his head toward me and gave me ... well, if not a smile then at least a look of recognition. If Billy was feeling impish he would address me as "Young Adelstein" or "Your Honor," but on this occasion he whispered the word "Clark" and let it go at that. I walked to his bedside and placed my hands lightly on his left forearm.

"How's business?"

"The *schmatte* business isn't what it used to be."

It was the beginning of every conversation I ever remember having with Billy. The only word I know in Yiddish is *schmatte*, rag. The *schmatte* business is the apparel business. Billy still puts in a long week at Antibes Men's Wear, First with the Finer Things of Fashion, in the lower lobby of the Antibes Hotel. He did until today.

"Maybe it's time to get out of the *schmatte* business."

He made a face, or tried to. "And do what? They're talking about closing Hialeah, you know. Gulfstream and Calder are all right, but they're not Hialeah." Billy's only leisure time activity, as far as I or anyone else knew, was the horses. "Move up to Boynton Beach and play shuffleboard?"

The answer to that was yes, you should move up to Boynton Beach and play shuffleboard, but now wasn't the time for that answer. "How are they treating you here?"

"Do you like Jell-O?"

Do I like Jell-O? "Well ...."

He didn't wait for the answer I didn't have. "Because if you like Jell-O, you'll love this place."

If he was complaining about the food he couldn't be in such bad shape, so I went along with him. "What flavor Jell-O?"

"Yellow. Orange. Green. A lot of green."

"Those are colors. They aren't flavors."

"You don't know how right you are." He was entitled to a courtesy laugh for that and I gave it to him. He was either very brave or not very ill or both. Having gotten his laugh, he moved on to one of his favorite questions: "So how are the criminals these days?"

Billy had always followed my legal career with a passionate interest, plying me with questions about the smallest details of every case. The day I became a judge was one of the biggest days of his life, but I had always sensed a little disappointment on his part that I was a judge in criminal court, not civil court. To Billy, criminal court judges decided the fate of criminals; civil court judges decided the fate of captains of industry, or at least of ordinary folks. He never came right out and said it, but I think Billy viewed criminal law as the service entrance to the edifice of Justice. If that was true, I had some good news for him. "No more criminals. I'm in civil court now."

I had done my good deed for the day. A tired old man with a tired old heart became – if only briefly – a happy old man with a happy old heart. He tried to pepper me with questions about the case over which I was presiding, but I didn't want him to wear himself out; in the few minutes that we had been chatting his voice had become a little raspy and breathing seemed to be more difficult than it had at first. So I launched into a narrative of the day's events, making no mention of the deaths of Boots Weber and Herman Bilstein but talking as much as I could about the case, occasionally patting him on the forearm to assure him that yes, he would get all the details, he needed to do no more than listen.

Listen he did, and intently. The effort seemed tiring for him, and toward the end of my narrative I thought that he was close to lapsing back to sleep. But when it was clear that I had no more to tell, he asked, "So, how do you like civil?"

"I don't know. It's much too soon to say."

"And why did you go there?" He paused. "Did you tell me that already?"

Yes, I had, but it didn't matter. "I'm hoping to apply for a federal judgeship. My application will be stronger if I've spent some time in civil court, learning that area of the law."

It was an answer that pleased Billy very much. "There's an old Jewish saying: Seek the company of those who are searching for truth, and avoid the company of those who have found it."

"That's an old Jewish saying?"

"All the old Jews say it." He was still holding up his end of the chatter. "So, these paintings, drawings, whatever they are. Are they the real thing? Did this guy Adler do them?"

"At this point I have no idea. Are you ready to get some rest?"

"Wait, not yet. How much is the whole thing worth, you said? Maybe a hundred million?" I nodded. Billy looked down and spent a few seconds fidgeting with the light blanket that covered him. "I never heard of Adler."

"Very few people have. I'm not sure I had ever heard of him till this morning."

Then Billy asked a strange question. "Where's he buried?"

Where's he buried? "I have no idea."

"I'll bet that's another one very few people know. He probably ended up in some unmarked, untended grave somewhere, decades ago, and now his stuff is going to be worth millions and millions. Justice, huh?"

I smiled. "There's an old saying in the law: The wheel of justice grinds slowly, but it grinds exceedingly fine."

"That's an old judge's saying?"

"All the old judges say it."

Billy wasn't up to a courtesy laugh, but he gave me a courtesy smile. Then he asked, "So is it true?"

"Is what true?"

"Your old saying. What you said, you know, that eventually in the end the wheel of justice comes rolling around, or whatever it was."

I shrugged. "I don't know."

Billy didn't like that answer. I was a judge, and in matters of justice he expected me to *know*. "What do you believe?" he asked.

I looked at my watch. It was late, and I was tired. Did I believe that there was some kind of objective, absolute justice out there in the universe, some kind of system of moral checks and balances built right into the whole gizmo? That justice, in an ultimate sense, was out there waiting to be done, and all we had to do was give it a chance to manifest itself? Probably not. "I don't know."

Billy shook his head. "It isn't a question of knowing. It's a question of faith. What do you believe?"

I didn't know much about any absolute variety of justice, but a lifetime in the courts was not much of a tonic for faith in the man-made variety. "What do you believe, Billy?"

He shook his head again, more emphatically. I was upsetting him. "What I believe doesn't matter. You're a judge.

What you believe about justice matters. So, do you have faith in justice? That the wheels of justice will come around in the end, or whatever the old saying is?" His voice had become very raspy.

"I believe ..." I looked at my watch again, "that it's time for you to get some rest, and for me to get some work done." He started to protest. He had seen, briefly, a night without end; and he wanted to be told that there was always a morning, that the sunshine would come at its appointed time. "Billy, please. Please rest. I'll come back in the next couple of days, we'll talk more. But not now."

He sank back into his pillow, nodded, sighed. I was right, at least for the present. "Thanks for the visit."

I patted his forearm again and smiled confidently. As I walked out a nurse was bringing a tray in. It bore pills of various kinds, and a cup of green-flavored Jell-O.

CHAPTER FOUR
TUESDAY

Back in those days I used to invest 30 or 40 minutes in the morning studying the actual paper copy of the *Miami Herald*. A judge, after all, ought to know what's going on in the world and in his community. Apparently all that was going on in the world, and particularly in my community, was the hearing on *Holtzman Museum v. Gumbiner* and the deaths that occurred in the middle of that hearing. So I skipped the paper and ended up getting to work about a half-hour early that morning.

It was quiet in chambers, and when the phone rang there was no one to answer it but me. It was Kay. I know this not because she said, "Hello," or "Hi, it's Kay," but because I know her voice. What she actually said was, "*State versus Ivan Vukovich and The Wet Spot*." This is not her usual greeting, so something was on her mind.

State versus Ivan Vukovich and The Wet Spot is, of course, the name of a case. It was one of the dozens and dozens of criminal cases in my division at the time my division became Floyd Kroh's division. The Wet Spot is a very pricey strip club in Coco Isles Beach, and Ivan Vukovich is its owner.

The case isn't scheduled for trial for weeks, perhaps months. "The case isn't scheduled for trial for weeks, perhaps months. What about it?"

"Trial's starting."

"What? When?"

"Now. This week."

"But ... how? That's impossible."

"There's been a change of defense counsel."

"A change of defense counsel? But Jon Holland always represents The Wet. He represents all those places."

"He had to list himself as a witness, so he's conflicted off the case. The Wet has a new lawyer."

"Who?"

"Sammy the Weasel."

Silence. Dead silence. Neither of us spoke. And then I realized why Kay had called me to ask, or to talk, about a case called *State versus Ivan Vukovich and The Wet Spot*. She had not called because she was angry at me. She had not called because she was troubled or had questions that needed answering.

She had called to laugh.

It was not a mean laugh, or even a loud laugh. Kay is too nice for a mean laugh, and too well-bred for a loud laugh. But she has a very girlish giggle for a woman of her age and place in life, and she was giggling now. She was laughing. I thought about why she was laughing, and I laughed too.

If you're not laughing, it's because I haven't told this story very well. Permit me to explain.

When the Soviet Union was dissolving, a bunch of Russian mob types, or people who wanted to be thought of as Russian mob types, decided to relocate to Coco Isles Beach. Coco Isles Beach is a small municipality in northeast Miami-Dade County, and no one is too sure how the Russian mob picked it, but pick it they did. The Wet Spot is, judging by what I see in the papers and hear in the Gerstein Building, the cultural capital of the Russian mob community. Rough-looking characters, speaking scarcely a word of English, will stop passersby on the streets in Coco Isles Beach at night to ask, "Vet? Vet?" and the locals will point them to The Wet Spot.

The locals, of course, are not too crazy about this arrangement. They were not invited to the meeting at which the Russian mob decided to relocate to Coco Isles Beach, and they didn't get a vote.

So the village council passed a series of ever-more-restrictive ordinances regulating stripping and related activities within the village limits of Coco Isles Beach. The ordinances were cast in language of general applicability, but everyone understood that they were directed at The Wet Spot. Every now and again someone will claim that a provision of one of the ordinances has been violated, and a prosecution will be instituted.

When that happens, The Wet Spot will be represented by Jon Holland. The Wet Spot is always represented by Jon Holland. Every strip joint, dirty book store, and escort service in South Florida is represented by Jon Holland. If you ever own a strip joint, a dirty book store, or an escort service, you will want your lawyer to be Jon Holland.

Jonathan G. M. Holland is originally from Philadelphia, where the Hollands have lived since the dawn of time, and where the Holland men have always been lawyers. There is, according to Carmen (I never ask how she knows these things), still an old-line white-shoe law firm in Philadelphia that bears a name like Somebody, Somebody Else, Holland, Fergus, and Jenkins.

Somewhere in Bala Cynwyd, at the end of the Main Line, a graying dowager still inhabits the ancestral Holland home. But the bloodline will end with her, because Jon Holland is the black sheep of the family and the Hollands of Philadelphia do not speak to or about Jon. Jon did not join the family firm. Jon did not remain in Philadelphia but moved to (of all places!) Miami. Jon represents strippers, hookers, and smut-merchants.

And worst of all: Jon's having fun.

Ask Jon what he does for a living and he'll tell you that he's a First Amendment lawyer. It's not that he's ashamed to tell you who he represents and what he does; he describes himself as a First Amendment lawyer because that is really, truly, sincerely what he believes. The First Amendment protects freedom of expression, and as far as Jon is concerned the front lines in the war for First Amendment freedom are to be found in dirty bookstores and peepshows. Let them start banning books and exotic dancing, says Jon, and book burning won't be far behind. Remember, says Jon with real depth of feeling, that James Joyce's Ulysses, arguably the greatest novel of the 20th century, was banned in this country for years.

I have no idea what the governors of the Bank of England look like, but I'd bet that they try to look like Jon Holland. Jon carries himself with a great deal of dignity and gravitas, particularly in court. His speaking voice is low, steady, measured in cadence. He is a big man, six feet or close to it and heavier than he needs to be, much heavier. But his bulk never detracts from his appearance. He comes to trial wearing hand-tailored suits and hand-crafted shoes, suspenders rather than a belt, and when he wants to know the time he takes a gold pocket watch slowly and ostentatiously out of a trouser-pocket. His hair is carefully combed, his nails neatly manicured. You keep expecting him to announce that he's representing General Motors or Lloyd's of London, not The Wet Spot or Ladies of the Evening Deluxe Escort Service.

Jon has his own law firm. He keeps an associate or two, but never very long, because if they stayed very long they'd ask him to make them partners, and Jon does not want partners. Partners are what they had at Somebody, Somebody Else, Holland, Fergus, and Jenkins, and what they had there is what Jon doesn't want. So when he bellies up to the podium to announce his appearance, Jon states, "Jonathan G. M. Holland, of The Law Offices of Jonathan G. M. Holland, on behalf of Defendants Oswald P. Riggelman and Honest Oswald's XXX Adult Book World." Somehow, he almost makes it sound like he's representing General Motors or Lloyd's of London.

Of course Jon takes a lot of ribbing from other lawyers. They leer, they make gestures, they ask him how the girls are and tell him what a lucky dog he is and wink when they talk about the one kind of legal fee that Uncle Sam can't tax. Just to have something to complain about Jon will claim that hookers are damn difficult clients, that they're always slow pay, and that he has to charge big fees because the girls won't respect him if they get more money for a few hour's work than he does. These complaints get him no sympathy, but then he isn't really looking for any. There's a story that used to go around the Gerstein Building every once in while about how once upon a time Jon was cross-examining a cop and the cop was giving Jon a very tough time, fighting him on every question and answer. At some point during the cross, the judge decided it was time to give the jury a 15-minute recess. During the recess Jon took the cop into the hallway and whispered one sentence in his ear. The cop turned white. When the trial resumed every question Jon asked was answered with a very respectful, "Yes, sir" or "No, sir." Supposedly what Jon had whispered was, "I can see to it that you never get laid in this town again." And the cop knew that Jon could make good on it.

According to Kay, Jon Holland was somehow a witness in the case of *State v. Ivan Vukovich and The Wet Spot*. What Jon had witnessed was anybody's guess, but of course he couldn't be a witness and a lawyer at the same time. So Ivan Vukovich and The Wet Spot had gotten themselves another lawyer.

They had gotten Sammy the Weasel.

There are new lawyers and judges in the Gerstein Building who do not know Sammy the Weasel's surname. They may work for weeks or even months, seeing Sammy in court on a very regular basis, before his real name sticks with them. One of my fellow-judges – I won't say which one – must have been trying to keep too many things in mind at once when he looked over his half-glasses at Sammy and started to ask, "Yes, Mr. We ...." The judge turned red, his mind went into lock-down, and it was several painful, paralyzing seconds before the clerk of court slipped him a note on which she had written, "Samuel Manheim."

Samuel Manheim knows that other people call him Sammy the Weasel. He doesn't care. He calls other people much worse things than that, both in court and outside of it. He comes into a courtroom a few minutes after his musk-based aftershave does, his hair shiny with pomade, his cowboy boots shiny with polish, his heavy gold rings and wristwatch shiny with diamond baguettes. Let lawyers call him Sammy the Weasel. His clients love him. They love him for defying judges. They love him for defying prosecutors. They love him for defying good taste. And Sammy loves to defy all these things.

So Kay had called to tell me about Floyd Kroh's first day on the job. Floyd had hoped to get into being a criminal court judge as he might get into a hot bath: slowly and oh, so gingerly. Instead he was in for the Gerstein Building's version of fraternity hazing. He would preside over the trial of a strip joint. The witnesses would include exotic dancers (strippers always identify themselves in court as exotic dancers). There would be references to, and depictions of, body parts and sexual movements that were anatomically correct but oh my, very politically incorrect. Floyd would be without the soothing and stabilizing influence of Jon Holland's dignity, because Jon was no longer the lawyer in the case.

In Jon's place would be Sammy the Weasel, who was to dignity what Twinkies are to nutrition. And worst of all, Floyd had no idea what he was in for; because Floyd, having served only in civil court, had no idea who Sammy the Weasel was.

It was cruel of Kay and me to laugh. So we laughed for only a couple of minutes.

"But why does trial have to start this week?" I asked. The case, as I told Kay at the outset of our conversation, wasn't supposed to come up for trial for weeks at least.

"Jon and Sammy were in Floyd's courtroom" – my courtroom, but I didn't interrupt Kay to say so – "to move for substitution of counsel." Ordinarily a motion to substitute counsel is the simplest thing in the world. The lawyers tell the judge, Your Honor, Lawyer B is taking over for Lawyer A. The judge asks the client if that's his understanding, and if the client manages to nod his head, it's done. "The prosecutor on the case, Eleanor Hibbard, was there too. And you know how she and Sammy get along."

Eleanor T. Hibbard is the ranking prosecutor in my – well, Floyd's – courtroom. She has been a prosecutor since the day she left law school and will be a prosecutor till mandatory retirement catches up with her. She feels very strongly that the prosecutors are the good guys and everybody else is the bad guys. She is a physically large and imposing woman with a beautiful, radio-announcer voice. She isn't afraid to use her bulk, and she isn't afraid to raise her voice, in the pursuit of guilty verdicts. Jurors often find her intimidating. Judges sometimes do. Floyd almost certainly will.

Yes, I knew how she and Sammy get along. They make beautiful music together, like metal nails dragged across a blackboard. Sammy knows exactly where Eleanor's buttons are, and he loves to give them a push. He'll wait till the judge's attention is elsewhere, then whisper something quickly into Eleanor's ear. The something will be some kind of very crude reference to her weight or size, and after he's said it Sammy will treat himself to a big laugh. Too often Eleanor will lose all composure, which of course is just what Sammy wants. "Yes, I know how they get along," I said. "What was it this time?"

"Well, I wasn't there," said Kay, "but I can guess. So can you. While Floyd was granting the motion substituting Sammy for Jon as defendants' counsel, Sammy whispered something brilliantly witty, like 'Caution, wide load,' and things went downhill from there. Sammy dared Eleanor to try the case today, and Eleanor said how about right now, and Floyd ... oh, I don't know, Floyd probably hid under his chair for a while. Anyway, they're starting trial."

"What are you going to do?"

"Me? Well, tonight I'm going to bake sugar cookies and drop them off in Floyd's chambers tomorrow morning. After that he's pretty much on his own. If I have a chance I'll sneak into the public gallery and watch some of the trial, but I can't do more than watch."

Poor Floyd. "Poor Floyd."

Kay sighed. "Look, Clark, in a way it's for the best. In a way ... in a way this is the perfect case for Floyd to cut his teeth on. Really, what's the worst that can happen? If Vukovich and The Wet are acquitted, they'll be charged with something else sometime soon. And if they're convicted, it's not like Floyd can put The Wet in jail or sentence it to the electric chair. He'll put the defendants on probation, and if that's wrong the court of appeal can figure out why."

"Floyd might like putting a strip joint on probation. It'll give him a good story to tell his friends, and come election time he can pass himself off as a champion of public morality." I was musing aloud. I may even have chuckled aloud.

Kay told me she was glad she could start my day with a laugh, and I told her I was glad too, and we hung up. Yesterday I transferred to civil court, Uncle Billy had a heart attack, and two people died in the stairwell outside my courtroom. But in the justice system in Miami you take your laughs when you can get them.

Carmen must have arrived, because I heard some kind of racket coming from her end of my chambers suite. It wasn't the usual sounds of someone settling into work, so I walked out to investigate.

Standing next to her desk was Carmen. Standing immediately before her was a man whom she alternately embraced, then punched, then embraced, then punched. The punches were delivered to the man's shoulders, more a closed-fist slap than a real punch, not likely to do any harm. The hugging, however, was done with enough enthusiasm to be life-threatening. Throughout this process, Carmen was cursing in at least two languages. "... for two years *y pico,* you *pendejo*, you cockroach, and we didn't know if you were alive or dead, not that I care, *anormal, imbecil ...*" and more to the like effect.

Blackjack Sheridan was back in town.

I stood quietly in the doorway for a few seconds until Carmen noticed me. She immediately stopped beating Jack – I will be able to brag for years that I saved his life – and Jack turned to see what had captured her attention. He smiled at me. "Good morning, Judge."

"Well, well, well. I told Carmen if you ever came back to give you a sound thrashing. Has she carried out my instructions?"

"I'm in the process of being thrashed. Soundly"

"Spare a minute to have some coffee with me?"

Jack stroked his chin, as if the matter required serious consideration. "I hate to cut such a sound thrashing short, but ... well, you *are* the judge." I headed toward my private office, Jack following.

I had a seat at my desk and Jack took one of the chairs in front of it. He hooked a leg over a chair arm, looked around for a moment and commented, "You're getting up in the world, Clark. Civil courthouse, nice new chambers."

"Thanks. How's the shoulder?" He was rubbing where Carmen had been punching.

"I'll be sore tomorrow. I don't heal as well as I did when I was drinking."

We both smiled, and for just a minute no one said anything. I would have asked Carmen for coffee, but in the circumstances .... "So, what brings you to town, Jack?"

"Miriam."

"Miriam ...?"

"Miriam. Your wife. The lady who lets you sleep in her bed."

Miriam had never, ever approved of Jack. "Miriam ...?"

"Telephoned. She told me about Uncle Billy." Oh. Miriam had telephoned Jack and told him about Uncle Billy. "I think she just wanted me to give you a call. When I told her that I'd drive up, she didn't exactly offer to roll out the red carpet." Jack smiled; he knew that Miriam considered him the bad boy I shouldn't hang around with after school. "But here I am." Here *ah em*. "How are you, Clark? How's Billy?"

"I'm fine. He's ...." I told him about my visit last night. Jack asked a few questions, then sat silently. In the silence I began to unpack my trial bag, stacking documents from *Holtzman Museum v. Gumbiner* on my desk.

That, of course, prompted Jack to ask about the case. I gave him a detailed account of yesterday's hearing. He listened carefully, nodding his attention from time to time. When it was clear that I was finished, he asked to be remembered to Raul

Santos. Then, after a moment's reflection, he had a little story of his own to tell. "Way back before our time, I suppose in the '50's, a man named Sam Phillips owned a music company, maybe in Nashville or Memphis, called Sun Records. One day a skinny young fellow and his wife walk into Sun Records, hand Mr. Phillips a song -- words and music and all -- and tell him that the skinny young fellow wrote the song. Phillips looks the song over, and you know what he says? He says he's going to take the skinny fellow's wife downstairs to the coffee shop, and that it will take them about 45 minutes to have their coffee. He tells the skinny fellow that in the meantime, he's to write a song – words and music and all – about seeing an old flame and realizing that he's still in love with her.

"Well, naturally the young fellow and his wife want to know what in the wide world Phillips is talking about. So Phillips says, 'Son, I don't know you and you don't know me. You say you wrote that sheet music there and maybe I believe you. But if you could write a song as good as that one, you can write another one in 45 minutes.' And off he goes.

"When he comes back 45 minutes later, the skinny young fellow sings him a song. The song is called 'I can't help it if I'm still in love with you,' the skinny kid is named Hank Williams, and the sheet music is for 'Your cheatin' heart.'" Jack paused, then asked, "You *do* know who Hank Williams was, don't you, Clark?"

"I sure-enough do, partner. Is that a true story?"

That got me the good Blackjack smile. "You know what Al Guerrero would say."

Al Guerrero is another of Miami's legendary criminal defense attorneys, and I did know what he would say. "All my stories are true – especially the ones I make up." Jack smiled his agreement. "It's a good story, Jack, but it won't help me." I had picked up a couple of paper clips, not enough to build a chain, and I was fiddling with them. "I wish I could ask Ernst Adler to paint something for me. I wish I could ask him what to do with this mess. I wish I could, but I can't." I looked at my wristwatch absentmindedly. I hadn't meant it as a sign to Jack that I needed him to go, but I guess that he took it as one because he stood to leave. "Do you have a place to stay, Jack?" I asked.

"I still own my house on Bayshore. I never sold it."

"How long will you be in town?"

He ran a hand through his hair. "Well, maybe I'll go with you to see Billy in the next couple of days. So then I might as well stay for the Ace High Bar Association meeting on Friday."

So Jack's visit to Miami was not entirely a mission of mercy. Some years earlier, at the height of the cocaine gold rush in Miami, the top criminal lawyers in town had gotten in the habit of turning up at Al Guerrero's plush offices late Friday afternoon for drinks, a bull session, and a poker game. In time, this weekly smoker came to be referred to by the participants as the Ace High Bar Association. Membership in the Ace High Bar Association was as coveted as it was restricted. No lawyer could simply show up; he had to be invited. An invitation was the highest honor the criminal defense bar could convey to one of its own, the criminal lawyer's equivalent to the *croix de guerre*. Any young, up-and-coming lawyer who had a big, high-profile trial victory would race back to his office, hoping the call would come inviting him to this Friday's game.

The players were some of the most recklessly competitive human beings on earth, but the game was not about the money. On the contrary; Al had set dollar limits on bets years ago and never increased them. The winner didn't even get to keep his winnings. It was an invariable rule of the Ace High Bar Association that all winnings were promptly given to a charity, the choice of charity being the winner's privilege. Over the years the Ace High Bar Association had probably raised tens of thousands of dollars for the ACLU, a particular favorite. When Jack won, the money went – appropriately enough – to a home for wayward girls, so long as it could be shown that there really was a home for wayward girls and that it wasn't actually a whorehouse.

I, of course, have never been permitted even a glimpse into the meetings of the Ace High Bar Association. Playing poker with a mere judge would be considered beneath the dignity of a great criminal defense attorney.

Jack and I shook hands and said goodbye. I was making a pile of the pleadings and notes that I would take into the courtroom with me when I looked up to see him still in my doorway. "Clark, there's one thing I didn't quite understand about that case of yours."

"What's that?"

"I know that most commercial contracts have arbitration clauses in them, but that business about a ... what did you call it, that panel of rabbis?"

"A *bes din*. A rabbinic court."

"Yeah. Whose goofy idea was that?"

"Pardon?"

"Who came up with that fool idea? Which side wrote it into the contract, the doctor or the museum?"

I thought about it for a minute. I had no idea. "I have no idea."

Jack shrugged. "Well ... well, hell, it probably doesn't make a dime's worth of difference. What do I know about contract law anyway?"

About as much as I do, I thought. But he was gone.

Back in those days I used to invest 30 or 40 minutes in the morning studying the actual paper copy of the *Miami Herald*. A judge, after all, ought to know what's going on in the world and in his community. Apparently all that was going on in the world, and particularly in my community, was the hearing on *Holtzman Museum v. Gumbiner* and the deaths that occurred in the middle of that hearing. So I skipped the paper and ended up getting to work about a half-hour early that morning.

It was quiet in chambers, and when the phone rang there was no one to answer it but me. It was Kay. I know this not because she said, "Hello," or "Hi, it's Kay," but because I know her voice. What she actually said was, *"State versus Ivan Vukovich and The Wet Spot."* This is not her usual greeting, so something was on her mind.

State versus Ivan Vukovich and The Wet Spot is, of course, the name of a case. It was one of the dozens and dozens of criminal cases in my division at the time my division became Floyd Kroh's division. The Wet Spot is a very pricey strip club in Coco Isles Beach, and Ivan Vukovich is its owner.

The case isn't scheduled for trial for weeks, perhaps months. "The case isn't scheduled for trial for weeks, perhaps months. What about it?"

"Trial's starting."

"What? When?"

"Now. This week."

"But ... how? That's impossible."

"There's been a change of defense counsel."

"A change of defense counsel? But Jon Holland always represents The Wet. He represents all those places."

"He had to list himself as a witness, so he's conflicted off the case. The Wet has a new lawyer."

"Who?"

"Sammy the Weasel."

Silence. Dead silence. Neither of us spoke. And then I realized why Kay had called me to ask, or to talk, about a case called

State versus Ivan Vukovich and The Wet Spot. She had not called because she was angry at me. She had not called because she was troubled or had questions that needed answering.

She had called to laugh.

It was not a mean laugh, or even a loud laugh. Kay is too nice for a mean laugh, and too well-bred for a loud laugh. But she has a very girlish giggle for a woman of her age and place in life, and she was giggling now. She was laughing. I thought about why she was laughing, and I laughed too.

If you're not laughing, it's because I haven't told this story very well. Permit me to explain.

When the Soviet Union was dissolving, a bunch of Russian mob types, or people who wanted to be thought of as Russian mob types, decided to relocate to Coco Isles Beach. Coco Isles Beach is a small municipality in northeast Miami-Dade County, and no one is too sure how the Russian mob picked it, but pick it they did. The Wet Spot is, judging by what I see in the papers and hear in the Gerstein Building, the cultural capital of the Russian mob community. Rough-looking characters, speaking scarcely a word of English, will stop passersby on the streets in Coco Isles Beach at night to ask, "Vet? Vet?" and the locals will point them to The Wet Spot.

The locals, of course, are not too crazy about this arrangement. They were not invited to the meeting at which the Russian mob decided to relocate to Coco Isles Beach, and they didn't get a vote.

So the village council passed a series of ever-more-restrictive ordinances regulating stripping and related activities within the village limits of Coco Isles Beach. The ordinances were cast in language of general applicability, but everyone understood that they were directed at The Wet Spot. Every now and again someone will claim that a provision of one of the ordinances has been violated, and a prosecution will be instituted.

When that happens, The Wet Spot will be represented by Jon Holland. The Wet Spot is always represented by Jon Holland. Every strip joint, dirty book store, and escort service in South Florida is represented by Jon Holland. If you ever own a strip joint, a dirty book store, or an escort service, you will want your lawyer to be Jon Holland.

Jonathan G. M. Holland is originally from Philadelphia, where the Hollands have lived since the dawn of time, and where the Holland men have always been lawyers. There is, according to Carmen (I never ask how she knows these things), still an old-line white-shoe law firm in Philadelphia that bears a name like Somebody, Somebody Else, Holland, Fergus, and Jenkins. Somewhere in Bala Cynwyd, at the end of the Main Line, a graying dowager still inhabits the ancestral Holland home. But the bloodline will end with her, because Jon Holland is the black sheep of the family and the Hollands of Philadelphia do not speak to or about Jon. Jon did not join the family firm. Jon did not remain in Philadelphia but moved to (of all places!) Miami. Jon represents strippers, hookers, and smut-merchants.

And worst of all: Jon's having fun.

Ask Jon what he does for a living and he'll tell you that he's a First Amendment lawyer. It's not that he's ashamed to tell you who he represents and what he does; he describes himself as a First Amendment lawyer because that is really, truly, sincerely what he believes. The First Amendment protects freedom of expression, and as far as Jon is concerned the front lines in the war for First Amendment freedom are to be found in dirty bookstores and peepshows. Let them start banning books and exotic dancing, says Jon, and book burning won't be far behind. Remember, says Jon with real depth of feeling, that James Joyce's Ulysses, arguably the greatest novel of the 20th century, was banned in this country for years.

I have no idea what the governors of the Bank of England look like, but I'd bet that they try to look like Jon Holland. Jon carries himself with a great deal of dignity and gravitas, particularly in court. His speaking voice is low, steady, measured in cadence. He is a big man, six feet or close to it and heavier than he needs to be, much heavier. But his bulk never detracts from his appearance. He comes to trial wearing hand-tailored suits and hand-crafted shoes, suspenders rather than a belt, and when he wants to know the time he takes a gold pocket watch slowly and ostentatiously out of a trouser-pocket. His hair is carefully combed, his nails neatly manicured. You keep expecting him to announce that he's representing General Motors or Lloyd's of London, not The Wet Spot or Ladies of the Evening Deluxe Escort Service.

Jon has his own law firm. He keeps an associate or two, but never very long, because if they stayed very long they'd ask him to make them partners, and Jon does not want partners. Partners are what they had at Somebody, Somebody Else, Holland, Fergus, and Jenkins, and what they had there is what Jon doesn't want. So when he bellies up to the podium to announce his appearance, Jon states, "Jonathan G. M. Holland, of The Law Offices of Jonathan G. M. Holland, on behalf of Defendants Oswald P. Riggelman and Honest Oswald's XXX Adult Book World." Somehow, he almost makes it sound like he's representing General Motors or Lloyd's of London.

Of course Jon takes a lot of ribbing from other lawyers. They leer, they make gestures, they ask him how the girls are and tell him what a lucky dog he is and wink when they talk about the one kind of legal fee that Uncle Sam can't tax. Just to have something to complain about Jon will claim that hookers are damn difficult clients, that they're always slow pay, and that he has to charge big fees because the girls won't respect him if they get more money for a few hour's work than he does. These complaints get him no sympathy, but then he isn't really looking for any. There's a story that used to go around the Gerstein Building every once in while about how once upon a time Jon was cross-examining a cop and the cop was giving Jon a very tough time, fighting him on every question and answer. At some point during the cross, the judge decided it was time to give the jury a 15-minute recess. During the recess Jon took the cop into the hallway and whispered one sentence in his ear. The cop turned white. When the trial resumed every question Jon asked was answered with a very respectful, "Yes, sir" or "No, sir." Supposedly what Jon had whispered was, "I can see to it that you never get laid in this town again." And the cop knew that Jon could make good on it.

According to Kay, Jon Holland was somehow a witness in the case of *State v. Ivan Vukovich and The Wet Spot*. What Jon had witnessed was anybody's guess, but of course he couldn't be a witness and a lawyer at the same time. So Ivan Vukovich and The Wet Spot had gotten themselves another lawyer.

They had gotten Sammy the Weasel.

There are new lawyers and judges in the Gerstein Building who do not know Sammy the Weasel's surname. They may work for weeks or even months, seeing Sammy in court on a very regular basis, before his real name sticks with them. One of my fellow-judges – I won't say which one – must have been trying to keep too many things in mind at once when he looked over his half-glasses at Sammy and started to ask, "Yes, Mr. We ...." The judge turned red, his mind went into lock-down, and it was several painful, paralyzing seconds before the clerk of court slipped him a note on which she had written, "Samuel Manheim."

Samuel Manheim knows that other people call him Sammy the Weasel. He doesn't care. He calls other people much worse things than that, both in court and outside of it. He comes into a courtroom a few minutes after his musk-based aftershave does, his hair shiny with pomade, his cowboy boots shiny with polish, his heavy gold rings and wristwatch shiny with diamond baguettes. Let lawyers call him Sammy the Weasel. His clients love him. They love him for defying judges. They love him for defying prosecutors. They love him for defying good taste. And Sammy loves to defy all these things.

So Kay had called to tell me about Floyd Kroh's first day on the job. Floyd had hoped to get into being a criminal court judge as he might get into a hot bath: slowly and oh, so gingerly. Instead he was in for the Gerstein Building's version of fraternity hazing. He would preside over the trial of a strip joint. The witnesses would include exotic dancers (strippers always identify themselves in court as exotic dancers). There would be references to, and depictions of, body parts and sexual movements that were anatomically correct but oh my, very politically incorrect. Floyd would be without the soothing and stabilizing influence of Jon Holland's dignity, because Jon was no longer the lawyer in the case. In Jon's place would be Sammy the Weasel, who was to dignity what Twinkies are to nutrition. And worst of all, Floyd had no idea what he was in for; because Floyd, having served only in civil court, had no idea who Sammy the Weasel was.

It was cruel of Kay and me to laugh. So we laughed for only a couple of minutes.

"But why does trial have to start this week?" I asked. The case, as I told Kay at the outset of our conversation, wasn't supposed to come up for trial for weeks at least.

"Jon and Sammy were in Floyd's courtroom" – my courtroom, but I didn't interrupt Kay to say so – "to move for substitution of counsel." Ordinarily a motion to substitute counsel is the simplest thing in the world. The lawyers tell the judge, Your Honor, Lawyer B is taking over for Lawyer A. The judge asks the client if that's his understanding, and if the client manages to nod his head, it's done. "The prosecutor on the case, Eleanor Hibbard, was there too. And you know how she and Sammy get along."

Eleanor T. Hibbard is the ranking prosecutor in my – well, Floyd's – courtroom. She has been a prosecutor since the day she left law school and will be a prosecutor till mandatory retirement catches up with her. She feels very strongly that the prosecutors are the good guys and everybody else is the bad guys. She is a physically large and imposing woman with a beautiful, radio-announcer voice. She isn't afraid to use her bulk, and she isn't afraid to raise her voice, in the pursuit of guilty verdicts. Jurors often find her intimidating. Judges sometimes do. Floyd almost certainly will.

Yes, I knew how she and Sammy get along. They make beautiful music together, like metal nails dragged across a blackboard. Sammy knows exactly where Eleanor's buttons are, and he loves to give them a push. He'll wait till the judge's attention is elsewhere, then whisper something quickly into Eleanor's ear. The something will be some kind of very crude reference to her weight or size, and after he's said it Sammy will treat himself to a big laugh. Too often Eleanor will lose all composure, which of course is just what Sammy wants. "Yes, I know how they get along," I said. "What was it this time?"

"Well, I wasn't there," said Kay, "but I can guess. So can you. While Floyd was granting the motion substituting Sammy for Jon as defendants' counsel, Sammy whispered something brilliantly witty, like 'Caution, wide load,' and things went downhill from there. Sammy dared Eleanor to try the case today, and Eleanor said how about right now, and Floyd ... oh, I don't know, Floyd probably hid under his chair for a while. Anyway, they're starting trial."

"What are you going to do?"

"Me? Well, tonight I'm going to bake sugar cookies and drop them off in Floyd's chambers tomorrow morning. After that he's pretty much on his own. If I have a chance I'll sneak into the public gallery and watch some of the trial, but I can't do more than watch."

Poor Floyd. "Poor Floyd."

Kay sighed. "Look, Clark, in a way it's for the best. In a way ... in a way this is the perfect case for Floyd to cut his teeth on. Really, what's the worst that can happen? If Vukovich and The Wet are acquitted, they'll be charged with something else sometime soon. And if they're convicted, it's not like Floyd can put The Wet in jail or sentence it to the electric chair. He'll put the defendants on probation, and if that's wrong the court of appeal can figure out why."

"Floyd might like putting a strip joint on probation. It'll give him a good story to tell his friends, and come election time he can pass himself off as a champion of public morality." I was musing aloud. I may even have chuckled aloud.

Kay told me she was glad she could start my day with a laugh, and I told her I was glad too, and we hung up. Yesterday I transferred to civil court, Uncle Billy had a heart attack, and two people died in the stairwell outside my courtroom. But in the justice system in Miami you take your laughs when you can get them.

Carmen must have arrived, because I heard some kind of racket coming from her end of my chambers suite. It wasn't the usual sounds of someone settling into work, so I walked out to investigate.

Standing next to her desk was Carmen. Standing immediately before her was a man whom she alternately embraced, then punched, then embraced, then punched. The punches were delivered to the man's shoulders, more a closed-fist slap than a real punch, not likely to do any harm. The hugging, however, was done with enough enthusiasm to be life-threatening. Throughout this process, Carmen was cursing in at least two languages. "... for two years *y pico,* you *pendejo,* you cockroach, and we didn't know if you were alive or dead, not that I care, *anormal, imbecil* ..." and more to the like effect.

Blackjack Sheridan was back in town.

I stood quietly in the doorway for a few seconds until Carmen noticed me. She immediately stopped beating Jack – I will be able to brag for years that I saved his life – and Jack turned to see what had captured her attention. He smiled at me. "Good morning, Judge."

"Well, well, well. I told Carmen if you ever came back to give you a sound thrashing. Has she carried out my instructions?"

"I'm in the process of being thrashed. Soundly"

"Spare a minute to have some coffee with me?"

Jack stroked his chin, as if the matter required serious consideration. "I hate to cut such a sound thrashing short, but ... well, you *are* the judge." I headed toward my private office, Jack following.

I had a seat at my desk and Jack took one of the chairs in front of it. He hooked a leg over a chair arm, looked around for a moment and commented, "You're getting up in the world, Clark. Civil courthouse, nice new chambers."

"Thanks. How's the shoulder?" He was rubbing where Carmen had been punching.

"I'll be sore tomorrow. I don't heal as well as I did when I was drinking."

We both smiled, and for just a minute no one said anything. I would have asked Carmen for coffee, but in the circumstances .... "So, what brings you to town, Jack?"

"Miriam."

"Miriam ...?"

"Miriam. Your wife. The lady who lets you sleep in her bed."

Miriam had never, ever approved of Jack. "Miriam ...?"

"Telephoned. She told me about Uncle Billy." Oh. Miriam had telephoned Jack and told him about Uncle Billy. "I think she just wanted me to give you a call. When I told her that I'd drive up, she didn't exactly offer to roll out the red carpet." Jack smiled; he knew that Miriam considered him the bad boy I shouldn't hang around with after school. "But here I am." Here *ah em*. "How are you, Clark? How's Billy?"

"I'm fine. He's ...." I told him about my visit last night. Jack asked a few questions, then sat silently. In the silence I began to unpack my trial bag, stacking documents from *Holtzman Museum v. Gumbiner* on my desk.

That, of course, prompted Jack to ask about the case. I gave him a detailed account of yesterday's hearing. He listened carefully, nodding his attention from time to time. When it was clear that I was finished, he asked to be remembered to Raul Santos. Then, after a moment's reflection, he had a little story of his own to tell. "Way back before our time, I suppose in the '50's, a man named Sam Phillips owned a music company, maybe in Nashville or Memphis, called Sun Records. One day a skinny young fellow and his wife walk into Sun Records, hand Mr. Phillips a song -- words and music and all -- and tell him that the skinny young fellow wrote the song. Phillips looks the song over, and you know what he says? He says he's going to take the skinny fellow's wife downstairs to the coffee shop, and that it will take them about 45 minutes to have their coffee. He tells the skinny fellow that in the meantime, he's to write a song – words and music and all – about seeing an old flame and realizing that he's still in love with her.

"Well, naturally the young fellow and his wife want to know what in the wide world Phillips is talking about. So Phillips says, 'Son, I don't know you and you don't know me. You say you wrote that sheet music there and maybe I believe you. But if you could write a song as good as that one, you can write another one in 45 minutes.' And off he goes.

"When he comes back 45 minutes later, the skinny young fellow sings him a song. The song is called 'I can't help it if I'm still in love with you,' the skinny kid is named Hank Williams, and the sheet music is for 'Your cheatin' heart.'" Jack paused, then asked, "You *do* know who Hank Williams was, don't you, Clark?"

"I sure-enough do, partner. Is that a true story?"

That got me the good Blackjack smile. "You know what Al Guerrero would say."

Al Guerrero is another of Miami's legendary criminal defense attorneys, and I did know what he would say. "All my stories are true – especially the ones I make up." Jack smiled his agreement. "It's a good story, Jack, but it won't help me." I had picked up a couple of paper clips, not enough to build a chain, and I was fiddling with them. "I wish I could ask Ernst Adler to paint something for me. I wish I could ask him what to do with this mess. I wish I could, but I can't." I looked at my wristwatch absentmindedly. I hadn't meant it as a sign to Jack that I needed him to go, but I guess that he took it as one because he stood to leave. "Do you have a place to stay, Jack?" I asked.

"I still own my house on Bayshore. I never sold it."

"How long will you be in town?"

He ran a hand through his hair. "Well, maybe I'll go with you to see Billy in the next couple of days. So then I might as well stay for the Ace High Bar Association meeting on Friday."

So Jack's visit to Miami was not entirely a mission of mercy. Some years earlier, at the height of the cocaine gold rush in Miami, the top criminal lawyers in town had gotten in the habit of turning up at Al Guerrero's plush offices late Friday afternoon for drinks, a bull session, and a poker game. In time, this weekly smoker came to be referred to by the participants as the Ace High Bar Association. Membership in the Ace High Bar Association was as coveted as it was restricted. No lawyer could simply show up; he had to be invited. An invitation was the highest honor the criminal defense bar could convey to one of its own, the criminal lawyer's equivalent to the *croix de guerre*. Any young, up-and-coming lawyer who had a big, high-profile trial victory would race back to his office, hoping the call would come inviting him to this Friday's game.

The players were some of the most recklessly competitive human beings on earth, but the game was not about the money. On the contrary; Al had set dollar limits on bets years ago and never increased them. The winner didn't even get to keep his winnings. It was an invariable rule of the Ace High Bar Association that all winnings were promptly given to a charity, the choice of charity being the winner's privilege. Over the years the Ace High Bar Association had probably raised tens of thousands of dollars for the ACLU, a particular favorite. When Jack won, the money went – appropriately enough – to a home for wayward girls, so long as it could be shown that there really was a home for wayward girls and that it wasn't actually a whorehouse.

I, of course, have never been permitted even a glimpse into the meetings of the Ace High Bar Association. Playing poker with a mere judge would be considered beneath the dignity of a great criminal defense attorney.

Jack and I shook hands and said goodbye. I was making a pile of the pleadings and notes that I would take into the courtroom with me when I looked up to see him still in my doorway. "Clark, there's one thing I didn't quite understand about that case of yours."

"What's that?"

"I know that most commercial contracts have arbitration clauses in them, but that business about a ... what did you call it, that panel of rabbis?"

"A *bes din*. A rabbinic court."

"Yeah. Whose goofy idea was that?"

"Pardon?"

"Who came up with that fool idea? Which side wrote it into the contract, the doctor or the museum?"

I thought about it for a minute. I had no idea. "I have no idea."

Jack shrugged. "Well ... well, hell, it probably doesn't make a dime's worth of difference. What do I know about contract law anyway?"

About as much as I do, I thought. But he was gone.

• • •

Carmen tried to hand me phone messages from the New York Times, the London Times, *Le Monde*, *Corriere della Sera*, *Ha-Aretz*, and two German papers the names of which she wasn't sure about. I told her that however difficult it might be for her, I was sticking to the party line and I expected her to do the same: I could not, would not, comment on a case presently pending before me. I took the bench a couple of minutes before 10:00.

It seemed, somehow, that the courtroom was packed tighter than it had been yesterday. The thought had no sooner occurred to me than I dismissed it as impossible; every inch of the visitors' gallery had been filled yesterday. Yet there was something about the courtroom when I entered it, a sense that it was filled to bursting. I felt -- this seems so silly to say -- I felt like a cowboy watching a herd of cattle about to stampede.

I didn't wait for the bailiff to call for order. He wouldn't have gotten it, which would only have made matters worse. I gestured toward Raul, indicating that he should proceed with his next witness.

He stood. "I call Dr. Bernard Gumbiner."

I think that I managed to contain any reaction I felt to that announcement. In criminal court the prosecution cannot call the defendant as a witness. The defendant has an absolute right to refrain from testifying, and if he chooses to exercise that right the prosecution may not even comment to the jury about the defendant's failure to testify. But this was civil court, and Dr. Gumbiner was fair game. Raul could call him as a witness. And because Dr. Gumbiner was the adverse party, Raul could call him expressly to cross-examine him.

Gumbiner was, I suppose, not an old man. But he conveyed an impression of general ill-health: the skin of his face was pale, sallow, and sagged as if it fit him loosely. From what little I knew of him he was no doubt a man of great intelligence and scholarly interests, but he wore no expression at all, almost as if he were dazed or sleepy. He walked the few steps to the witness stand with no particular energy. The voice in which he took the oath was audible, but barely so.

Raul wasted no time. He approached the witness with the contract – Exhibit A to the museum's Complaint – and directed Dr. Gumbiner to the signature page at the end. "You recognize this contract, do you not, Doctor?"

"Yes."

"And you recognize your signature" – Raul pointed to it – "there?"

"Yes."

"And beneath your signature, the signatures of your lawyers?"

"Yes."

"At the time you signed this document, you intended to loan the Adler collection to the Holtzman Museum of Judaica?"

"Yes. And I still hope to do so."

"We'll get to the subject of hopes in due course, Doctor, but the fact is that you have *not* loaned the Adler collection to the Holtzman Museum, have you?"

"Through no fault of my own, I have not." The sickly-looking doctor was full of spunky answers.

"If I ask you to honor your contract and loan the Adler collection to the museum today, you won't do so, will you, doctor?"

"Not if the museum persists in its baseless insistence on an unnecessary and potentially damaging examination of priceless art treasures."

Raul had a good poker face, one of the best, but he seemed somehow pleased with the answer. "You object to what you term an unnecessary and potentially damaging examination?"

"Yes. I do."

"And that is the reason that you have failed to loan the Adler collection to the Holtzman – your objection to an unnecessary and potentially damaging examination?"

"Yes."

"If it were not for the unnecessary and potentially damaging examinations, you would have no objection to loaning the Adler collection to the Holtzman?"

"No."

"Let's talk first, sir, about the 'unnecessary' feature of these examinations. The Adler collection is presently kept in your home, isn't it?"

"Yes."

"You get many requests for permission to view the collection?"

"Yes."

"Requests from art critics, art collectors, art experts?"

"Yes."

"But it is not your practice to grant those requests, is it?"

"No."

"Other than to a few private friends, you have never displayed the Adler collection?"

"No."

"And you have never permitted any expert or art authority to see the collection?"

"Mr. Santos, if I started permitting one so-called art expert to see the Adler collection, I would have no basis not to permit every so-called art expert to see it. I see no reason for me to do so. I certainly don't intend to turn my home into a circus tent."

Raul looked troubled. "I apologize, Doctor. I did not intend to make the question unduly complex, and I'm very sorry if I have done so. What I meant to ask – and again, I'm sorry if I was unclear – is simply this." Raul slowed the pace of his speech, as if addressing someone possessed of limited English-language skills. "You have never permitted any art expert to see the Adler collection, have you?"

Different lawyers take different approaches to cross-examination. I had heard about Raul's approach. When a witness gave an answer that wandered away from where Raul wanted the answer to go, Raul treated the whole thing as a misunderstanding. He apologized elaborately, taking the position that the witness, through no fault of his own, had misconceived what must have been a poorly-phrased question. He made a great show of blaming himself, and of attempting to re-state the question. He then posed the question in almost the identical words he had used the first time.

It was not a technique that would have worked for many lawyers. In most lawyers it would have been seen by the jury as a sarcastic affectation. But for Raul it was no affectation at all. He was a gentleman of the old school, *muy caballero*, and the more offensive a witness became, the more scrupulously politely Raul treated him. Some witnesses were shamed by this technique into docile compliance. When Raul was very lucky, the witness was so foolish as to treat Raul's kindness as weakness, and to bluster all the more. Juries respected Raul, and they usually disliked witnesses who disrespected Raul. Many such a witness had walked away from the witness stand believing that he had bulldozed Mr. Santos, later to read a very different lesson in the jury verdict.

Dr. Gumbiner opted for compliance. "No."

"You have never taken and published photos of the collection?"

"No."

"Nor permitted anyone else to do so?"

"No."

"You have performed no scientific tests to determine if the pieces in the Adler collection are all authentic?"

"They are all authentic!" The soporific doctor showed some signs of life.

"My question must have been unclear, Doctor. And I apologize for that. What I meant to ask was" – now the slow, measured, words – "*You* ... have performed ... no scientific tests ... to determine if the pieces ... in the Adler collection ... are all authentic?"

"No. I haven't."

"Although you are a very skilled physician, you are not trained to perform such scientific tests – tests for the authenticity of works of art?"

"No. I'm not."

"As I understand it, Doctor, the Adler collection consists of dozens of individual works of art, is that correct?"

"Yes."

"These individual works of art are of a variety of different sizes?"

"Yes."

"They are drawn or painted on a variety of different kinds of surfaces?"

"Yes."

"Using a variety of different implements?"

"Yes."

"No two of these individual works of art are exactly alike?"

"No. Not exactly, although several are very similar to one another."

I thought that we were in for one of Raul's lengthy apologies, but apparently, he was satisfied with the answer. "Doctor, is it possible – barely possible – that out of all these dozens of individual art objects, one – just one – is *not* the work of Ernst Adler?"

For a moment Gumbiner said nothing. He was an intelligent man, a respected doctor, and he did not want to make himself and his cause look foolish. If it was possible for one piece in the Adler collection to be inauthentic, then it was possible for two pieces, or three, or half the collection. But to say that it was impossible, categorically impossible, for even one piece to be inauthentic when no part of the collection had ever been examined or tested was to risk a complete loss of credibility.

When he spoke, he doled out his words carefully. "I suppose, Mr. Santos ... I suppose that it is possible, in the same sense and to the same degree that it is possible that the Mona Lisa, or the Chagall Windows, could be in some small particular inauthentic."

It was a very disarming answer, but Raul was not disarmed. "And do you know, Doctor, whether, or how many times, the Mona Lisa and the Chagall Windows have been examined by art experts or scientists?"

"No," he conceded. "I don't."

"But you do know that the Mona Lisa and the Chagall Windows are displayed publicly?"

"Yes."

"And have been displayed publicly for many years?"

"Yes."

"And that they are visited by art teachers, art critics, art students, on an almost daily basis?"

"I suppose so."

"Unlike the Adler collection, which has never been examined at all?

"No. It hasn't."

"And do you persist, Doctor, in maintaining that the examinations and inspections which the Holtzman Museum proposes to make of the Adler collection are unnecessary?"

"Yes." He was about to say something else, then caught himself; "Yes I do."

Raul turned a page. He seemed never to look at his notes, and it occurred to me that he was turning the page for effect, for metaphoric value, to signal that he was moving on to another area of his examination. "Now, Doctor, in addition to maintaining that the examination of the Adler collection is unnecessary, you also maintain that it will be damaging?"

"Yes. I am very concerned about that."

"I take it that you're referring to the scientific examination of the collection?"

"Yes."

"You're not suggesting that just letting Mr. Arnovitz and his colleagues *look* at the collection could damage anything, are you?"

"No."

"You testified earlier that you are not trained to perform the kinds of scientific examinations that can determine the authenticity of the Adler collection, is that right?"

"Yes."

"Have you ever watched such examinations being done?"

"Have I ... no, I have not."

"Do you know if all of the scientific tests currently in use are chemical tests?"

"It's my understanding that the testing process will involve removing small amounts of paint, or fabric, or something, from the object to be tested, and subjecting that something to chemical or other kinds of tests. And as you point out, Mr. Santos" – the doctor leaned forward slightly, raised his voice slightly, in what for him must have been a meteor shower of energy and emotion – "establishing the authenticity of one, or some, or even most of the objects in the collection would not establish the authenticity of all. Every single one of these priceless art treasures would have to be prodded, picked at, and pulled apart."

Raul looked wounded. "Doctor, this is entirely my fault, my question was unclear. I apologize for the confusion. Permit me to rephrase the question: Do *you* know ... if all the scientific techniques ... currently used to examine art objects ... are *chemical* tests or techniques?"

"No." Gumbiner still had some fight in him. "I think that some of them involve chemical analysis."

"Do you know if some of them simply involve microscopic analysis?"

"I don't know."

"You have no reason to believe that looking at a work of art under a microscope would damage that work of art, do you?"

"I don't know."

"Do you know if some of the current scientific techniques involve the use of ultra-violet or infra-red light?"

"I don't know."

"You have no reason to believe that looking at a work of art with ultra-violet or infra-red light would damage that work of art, do you?"

"I don't know."

"And as long as no damage is done to any of the pieces, you have no objection to their being examined?"

Zachary Davis objected, claiming that Raul was mischaracterizing the witness's testimony and that the question was speculative and hypothetical. I sustained the objection without saying why, but mostly because Raul had made his point and was probably finished with his examination anyway. After a quick consultation with his colleagues Raul announced that he had no further questions of the witness at this time and sat down.

Davis stood to repair the damage. He began by taking Dr. Gumbiner through his personal and professional history. It was not particularly riveting testimony, and it was only marginally relevant to the case, but it was useful to Davis because a witness – like anyone else – is generally most at ease talking about himself. Gumbiner was a very wealthy and successful physician and not ashamed to say so. He told us about his medical credentials. He told us about his devotion to art collection, and particularly to the Adler collection.

"Doctor," asked Zachary Davis, "have you given any thought to what you want to see happen to the Adler collection?"

"My wife passed away much too young, Mr. Davis. We have no children to whom to leave our art objects. The Adler collection is one of the great and triumphant artistic achievements of modern times. It belongs in a museum that can afford it the care and the exposure that it deserves."

"And is that why you negotiated the loan of the Adler collection to the Holtzman?"

"Yes. I had hoped – and been led to believe – that the Holtzman would devote a special wing to the Adler collection, perhaps to be named the 'Adler Wing,' or the 'Adler/Gumbiner Wing.'"

Gumbiner's obvious desire to have a wing of a museum named after him evoked some smirks among the spectators and even from one of the attorneys at the Williams, Santos table – not Raul, of course – but Davis moved smoothly past it. Approaching the witness, he gestured toward the contract. "Now Doctor, you freely acknowledge having signed that contract, don't you?"

"Of course I do."

"And clearly it provides for examination of the Adler collection by the museum?"

"I suppose so. What's clear to me, Mr. Davis, is this: Any disputes that arose under the contract were to be referred to arbitration, not dragged into court as has been done here." Gumbiner spoke with as much emphasis as he seemed capable of.

Davis gestured toward me. "Dr. Gumbiner, tell the Court in your own words why you are unwilling to submit the Adler collection to the various examinations demanded by the Holtzman Museum."

Gumbiner didn't look at me. His face was pinched with concentration, but he was staring at nothing in particular when he said, "Because it is demeaning. Because it is unnecessary, pointless. No serious, sentient student of art, particularly of art of the Holocaust, doubts the authenticity of the Adler collection. To demand that it be subjected to any testing at all is Hitler's revenge. Ernst Adler, and those inmates of Weeghman in whose presence he created his extraordinary paintings, drawings, and sketches, were history's most tragic victims. The Adler collection is their triumph over victimization. To test, even to question, the authenticity of the Adler collection is to renew that victimization. Art does not require it. History will not allow it."

I suspected that this answer was something Gumbiner had worked out in advance, something he had planned, scripted, memorized. Still, its force was felt in the courtroom. Davis had the good judgment to say nothing, to do nothing, to stand stock-still for several seconds. At first the gallery was silent. Then a noise, composed of whispers, the shifting of weight, the shuffling of position, the scribbling of notes, began to form. It built slowly but steadily. Davis was too wise to do anything but wait until I had no choice but to ask the bailiff for quiet. Then and only then did he resume his examination.

"Doctor," he asked. "What, exactly, do you want to happen now?"

"My agreement with the Holtzman," he gestured toward the contract, "provides that any disputes shall be submitted to arbitration. The arbitrating body is the *bes din* of Miami Beach. Clearly, we have a dispute. The Holtzman, not I, filed the lawsuit that brings us here today. Let the agreement be honored. Let this dispute be submitted to the *bes din*."

"But doctor, suppose the *bes din* determines that the Adler collection must be subjected to examination, as the Holtzman maintains? What will your position be then?"

Gumbiner raised his gaze slightly, casting his words – it seemed to me – over Davis's head, toward some unseen interlocutor. "The *bes din*, Mr. Davis, will not do that. It will treat the Adler collection with the reverence and respect it deserves. But to answer your question: If the *bes din* determines that the Adler collection must be subjected to the demeaning examinations required by the Holtzman, I will, of course, respect that determination."

It was a very forcible answer, the culmination of very forcible testimony. Davis paused at the lectern; and when he could not justifiably do so any longer, said only, "Nothing further, Your Honor."

Raul stood to announce that he had no redirect. Dr. Gumbiner shuffled slowly back to his seat between Zachary Taylor Davis and Aimee Arrants. We had, it appeared, gotten about as far as we would be getting for the time being. I gave a couple of half-hearted taps with my gavel and headed for chambers.

• • •

I had told Doc Riggs when he was in my office that I had business to be about, and in truth I had business to be about, but I had no desire to be about it. My business consisted of reviewing and ruling upon the dozens and dozens of motions in the dozens and dozens of cases assigned to me. The cases, of course, were civil cases: claims for personal injury or breach of contract, one much like the next. They were, no doubt, of surpassing importance to the parties involved. But with my mind filled with the circumstances of Herman Bilstein's death, these civil cases seemed boring and annoying, nothing more than boring and annoying, to me.

Once upon a time it made sense, I suppose, to resolve every complaint between man and man via the jury trial system. It was better than permitting such complaints to be resolved by sticks and stones, or swords, or guns. Today the civil justice system has become a national lottery. If you slip and fall in the supermarket you file a lawsuit; in effect, you are given a lottery ticket. It is one of thousands upon thousands of lottery tickets, and the drawing for the winner won't take place for years. When it does, odds are you'll come away with little or nothing. But there's always that chance you'll hit the jackpot.

Many countries – even many countries with which we share our legal heritage – have done away with jury trials in civil cases. Personal injury claims are handled administratively, more or less the way we handle worker's compensation claims in this country. But litigation, like baseball, has become America's national pastime, our favorite spectator sport, and an industry in which wealthy and powerful interests are heavily invested. So I, a newly-minted civil judge, would spend this afternoon, and likely spend many, many afternoons, reading and resolving pretrial motions in cases claiming injury from a slip and fall, or a rear-end collision, or a breach of contract, or medical malpractice. The cases, and the motions, would take on a paralyzing sameness.

And I had better learn to like it. I came to civil court because it is here, among the endless piles of Motions to Enforce the Order Granting the Previous Motion, and Memoranda in Support of Plaintiff's Interrogatory Number Sixty-Three, that the road to promotion begins. Here money and power congregate, demanding justice, or demanding what they can get and calling it justice. Here, and not in the criminal courthouse. The Gerstein Building, the down-at-the-heels criminal court where I had spent my professional life until this week, offers none of the trappings of money or power. It does, however, offer a certain . . . clarity.

I don't mean clarity. I don't claim, I can't claim that it was always clear to me whether the defendant really did it, whatever "it" was; or that it was clear to me where the defense attorney was going with his cross-examination, or what the prosecutor meant by her objection. What was clear to me was the reality, the consequence, of what we were doing. Preside over the trial of, say, the man accused of raping a troop of Girl Scouts and you never find yourself wondering if it really matters, if we really ought to care. Perhaps, if I spend enough time in civil court, I'll learn to derive that same feeling of clarity from resolving the next Motion to Enforce the Order Granting the Previous Motion, or the next Memorandum in Support of Plaintiff's Interrogatory Number Sixty-Three. Perhaps I will.

I had been waltzing legal documents around my desk unenthusiastically for almost two hours when Jack Sheridan walked in. Jack could be the most silent of men, in both his speech and the movements of his body; and I did not notice his presence until he was actually seating himself in one of the chairs opposite my desk and hooking a leg over a chair arm. If he had visited with Carmen first he had done so in tones so hushed that I was unaware of it.

We sat in silence for a moment or two. That, I think, was one of the things I had come to miss most during Jack's self-imposed exile: casual friendship may lie in the ability to make conversation, but true friendship includes the ability to refrain from conversation. You only get two or three friends like that.

A couple of minutes later Jack stood up. "I think I'd like to get out of here and maybe go see Uncle Billy. Would you like to get out of here and go see Uncle Billy?"

I stood up too. Yes, I would like to get out of here. And go see Uncle Billy.

The outer office, Carmen's work area, was a place transformed. Order had been imposed upon chaos. There was nothing on the floor but the carpet. There was nothing on the chairs at all. All that remained of the manila folders and accordion files that had been scattered about were two or three case files on Carmen's desk which she was beating into submission.

During the – was it 24 hours? a little more, perhaps? – since the deaths of Herman Bilstein and Boots Weber the torrent of telephone calls from the press had reached flood tide. Carmen handled each call with the same patient firmness. All inquiries were referred to the police department's public information office. Judge Addison was unavailable for comment. No meant no.

Her phone rang yet again as Jack and I were about to leave. We were heading for the outer door when Carmen made an urgent "come here!" gesture and said "One moment, please" to whoever was on the line. She covered the phone with one hand, said, "It's Judge Kroh," and handed the call to me.

"Hello."

"Clark, this is Floyd. This is tragic, absolutely tragic."

I had judged Floyd Kroh unfairly. Whatever his shortcomings, he was a decent man, a very decent man. I had taken over Floyd's courtroom and Floyd's cases on the day two people's lives happened to end outside of Floyd's courtroom in the midst of one of Floyd's cases. These circumstances were not of Floyd's making, and there was nothing he could or should have done to spare me from them. "Of course it is, Floyd. But it's very good of you to call. I appreciate it. I suppose everyone at the Gerstein Building is buzzing about it?"

"Well ... I don't know. I didn't see any reason to talk about it to anyone but you."

"That was very discreet of you."

"I mean, I've got another call in to the Administrative Office of the Court, but they've been useless. It's their fault in the first place."

"Floyd, I don't see how you can say it's anyone's fault. These things happen." Were the building services people supposed to have kept the doors to the stairwell locked except in case of emergency?

He responded with an energy, an indignation unusual for him. “It’s not good enough to say that these things happen, Clark. We’re talking about something special and precious.”

I had, indeed, misjudged Floyd Kroh. Every human life – whether that of a colleague in the judicial system or that of an octogenarian stranger – is, as Floyd said, special and precious. Floyd would make a fine criminal court judge after all.

“Clark,” he went on, “the Lorillard Snuff Mill operated from 1792 to 1870. It was located on the Bronx River in New York, on a part of the Lorillard estate that is now included in New York’s Botanical Garden. The commemorative ashtray was one of kind. I really don’t know if there’s another one like it in the world. And it was one of Dad’s favorites. It’s square in shape but with rounded corners, large – oh, I’d say about seven inches or so on each side – and very heavy. It bears a beautiful depiction of the snuff mill itself. I just don’t understand how they could lose such a thing. I’m at my wit’s end. I’d like to come over and look for it myself. Would it be convenient if I came over now? Clark? Clark, are you there?”

I was there. “Floyd,” I said slowly, “two people died in the middle of our proceedings yesterday.”

“Oh,” said Floyd. “Well, of course, ... of course that’s bad too.” He thought deeply for a moment; I heard a humming noise. “Perhaps it would be better if I came another day?”

“Goodbye, Floyd.”

Jack and I almost made it out of chambers, but the doorway was blocked. It was blocked entirely. The thing blocking it was Carlos Benitez.

Carlos Benitez went to the University of Florida on a football scholarship. He was an indifferent student but a terrific football player, with real prospects of being drafted into the NFL. Then came the knee injury.

It must be a hard thing for 19- or 20-year-old kid to wake up in a hospital room and be told that he would never again do the only thing he had ever wanted to do. It was a hard thing for Carlos. Football was all that had kept him in school, and without football there was nothing to keep him there. He drifted back to Miami, and when he got here he kept drifting. Mostly he drifted into drinking, and drugs, that sort of thing.

But bad habits are just as expensive to support as good ones – no, more so – and Carlos had to pick up some money somewhere. He was still a big, powerful kid, still a weightlifter, and a friend of a friend told him about a bail bondsman who could give him work and pay him in cash.

A bail bondsman promises the court that he will produce a criminal defendant for trial when that defendant is needed. In exchange for this promise, the court lets the defendant out of jail and the defendant pays the bondsman a fee. If all his defendants show up for court as scheduled, the bail bondsman will make a nice living. If a defendant fails to show up, the bondsman must pay the court the amount of the bail bond. If many defendants fail to show up, the bondsman will go broke. To prevent that from happening – to assist the bondsman in making sure that defendants show up – the law provides that the bondsman may use "reasonable force" to make sure the defendants show up. How much force is reasonable is something about which defendants and bondsmen may differ, with the courts usually siding with the bondsmen.

For his part, Carlos was surprised and delighted to learn that someone would actually pay him good cash money to tackle fugitive defendants, truss them up like Christmas turkeys, toss them in the trunk of his car, and deliver them to the county jail. In due course Carlos got his own license as a bail bondsman. It wasn't as good as football, but it was a living. It left him with the time and the money to do drugs, drink, life weights, and chase girls. Really, what more was there to life?

The answer to that question came to Carlos in the form of an epiphany. That's not a figure of speech. Carlos had a true religious revelation.

The Dalai Lama was appearing in Miami, and a girl whom Carlos had just started to date asked him if he wanted to go. Carlos had no idea what the Dalai Lama was – he naturally assumed it was a rock band, and just as naturally assumed that after the performance he and the girl would go home and get naked – but he agreed to go. It was the event that changed his life.

Carlos Benitez became a passionate adherent of Tibetan Buddhism. He gave up drinking, drugs, even meat, because it was wrong to eat a living creature. (He still lifted weights and chased girls. The Dalai Lama hadn't mentioned those things specifically.) Now when he takes a defendant out on bail, he sits that defendant down for a long and very earnest lecture on the defendant's spiritual obligations. Defendants are very attentive to lectures about their spiritual obligations when the lecturer is 6 foot 4 by 245 pounds and lawfully entitled to put them back in jail. A number of these defendants have themselves converted to Tibetan Buddhism, and given up all violent crimes. (Operating a marijuana grow house, or jacking a car, things like that, are entirely non-violent and involve no harm to living creatures.) Carlos has become the stuff of legend in the Miami criminal-justice community.

You will understand, then, that what was blocking my chambers doorway was larger than life in more ways than one. I've never asked Carlos if he ever cheats on his diet and has a little steak and I'm never going to; but if he's eating nothing but fruits and vegetables he's eating an awful lot of them. Carlos is still football-player big and weightlifter built. When he saw Jack he broke into a big grin – apparently Carlos hadn't known that Jack was back from wherever he had been – and gave Jack a hug that probably did damage to the ribcage. I got off easy; he said hello Your Honor and shook my hand. Then he asked if he could talk to us for a moment, so we headed back to my office. I was reminded that Carlos walks with a limp so slight as to be almost imperceptible. You wouldn't notice it if you didn't know about what happened to him in college.

We chatted about this and that for a few minutes, and then Carlos got a serious look on his face. "Your Honor," he asked, "is it true that Rabbi Stein will be in your courtroom this week?"

"So it appears."

The serious look on Carlos's face turned to one of admiration, of awe. "Is it true that he personally met Kundun, met Yeshe Norbu?"

I have no idea what look was on my face, but apparently it told Carlos that I didn't know who Kundun or Yeshe Norbu were.

"The Presence," he explained. "The Wish-Fulfilling Gem." He paused, waiting for some sign of recognition. "His Holiness, the Dalai Lama."

Ah, yes. "I don't know. That's what everyone says."

Carlos was clearly wowed. He shook his head slightly, then closed his eyes and whispered, "*Om mani padme hum*." He whispered it a couple of times. Then he opened his eyes again and asked me, "Judge, do you think I could talk to him? To Rabbi Stein?"

"It's really not up to me, Carlos. I expect he'll be here till this hearing concludes. If you come by during a break, I imagine you could introduce yourself to him." I wanted to be helpful to Carlos, who was so very eager to meet the rabbi; but there was a limit to the extent I could get involved. Rabbi Stein was, according to Dr. Gumbiner's lawyers, going to be a witness before me, and it wouldn't be right for a judge to be acting as a social secretary for a witness in his courtroom.

In any event, Carlos seemed satisfied. He would return, in hopes of meeting a man who had spoken as friend and equal to the Dalai Lama himself.

Carlos stood to go. There was, however, one more thing he wanted to share with us. "For as long as space endures/And for as long as living beings remain/Until then may I too abide/ To dispel the misery of the world."

I wasn't sure what to say to that – "Have a nice day" seemed a little inadequate – so I nodded very gravely, the serious face I use in court, then extended my hand and shook Carlos's. He turned and left.

It wasn't until he was gone that Jack spoke. "Hey Clark?"

"Yes."

"What does that mean? That, *hum-manny-panny-hum*."

"I'm not sure. Something about a jewel inside a lotus."

Jack thought it over. "There's a jewel inside a lotus?"

"Something like that."

Jack thought it over some more. He took his time about it. Then he said, "Go see Uncle Billy?"

"Yeah."

• • •

I was driving, Jack was in the front passenger seat, and we were inching our way through the 24-hour-a-day rush hour that is Miami. "Whatever became of, uh, ...?" I started to ask, and then stopped.

I had been on the threshold of a very stupid question. I was about to ask Jack about Teresa Rodriguez. Teresa Rodriguez was a woman like no other. She was the woman for whom Jack had betrayed a client and subverted the criminal justice process. She was the woman for whom Jack had thrown away everything of value to him. She was the reason he no longer lived in Miami, no longer practiced law, no longer – I suppose this is the ironic part –

drank. When Jack left, those of us who knew him and wondered where he went wondered if Teresa Rodriguez had gone with him. We never really found out.

When we were young lawyers, Jack had explained to me the theory of "znargh." Jack was a man of many theories, but "znargh" was one of his best. "Think about it, Clark," he would say, affecting a look of deep philosophical reflection. "When you first heard about sex, you were amazed to find out that something everyone was doing had been kept secret from you for so many years. And when you first tried it – you have tried it, haven't you, Clark? – you were *really* surprised. Now suppose, just suppose, that fifty years or so from now when we're all sitting around the 'Threshold of Thrombosis Senior Living Center' in Boynton Beach, someone says, 'Damn, I sure miss sex.' And then someone else says, 'Yes, but goddamn, I sure miss znargh even more.' And everyone nods and rocks back and forth in their rockers, yes, yes, znargh sure was the best. And you, Clark, you look up and say, 'Znargh? What's znargh?' Everyone stops rocking. Their jaws drop open and their teeth fall out. They stare at you. Finally, one of them croaks, 'Znargh ... you know, the thing that's better than sex, the thing you learn about after they let you learn about sex. You had znargh, right?' And everybody's looking at you, thinking, oh my God, this fool never had znargh. I worry about that all the time, Clark. I worry that znargh exists and I'm not getting it."

Jack was relentless in his pursuit of znargh. He dated all the pretty girls, and once in a while he'd remark – by way of complimenting the technique of the girlfriend *du jour* – that he'd been plowed under by a love tractor. But he never claimed to have achieved znargh. Maybe that what was set Teresa Rodriguez apart. Maybe she gave znargh.

Jack spoke. "She was liberated by her failure. I was enslaved by my mediocrity." To a stranger, it would have been gibberish. To me it meant all kinds of things. It was the answer to the question I had almost asked, the question he knew I meant to ask. It meant that she was gone, that she had left him, that he didn't want to talk about it. It was a canned answer, one that rolled trippingly off the tongue but had no real content. He would use it to put off the question, and the questioner, every time he was asked: what happened to Teresa?

We drove north on Biscayne Boulevard, and the federal courthouse complex was visible a block or so to our left. "I've got an appointment tomorrow with Bob Aguilar," I mentioned. Jack made a face. "I'm going to be putting in for a federal judgeship, Jack, and Bob might be able to help."

"What's in it for him?"

"Nothing."

"Then he won't help." Jack shifted in his seat, stared out at the bay to his right. "Why in hell do you want to be a federal judge anyway, Clark? You wouldn't like it."

Because federal judges are lifetime appointees. Because federal judges don't have to run for election. Because a federal judge's orders carry the force of the federal government. Because federal judges make more money, work in nicer quarters, deal with a better class of cases and litigants. Why wouldn't I like it? "Why wouldn't I like it?"

Jack sighed. "You think that federal judges have power, don't you, Clark?" He made a chuckling noise, or something like it. "All you judges in state court think that the big boys" – *big bauys*, he said, because his Southern was flaring up -- "over in federal court have the power. Well, they have power, but it's only one kind of power: the power to hurt people, to put them in prison till the next ice age. They don't have power to help anyone. When federal prosecutors are driving the guilty train down the guilty tracks to Guiltyville, a federal judge's job is to make sure the defendant is tied good and tight to those tracks."

"That wouldn't be a criminal defense attorney's point of view, would it?"

"Yes. It's none the less true for that." Jack thought for a moment. "Let's say a defendant is charged in federal court with littering in a national park and homicide of a federal agent. We go to trial and I get him acquitted of the homicide. Not the littering, though; he's convicted of that. Now you know what happens come sentencing time? The judge looks down at him and says, 'Well now, I know that the jury acquitted you of homicide, but I heard the evidence too, and I think you're guilty. Maybe not guilty beyond all reasonable doubt, but guilty enough. So in sentencing you on the littering, I'm going to take into account the fact that I think you should have been convicted of the homicide and give you the maximum sentence allowed by law for the crime of conviction.' 'But Judge,' sputters the poor dumb son of a bitch defendant, 'a jury of my peers acquitted me of the homicide! I have a jury verdict of not guilty! What good is my constitutional right to trial by jury if you can ignore the jury's verdict?' 'Why, I'm not ignoring it at all,' says the judge. 'The jury's verdict will be duly noted in the record of these proceedings. When you're up in Atlanta Penitentiary, where I'm about to send you, if any of your fellow inmates ask if you've ever been convicted of a homicide, you look 'em right in the eye and tell them no. You see, verdicts are for juries. But sentencing is for me. Marshal, take him away.' And away he goes."

"You wouldn't be exaggerating, would you, Jack?"

"Tell you what, Clark. When you're having teatime with your pal Bob Aguilar tomorrow, you just ask him. You ask him if that's any exaggeration."

"Sounds to me like ...." I was cut off – literally – in mid-sentence by a driver in the left-hand turn lane who made a right-hand turn in front of me. As is customary practice on Miami's roads and highways, he did this while talking animatedly on a cell phone. I managed to slam on the brakes and, fortunately, so did the driver behind me and the drivers behind him. There being nothing out of the ordinary in Miami about making a right-hand turn from the left-hand turn lane, no one bothered to honk, curse, or even shoot. "Sounds to me like you're ready to return to the practice of law."

"I don't know," said Jack. And then, very seriously, he asked: "It would make things harder for you, wouldn't it?"

I didn't have to ask what he meant. Jack was just what he had called himself when we chatted in the Albatross bar: my little moral dilemma. If he returned to Miami, returned to the practice of law, I would see him often. I would see him in court, I would see him socially, I would see him in the company of mutual friends and colleagues. And each time I saw him I would think, 'Here is a prominent lawyer, a gifted and successful lawyer, who willfully obstructed justice by fixing a criminal trial. And I am a judge, a well-respected judge, who knows what he did and said nothing.'

I didn't answer Jack's question. I suppose he took my silence for a "yes." For a while no one spoke. Now the car driving in front of me was a late-model Mercedes, beautifully polished. It bore a bumper sticker that read, "My kid was prisoner of the month at Miami-Dade County Jail."

When I had visited Jack in Key West I had quoted an old common-law maxim to him: the wheel of justice grinds slowly, but it grinds exceedingly fine. The saying was not about human justice, not about what went on in the criminal or civil courts. It was about Justice writ large, empyreal justice, natural justice. It was the notion that there was a system of checks and balances built right into the universe, that the hinges upon which life turned were oiled with justice, that justice was one of the symbols in the big equation. It was the notion that somewhere, somehow, sometime, both our good deeds and our bad would catch up to us. If it was true, then by trying to create justice on earth, human justice, we were bringing ourselves and our lives in alignment with the pattern and rhythm of the universe. Or perhaps if it was true, then our attempts at human justice are inconsequential; justice will be done to us no matter what we do to ourselves. I thought of my visit to the Albatross. On the wall there hung a passage from The Rhyme of the Ancient Mariner; and I thought of a later passage from that same poem: "The man hath penance done/ and penance more will do." Jack had, I suppose, done penance for his crime. He had thrown away the life he loved, and then lost the woman for whom he had thrown it away. He had penance done, and penance more would do. Had the wheel of justice caught up to Jack? And if it had, did that relieve me of the burden of my moral dilemma?

Was that it -- was I just looking for a way off the hook? Since when was I a man of faith, a believer in the ultimate justice of the universe?

Jack broke in on my musings with more practical thoughts. "You haven't said anything to Uncle Billy about the two people who died in the stairwell, have you?"

"No, no. He hasn't heard it from me, and I doubt that he's heard about it at all. Let's see if we can keep it that way."

Jack nodded. "Let's."

• • •

Billy today was better in every way than Billy yesterday. He had been moved out of the cardiac care unit into a small private room. His bed faced west, faced a large window through which bright, healthy Miami sunshine poured in abundance. The walls of the small room were painted in a dark yellow color, undecorated but not drab, bordered by white floor boards below and white crown molding above. In the corner to the right of the window a television was affixed to the wall, and the remote control lay inches from Billy's right hand. His left hand was equally close to a panel of controls for the bed itself, so that he could raise or lower his feet, his knees, his head, each independently. On a rolling tray that he had pushed aside were the remnants of a meal: no Jell-O.

He was still dressed in one of those absurd hospital gowns, still connected to various wires and tubes. But as he sat slumped in his bed, daydreaming till we walked in the door, his face and arms were the color of a normal, healthy human being, not the pallid color of hospital flesh. He grinned broadly, the grin of a kid, when he saw us.

I read once, somewhere, that a man's nose and ears continue to grow slightly throughout his life. It made sense to me when I read it, because you see so many old men whose withered heads seem barely capable of supporting the weight of the nose hanging like a huge third elbow off the front of the face and the enormous ears unsteadily balancing each other on the sides. Billy is nothing like that. As the years passed whatever weight he has gained has gone to his face. His body is still relatively trim, but his face is wide and fleshy. His nose seems trivial in the expanse of his face, nothing more than a speed bump between his cheeks. When he smiled the cheeks gathered in thick rolls.

So we stood there grinning at each other, and Jack said, "How's the *schmatte* business these days, Billy?"

And Billy made a face as if something smelled bad and said, "The *schmatte* business isn't what it used to be."

The least you can do for Billy is ask him about the *schmatte* business, the clothing business in which he has worked all of his adult life. He will tell you that the *schmatte* business isn't what it used to be. Apparently the *schmatte* business was never what it used to be, and never will be. That is not the point. The point is that you asked him, and you gave him a chance to tell you.

I said that I'd go try to find a couple of chairs – for some reason there were none in Billy's room – and left the two of them to gab. Billy always liked shooting the breeze with Jack. It's not that Billy likes Jack so much – sometimes he only puts up with Jack for my sake – but Jack usually has a joke or a dirty story, and can hold his end up in just about any conversation that a couple of guys might want to have. That was a role I could never fill for Billy. After my father died he had been a father to me, but I had probably never asked him to teach me how to spit, or tie knots, any of the kinds of things that a man teaches a boy. When I became a lawyer he was proud, and when I became a judge he was prouder, but every once in a while, pride needs to be interrupted with a story about the traveling salesman and the farmer's daughter, or an argument about whether Jason Veritek was as good a catcher as Yogi Berra was ("As good as Berra? Oh, you're full of canal juice!"). That's where Jack comes in.

At the end of a corridor I found two metal folding chairs. I tucked one under each arm and walked back to Billy's room.

"Looks like the food's pretty good here," said Jack, pointing to Billy's mostly-empty plate.

It was a gift, and it was meant to be. It gave Billy a chance to complain. What more could an old man be offered?

"There are two places never to eat if you can help it," pronounced Billy. "A hospital, and anyplace called 'Mom's'."

Jack was in a gift-giving mood. "Why anyplace called 'Mom's'?"

"'Mom' won't be my mom. And she might be Albanian. They eat raw rabbits." Billy worked the bed controls and brought himself to a more upright sitting position. I unfolded the chairs and Jack and I sat. "I learned that in my traveling salesman days. Albanians eat raw rabbit sometimes. You don't eat at a place called 'Mom's', just like you don't play poker with a guy named 'Doc'."

Jack nodded, taking in Billy's life lessons. "If you're ever accused of subtlety, I'll testify for the defense," he said.

I asked Billy if he was thirsty, offered to try to find him some juice. He declined. "But tell me about your case. The one about artwork. You started to tell me the other day ... when was that?"

"It was yesterday."

He seemed surprised; a little surprised. "Yesterday. Well ... I didn't get it all. Tell me about it."

So I told him about it. I told him about Ernst Adler's life and work, about his suffering and his artistic triumph. I told him about the Holtzman Museum of Judaica and its contract with Dr. Bernard

Gumbiner. I told him about the witnesses who had testified, and about those who were going to testify. I did not tell him about Bootsie Weber. Of course I did not tell him about Herman Bilstein.

Billy grimaced when I spoke about the *bes din* and the Orthodox rabbis who comprise it. Billy does not like the Orthodox. He was born in this country, the son of immigrants, and his was the generation of American Jews determined to prove that they were more American than the Americans. He was 15 when the Korean war broke out – I have heard this story many times – but he was big for his age and had little trouble talking the recruiter into letting him enlist in the Navy. He served throughout the war, and he has a large scar and two large medals to show for it. The scar, and the medals, were proof that he was as American as any American. The Orthodox Jewish community, with its distinctive dress and customs, was old-world. Its members were Jewish-Americans who drew a line between Jewish and American. To Billy, the separateness of the Orthodox made it more difficult for all American Jews to be accepted as Americans. I never heard Billy speak a word of prejudice against any ethnic or religious group, with one exception: he did not like Orthodox Jews.

For that reason, or another, Billy offered little response to my narrative. Instead, he turned to Jack. "So how are the criminals these days?"

"I couldn't tell you, Billy. I'm out of the business."

Billy winced; not to learn that Jack was out of the business, but because he had known that Jack was out of the business and had forgotten. At his age any little evidence of forgetfulness could be a sign that senility is lurking just around the corner. Children do not rage at themselves over a small thing forgotten. "So what are you doing for a living these days?" he asked, to have something to ask.

Jack smiled. "I do a little bartending down in Key West."

Billy smiled. "Were you smart with money, when you were making it?"

Jack's smile broadened; the good smile, the jury smile. "My money's all tied up in cash." *Mah muney,* he said, because the good smile and southern went together. "See, back when I was practicing law, I put a dime in a jar" – *a dahm in a jah* – "every time a witness lied to me, and took a dollar out every time I lied to someone else. I believe I'll be able to live off that jar the rest of my life."

Billy worked the controls and sat himself up a little straighter in bed. "All those drug cases made you a rich big-shot." It was not an accusation. He was still smiling.

Jack turned in his chair and looked away, looked without blinking into the sunlight streaming in from the window. "Well I'll tell you, Billy," he said. "Once upon a time the practice of criminal law was a beautiful business. A criminal lawyer was a member of a learned profession and was treated accordingly. Prosecutors and defense attorneys viewed themselves as members of the same fraternity, and they acted toward one another with courtesy and cordiality. Then the drugs and the drug money came along." Jack turned again, facing Billy. "Yes, I made a lot of money. Good lawyers, and some not so good, made a lot of money. But the drug gold rush brought the war on drugs, and the war on drugs turned out to be a war on the Constitution and a war on the courts and a war on common sense. It wasn't a war anybody wanted, and it wasn't a war anybody meant to win. The American people spent millions of dollars buying Columbian drugs and the American government spent millions of dollars punishing the Columbians for selling us their drugs. We put more people in more prisons for more years than any society in the history of the world. And when we were done – when prosecutors and criminal defense lawyers were no longer speaking to one another, and federal judges had been reduced to dungeon-keepers, and the Bill of Rights had been fed to the paper-shredder – we had solved no problems and won no war."

Jack was standing up. He stopped speaking for a moment, and realized that he was standing up, and sat down. He had probably been on the verge of asking the ladies and gentlemen of the jury for a verdict of not guilty, and maybe he felt a little silly, or maybe he didn't. He glanced back out the window at the setting sun, and then turned back to Billy and me. "Hell, it doesn't matter to me anymore. I'm out of the business." He smiled. "I only got in the business in the first place because I was seduced and betrayed by a blindfold goddess with scales and a sword."

Billy sighed, and worked the gizmo to bring his knees up a little higher. I don't know whether he really felt more comfortable with his knees higher, but he was enjoying working the gizmo. "When I first moved down here there was a nice citrus industry, but what with citrus canker and the cost of land it's all moved away," said Billy. "There was a tourist industry in Miami, too, but that's all moved to Orlando ... you know, Mickey Mouse .... And the drug trade was actually pretty good for business for a while, because the hotels on Miami Beach were always full and people were buying for cash. I sold some guy who didn't speak English the same pair of golf slacks in four colors and two sizes. Cash."

This struck Jack as funny for some reason, and he started to chuckle. Billy didn't mind getting a laugh – I think he appreciated it – but he wagged a finger at Jack just the same. "Listen, smart guy, don't ever monkey around with an old man's memories."

"All your stories are true, especially the ones you make up?" asked Jack, still chuckling just a little.

Billy knew Al Guerrero's favorite saying. "Especially the ones I make up. An old man's stories are his identity. Question his stories and you tell him he didn't exist."

Jack put his hands together and bowed his head, a gesture of repentance. Billy asked me about Miriam and the kids, and that gave us something to talk about for 15 minutes or so. He even asked me about Carmen, or tried to. He couldn't remember her name for a moment, and in his frustration referred to her as "your secretary, ah, the one ... the one who was built back when there was no shortage of materials."

But Jack found something else to talk about. "Clark," said Jack, "you remember the Albatross, where I tend bar?" Sure I did. It's around the corner from Duval Street, which is the main drag in Key West. There's a bookstore there that used to be called the Duval Street Bookstore, or something like that. The bookstore did about enough business to get by, not much more than that.

"Maybe you know that Ernest Hemingway is the guy who put Key West on the tourist map. He wrote stories about the Florida Keys, and he had a home in Key West for a good long time. It's still on all the tours. Tourists get to see the filthy cats that live there because they're supposed to be descended from Hemingway's cats, although how you can tell if one filthy cat is descended from another is anybody's guess." Jack is not a cat person.

"Well, one day the guy who owns the Duval Street Bookstore comes across a couple of author-autographed copies of Hemingway novels. He puts them in the front window and they sell in two seconds, for good prices. It dawns on the guy that the Hemingway connection is the key to success for his bookstore. He scours catalogues, estate sales, whatever bookstore owners do to get old books to find Hemingway-autographed copies, and sure enough, they sell for big mark-ups. But it's hard to find author-autographed Hemingways, and when you find them they cost a lot.

"Now I don't know how it happened – this part of the story I never really got – but the bookstore owner in Key West somehow crosses paths with a ... Clark, what do you call those Orthodox Jews who spend all day writing out those scrolls, you know, ..."

"You're talking about a *torah* scribe? A *sofer*?"

"Yeah, whatever. They have them on Miami Beach, right?"

I shrugged my shoulders. I knew, vaguely, that a *torah* scribe is a very observant Jew who is trained, highly trained, to copy out the *torah*, the scroll of the first five books of the Bible that is kept in the sanctuary of every synagogue. That was about all I knew.

"I don't know how they got together, but the bookstore owner figures out that for the scribe to copy Hemingway's signature on any old Hemingway novel is a piece of cake. The scribe is a very religious guy, his work is a sacred trust, but if some Gentile in Key West wants to pay him a lot of money to copy some dead Gentile's signature on a ratty old edition of *To Have and Have Not*, well, that doesn't violate any sacred trust." Billy made a kind of snorting noise to indicate his general disgust with religious hypocrites, particularly Jewish ones, but he didn't interrupt Jack's story.

"The bookstore guy changes the name of his store to 'The Old Man and the Sea'." He can easily scoop up old copies of Hemingway novels, scoop them up for a song, because the worse beat-up they are, the better he likes them. He ships them off to the scribe with notes about what inscriptions to use, you know, 'To Charlie, the best damn bartender in this town, Ernie Hemingway'." Of course he knows better than to use the same inscription twice, and he always reminds the scribe to use a variety of different pens or other writing implements. Apparently compared to copying out those Bible scrolls, this is child's play for the scribe – his Hemingway signature is every bit as good as Hemingway's, maybe better.

"Well, the money is rolling in. Tourists get off the cruise ships, stroll down Duval Street, and see the sign for 'the largest and finest collection of Hemingway-autographed literature in the world' or some such thing, and the next thing you know someone from Iowa or England is laying out a hundred bucks for a dog-eared old copy of *The Sun Also Rises*. The bookstore guy is happy, the scribe is happy, and the tourist – he's never going to know the difference – is happy.

"The only problem is that now there's so much inventory that it's starting to look like Papa Hemingway had no time to write books, he was so busy autographing them. So the bookstore guy has another bright idea. Hemingway was supposed to be this hairy-chested outdoorsman, right? So the bookstore guy buys up a bunch of old, beat-up hunting hats and fisherman's hats – he has the good sense to buy them from far away, not locally – and sends them to the scribe with the same instructions. I mean, the inscriptions are like, 'To my pal Charlie, who knows the best damn fishing holes in the river, Ernie Hemingway,' that sort of thing, but it's the same idea. And it's all the same to the scribe whether he's writing on an old book or an old hat. Now the sign in the front window reads, "the largest and finest collection of Hemingway-autographed memorabilia in the world.'

"Last I heard, they were branching out to Steinbeck-autographed and Faulkner-autographed stuff. Of course those guys aren't identified with Key West the way Hemingway was, but they were good too, right? And anyway, the scribe was getting tired of Hemingway signatures and was looking for something new."

Billy snorted again. I took the opportunity to interrupt. "Jack, I know that all your stories are true, especially the ones you make up, but how do you know all this? I mean, if you know it, don't other people know it? And if other people know it, aren't the bookstore owner and the scribe going to be sued or prosecuted or both?"

Jack smiled. "I learned all this in strictest confidence. The bookstore guy does his drinking at the Albatross, and I'm his bartender. Attorney-client privilege may be strict, Clark, but bartender-customer privilege is inviolable. Especially in Key West." I learn things from Jack all the time.

Then a nurse or orderly – a heavy, sullen, slow-moving creature – came into Billy's room to remove the tray from his last meal, and somehow that meant that it was time for us to go.

• • •

Jack and I were across the bridge and back on the City of Miami side of Biscayne Bay before Jack started to tell another story. This one was a story about a horse, a horse that worked in a factory town in New England in the old days. Every day the horse was hitched to a mill – Jack didn't recall exactly what the horse was hitched to, some contraption, but I assume it was a mill – and made to walk around in a circle till the factory whistle blew. When the horse got old the factory owner decided that the horse shouldn't have to work anymore, that it should be turned out in some nice pasture to graze and spend a leisurely last few years on earth. Well, after a few weeks the factory owner thought he'd just stop by to see how the horse was enjoying its retirement. When he got to the pasture, you know what he saw? He saw the horse walking slowly around an old tree stump, around and around in a circle, just like it used to do. And the horse kept on walking till sundown, when it heard the sound of a far-away factory whistle.

Jack was a good storyteller, but this was not his good stuff. I couldn't imagine how telling that story in defense of a drug dealer or a bank robber would put Jack in a position to ask the jury for an acquittal.

"Miriam and I have told Billy he ought to move up to Boynton Beach or Delray, into one of those retirement communities. He's not rich, but he's got enough. You figure he's just a workhorse who wants to stay in harness?"

The brunt of rush hour had passed. We were moving along Biscayne Boulevard, not rapidly but at something better than the usual inch by inch pace. Jack didn't answer right away. Then he said, "I don't know. I wasn't thinking about Uncle Billy."

It was, apparently, my day to ask stupid questions. Jack hadn't been talking about Billy; he had been talking about himself.

Jack looked straight ahead, looking south down the Boulevard. The city fathers tell us from time to time that someday there will be an elevated train, or a trolley, or a pedestrian mall on Biscayne Boulevard. Someday, but no day in particular. "Remember that old legal maxim, Clark, that the wheel of justice grinds slowly but it grinds exceedingly fine? Well there's a wheel, Clark, but not of justice. Justice is only a name we give things. One man falls into a pile of shit and another falls into a pile of gold. If we don't like the first fellow but we like the second, we say it's justice. If we like the first fellow but we don't like the second, we say it's injustice. The pile of shit and the pile of gold know nothing about justice, because justice and injustice don't exist till we say they do. The wheel that keeps rolling along is just life, Clark, or circumstances, or whatever you want to call the things that happen. But it makes us sad to think of life that way. So we make up justice, and then say that we didn't make it up at all, that it was always out there waiting for us to find it."

We were stopped at a light. To the left was the bayfront park, and beyond that the bay itself. Office towers lined the boulevard on our right, and the sun had all but set behind them. The rays of sunlight that slipped between the buildings, the last rays of sunlight of the day, were bright and strong, so I could not turn toward the passenger seat to face Jack.

"I need to come back to Miami and practice criminal law, Clark. If that creates problems you can't handle, I need to know it." Cars were honking, but cars always honked in Miami. "Light's green, Clark." So it was.

We inched along in silence for a moment or two. I mentioned to Jack that there was some bar association reception scheduled for that evening, and that many of the lawyers and judges he used to know would be there.

"Where is it?"

"Lime Rickey, I think." Lime Rickey is a bar and restaurant, but mostly a bar. It's located a block or two west of Brickell Avenue,

Miami's financial district. It had been there when the neighborhood was a good neighborhood, and it had been there when the neighborhood was a bad neighborhood, and now that the neighborhood was a very good neighborhood it was still there. Kay Surrey claims that her father tended bar there long ago.

Jack made a face. "Rickey is a prosecutor's bar."

Add to the list of things I'd never know if Jack hadn't told me: there are prosecutor bars and defense lawyer bars. "There are prosecutor bars and defense lawyer bars?"

"Uh-huh."

"And Lime Rickey is a prosecutor bar?"

"Yep." Jack fiddled with his collar.

"Which are the defense lawyer bars?"

Jack thought, but not for long. "All the other ones."

A few blocks later I dropped Jack off at his car. He looked at me to see if I had something to say. I asked him if he was coming to dinner on Friday night.

The question itself was a reminder of old times, and it got a smile from Jack. Miriam was brought up in a somewhat religious household – not necessarily Orthodox, but religious – and has always been particular about Friday night dinner and the prayers and rituals that go with it. On the theory that Jack had no real home of his own – a house, perhaps, but not a home as far as Miriam was concerned – he was routinely invited to join us. He routinely declined. Friday night was one of seven excellent opportunities Jack made each week to chase drinks and women, and he was not about to squander it at the home of his Jewish friends taking part in their Jewish ceremonies. Still, each week Miriam insisted that I extend the invitation; and each week Jack turned it down.

So we sat there grinning for just a second, and then Jack said, "Sure. If the meeting of Ace High Bar Association doesn't run too late, I'll be there."

And rather than look out the window to see if an elevated train, or a trolley, or a pedestrian mall had materialized on Biscayne Boulevard, I said, "You're entitled to an answer, Jack. Give me till Friday night to think about it."

CHAPTER FIVE
WEDNESDAY

There used to be just one federal courthouse in Miami. For years, decades, there was just the one. The courtrooms were upstairs, and the post office was on the main floor. It is a beautiful building, coral rock walls and Spanish tile roof. There is an interior courtyard with more coral rock, more Spanish tiles, and palm trees. The main courtroom, the ceremonial courtroom on the second floor, has a magnificent mural depicting the history of Florida and the civilizing influence of the Rule of Law. In that courtroom, and in the smaller ones outlying it, offenses against the postal service or the customs service were tried. Before the drug dealers came that was about all there was.

The old federal courthouse is still there, still in use. Some years ago they built another courthouse adjacent to it, on its west side. The adjacent courthouse, known as the tower building, is as unlike the old building as two structures can be. The tower building is an 11-storey cement cylinder. It has all the charm and cachet of an impacted molar, but it would be a good place to hide during nuclear winter.

Across the street to the north is the third of Miami's federal courthouses, the James Lawrence King Federal Justice Center. Named for the former chief judge, the King building is finished almost entirely in green glass. From a distance it looks like a large, square bottle of Seven-Up with cement wings.

There is a fourth federal courthouse which in those days was under construction. It is made, or appears to be made, almost entirely of glass in varying shades of blue. It's supposed to look like a cruise ship if you glance down at it from I-95 as you drive by. I suppose some frat boy in the federal bureaucracy thought that was a big joke. A cruise ship, get it? We're going to send you up the river for the rest of your life, but hey, you're going on a cruise ship. Get it?

A federal judge enters the reserved parking area by driving past a security attendant, down a ramp into an underground parking lot. From there he travels by private elevator to his chambers. A visitor – a lawyer, a juror, a witness, anyone but a federal judge – will either hope to find a metered parking space on the street or take his chances squeezing into one of the outdoor parking lots a few blocks from the courthouse buildings. After he has walked from wherever he parked to the public entrance he must put his personal possessions, including the contents of his pockets, through an X-ray machine; and he must pass through a magnetometer. He must then wait patiently for the public elevator, which in the fullness of time will deliver him to his floor.

I am a mere visitor in the federal courts. In the fullness of time the public elevator delivered me to a floor on which the chambers of Judge Aguilar were located. I was conducted through the chambers suite – reception area, a series of small offices for law clerks, a conference room, that sort of thing – to the large corner office occupied by Judge Aguilar himself.

As I stood in the doorway I was scrutinized by a pair of green eyes, very deep green eyes. The eyes' possessor yawned, not out of sleepiness or for need of oxygen but as an expression of disdain; whoever I was, the eyes and the yawn said, I could not have been less important or interesting. The eyes' possessor was reposing on a sort of divan near a window on the east side of the office, a window through which warm sunlight was streaming. The eyes' possessor then licked one of its paws for a few seconds, gave me another desultory glance and, annoyed to see that I was still present, turned to the window and went back to sleep. Apparently low-carb diets don't work for felines, because the cat on Bob Aguilar's divan was grossly overweight, so obese that it appeared to be imprisoned in its own fat and all but incapable of movement. The cat's white fur, however, was luxuriant, and appeared from across the room to be silky to the touch. Bob had probably paid good money for the stupid thing. The cat probably had a pedigree, and Bob would pay good money to own something with a pedigree.

Bob was on the phone, but gesturing to catch my attention. He pointed toward a small coffee table flanked by wingback chairs at the far side of his office. There were chairs opposite his desk, but apparently, we would chat in the wingback chairs, next to the coffee table on the oriental rug.

"See you on the links, then," said Bob enthusiastically to the telephone; and hung up. He stood, smiling. "Clark, old man. How the hell are you?" Bob was about six feet tall and still very fit. He had a full head of hair, the color of which did not exist in nature. There was a sort of blondish sheen to Bob's hair, but you had the sense that at any moment the hair would morph back into the plain brown that nature had intended it to be. I know that Bob swam a great deal, so his hair came into contact with sea water or chlorine or both. It apparently came into contact with other things as well.

Bob gave me a good firm handshake, pointed toward the chairs, and we sat. I sat, actually, and Bob was about to sit when he got back up and walked over to the cat on the divan. "I saw you admiring Oliver here," he said to me. He picked the cat up in his arms; the cat, startled, attempted to react, but was so hampered by the weight of its own blubber and fur that it could do little more than look surprised and annoyed. Bob sat with the cat in his lap and stroked it a few times. "Oliver Wendell Holmes, you know. Lives here in chambers." The stroking was obviously pissing off the cat, and Bob stopped. "You probably remember that I'm related, on my mother's side, to the Holmes family."

A family connection to Oliver Wendell Holmes must have been a recent invention; he hadn't made that one up yet back when we were in law school. If I recalled correctly, his mother had been born on Isla de Pinas, the daughter of laborers. He was related to Oliver Wendell Holmes the Supreme Court justice like he was related Oliver Wendell Holmes the beer-bellied cat. "Yes, of course," I said.

That was the right answer. "It really is grand to see you, Clark. I don't know why we don't see each other more often."

I could think of several reasons, all good. "Well, perhaps we'll have a chance to see each other much more often." I wanted to get to the point of my visit.

Bob smiled. "Right you are." He then looked serious again. "Hell of thing about Tom Needham. Quiet fellow, not much to say, but a hell of a good old boy really. And a six handicap, at his age." Bob paused reflectively, considering the tragic death of a man who was a six handicap. "You ... you don't play, do you, Clark?"

"Golf? No. Never took it up."

He looked at me with an exaggerated sympathy, as if I had just told him that everyone on my block had pancreatic cancer. Perhaps Bob Aguilar would not want to be joined on the federal bench by someone who did not play golf; especially if that someone was taking over the courtroom of a six handicap. I felt the urge to say something, so I said, "Bob, mind if I ask you a question about procedure here in the federal courts?" He replied with a gesture; no, he didn't mind. "Someone told me that in federal court judges routinely base their sentencing decisions on charges for which the defendant has been acquitted, as well as those for which he's been convicted. That's not the case, is it?"

"Well, of course we consider all relevant evidence, old boy."

"But if a man's been acquitted, evidence of the charge for which he was acquitted is no longer relevant."

"The Supreme Court says it is. There's a case right on point. Weren't you the clever little fellow who remembered the names of all the Supreme Court cases?"

I shouldn't have, but I said it. "You're thinking of *United States v. Watts*."

"Well," he said indulgently, "there you have it."

I shouldn't be drawn into an argument. I knew that I shouldn't be drawn into an argument. "Bob, it's one thing for the Supreme Court to say that judges can consider a wide range of facts and evidence in fashioning a just sentence. It's another thing for judges to routinely ignore jury verdicts of acquittal and sentence defendants for conduct as to which they were found not guilty."

I shouldn't have said it. He looked peeved, as if I were a hopelessly rebellious and idealistic teenager with whom he, the *pater familias*, was obliged to deal. "Clark, look here. I have the highest regard for what you fellows do down at the Gerstein Building. I really do. Dealing with the wretched of the earth, armies of them, day in and day out, in that squalid building – I think you're entitled to all the credit in the world. Just maintaining some semblance of order is an achievement." Carefully, Bob set Oliver Wendell Holmes down on the floor. The cat lay there, exhausted by the ordeal of having been moved from lap to carpet. Bob looked at me, pursed his lips very gravely, nodded a few times. "I understand that you fellows must use any and every tool to maintain your shred of order, to prevent the state criminal justice system from plummeting into riot and chaos. One of the tools you must use is mythology. Old shibboleths such as 'the defendant is presumed innocent' or 'no defendant may be convicted absent proof beyond a reasonable doubt,' if not used too frequently, serve to persuade the rabble that you're really *about* something, that justice writ large is being done and they ought to behave themselves and respect the majesty of it. I understand that, old boy; believe me, I do.

"But if you're serious about coming over to federal court, you must understand that we are concerned here with the serious business of protecting society from serious crimes. It would be irresponsible for us to permit seventh-grade civics-class platitudes about guilty people being presumed innocent to hobble us in the discharge of our duty. The overwhelming majority of defendants who come into my courtroom have committed the crimes with which they are charged and will commit other crimes if given the chance to do so. I have the power to impose a sentence that will deprive them of that chance, and I would be wrong if I failed to exercise that power."

"Even by relying on conduct underlying charges for which a jury has returned a verdict of acquittal?"

Bob made a momentary display of overcoming his feelings of exasperation. "Sentencing typically takes place a couple of months after a trial concludes. The 12 retired postal carriers who made up the jury have gone home feeling that they did their little part in the process. They have told their friends and neighbors how justice was done. Sentencing is no concern of theirs. Just the opposite; it's a chance for me to rectify any mistakes they may have made."

So there was, after all, something Bob Aguilar believed in besides the aggrandizement of Bob Aguilar via his elevation to high places. He believed in the aggrandizement of Bob Aguilar via the exercise of the power given to those in high places. Other than that, Bob's little speech had taught me nothing I didn't already know. I knew that he was intelligent, that he could make a forcible and logical argument about the law. And I knew that no amount of civility or unction on his part or mine would ever cause me to like, respect, or agree with him.

It was an awkward moment, but that was something that Bob's civility and unction could fix. He smiled. "Did my staff give you a little tour of our chambers?" No, his staff had not given me a little tour of our chambers. So Bob himself showed me the sights. He even introduced me to one of his law clerks as "someone we hope will be joining us here on the federal bench very soon." Our tour ended up at the outer chambers door, from which point Bob made it clear that my visit was over. I was a little surprised. I had expected ... I don't know what, really. Being introduced to the other federal judges? Being taught the secret federal judges' handshake? Being given the key to the federal judges' men's room? "It was a great pleasure seeing you, old boy. If there's anything, anything at all that I can do to help, don't hesitate for a moment to call."

"Thanks very much, Bob." And I left, less certain why I had come than when I arrived.

• • •

I had assumed that I would be spending all morning in federal court, perhaps even be invited to stay for lunch. As it turned out I was back in my own chambers by mid-morning. That was good, and it was bad. It was good because it gave me time to work my way through the piles of files on my desk. It was bad because I didn't particularly feel like working my way through the piles of files on my desk. I had been at it for a very long hour when Carmen told me that Dr. Riggs was on the phone.

We didn't spend much time on pleasantries. I knew why he had called, I wanted to hear what he had to say, and I told him so.

So he said it. "He's a homicide, Clark. Blunt instrument trauma, above the left temple. A first-year medical student could get this one right."

"Any idea what he was hit with?"

"Not really. He was a frail old man, Clark. A blow that wouldn't have done real damage to a young, vigorous man might have been enough to kill Bilstein. Blunt instrument trauma, a single blow – that's about all I can say. He probably fell down the stairs afterward. There's little bruising, but then there wouldn't be if he was already dead. Of course it's harder to be certain about the bruising in a man of that age and condition."

I wanted to make sure that I understood. "So either a right-handed man was facing him and hit him, or a left-handed man was behind him and hit him."

"Provided you're not using the word 'man' in a gender-specific sense, that's probably correct. A woman could have hit him hard enough to kill him."

"Any idea which it was?"

"You mean was it a man or a woman?"

"No." No, that wasn't what I meant. "No, I mean was he struck from behind, or face-to-face?"

"I honestly don't know. Maybe someone stood to the side and hit him. Maybe someone backhanded him." I heard a sigh at the other end of the line. "Clark, you're not the prosecutor on this case. You're not even the judge. I called to give you this information as a courtesy, because we're old friends and because you'll be deluged with inquiries from the press. My advice to you is: be a civil judge, and let the police be the police."

It was good advice. "That's good advice. How about Bootsie Weber?"

He was starting to feel sorry that he had called, so I got less information about Bootsie than I had about Herman Bilstein. "About the same."

"Any idea who the lead investigator on this is?"

"Goodbye, Clark."

"Wait, Doc, wait, one more thing: do you have the inventory of his personal effects?"

I could almost feel him tugging at his moustache. "Clark, when this case is over, feel free to come by my office. I'll show you some nice new corpses and we'll have lunch. Goodbye." He hung up.

I thought about Dr. Riggs's good advice. Then I took another long look at the various pleadings piled upon my desk. Then I told Carmen to telephone whichever police property-room supervisor had custody of whatever personal property Herman Bilstein had on him at the time he died. In about three minutes I was talking to a sergeant.

"Passport issued by the State of Israel. U.S. currency, $119.31. Foreign currency, value not determined. Traveler's checks, various denominations. Brown wallet, contents ... what appear to be miscellaneous forms of identification in foreign language, some photos, ... also credit cards. Airplane ticket. Eyeglasses. Some prescription medication but we can't read the prescription, we're having that checked out. The ME's office has his clothing and his cane or walker or whatever it was. Mmm ... that's about it. Anything in particular you were looking for, Your Honor?"

No one took his cash, his ID or passport, his medications. Whoever killed him either didn't intend to rob him or was interrupted before robbing him. "The photos in his wallet ... what are they? Portrait photos, pictures of family members, that sort of thing?"

"Uh ... let's see ... yes. Yeah, just pictures of people, probably relatives, grandchildren, uh-huh."

"Old photos or new photos?"

"I really couldn't say, Judge. They're all color, no black-and-whites, so I guess they're pretty new." He paused, waiting for a sign that we were finished. He would not show impatience with a judge, even if he felt it. I asked quickly about Boots Weber's property, but there was none. The pockets of her clothing were empty at the time she was found. Her purse, with the usual items in it – wallet, cash, cellphone, cosmetics – was in her desk where she had left it, and nothing in it was impounded for evidence. Apparently, she hadn't planned to be gone long.

"Thank you, Sergeant, you've been most helpful. One more thing: who's the lead detective on this case?"

I heard a shuffle of paper. "Well, the property receipt was signed off by ...." He gave me a name: Lt. Cabrera.

I hung up with the sergeant and asked Carmen to get the detective on the phone. I knew Cabrera slightly. He was an experienced homicide investigator, a man at home with his work. He was courteous, quiet, expressionless. I had not seen him in some time, but I recalled him as a tall, thin man, with dark hair combed straight back.

Carmen had him on the line in minutes, and he answered my questions patiently if briefly: So far as the police knew, Herman Bilstein had no acquaintances in South Florida, including Boots Weber; Boots had a wide circle of friends, but no enemies, no one with a reason to wish her mortal harm. Yes, the police were attempting to identify and interview everyone known to have been in the area at the time. Of course the police had only begun to look into the matter. He would be happy to keep me informed. I thanked him.

I walked out of chambers to the right, down the empty corridor, turned right again and passed through the door into the stairwell. The walls were painted a tired and dirty beige. Each stair was finished with a rough, textured surface that appeared to be rubber, or something like rubber. The finish was intended to prevent accidents. Along the stairs ran a sturdy handrail; it, too, was there to prevent accidents. Every precaution had been taken to prevent anyone from slipping and falling as he, or she, went up, or down, the stairs. The landing on which I stood, like the landing half a floor below on which two bodies had been found, was poured cement painted a reddish brown.

I stood with my hands in my pockets. There was little to see and nothing to hear. The stairwell was silent, as it almost always was. Lawyers, burdened with trial files and briefcases, would use the elevator unless they were very pressed for time. Courthouse employees probably would use the elevator; they were seldom pressed for time. Strangers to the courthouse – witnesses, say, or jurors – would follow the crowd to the elevators. Did a smoker, hoping to catch an illicit puff or two without detection, slip into the stairwell and commit murder? Sure; or maybe a homicidal maniac with nothing much to do on his day off wandered into the civil courthouse, found his way into the stairwell, and killed Boots Weber. Sure; maybe Bilstein committed suicide by smashing himself in the head with his walker.

I wandered back to chambers.

Carmen was at her computer, typing furiously. I looked at my watch; it was almost noon. "Carmen, do you know why most of the judges prefer the civil courthouse to the criminal courthouse?" It wasn't a real question and she didn't treat it as one. But she did stop typing. "Because there aren't any good restaurants near the criminal courthouse, but there are lots of good restaurants around here. We've been here at the civil courthouse two and a half days. How about I take you to lunch?"

She looked me over carefully. "*You* want to go out to lunch?"

I nodded.

"And you're actually going to eat?"

I nodded again.

"Food. You're going to eat food?"

I nodded.

Carmen is the world's best secretary. She is a dear and loyal soul. She has other good qualities as well. But she will not see 40 again and spends no time looking in the rear-view mirror for it. She was young once, had her days of wine and roses, got married, had children. The children are gone but not too far away; the husband is gone and far away enough. The husband was a disappointment to Carmen. Food, on the other hand, is rarely a disappointment to Carmen. She considers eating to be serious business. Eating with me annoys her, because I do such a poor job of it and derive so little enjoyment from it.

Still, I was offering to buy lunch, and the alternative was whatever was in the brown paper bag she had brought to work with her. "Where?" she asked.

"That place across the street. You'll like it. All the lawyers and judges go there for lunch."

"What place across the street?"

"The ... uh ... the one that all the judges and lawyers go to." Carmen's face was a picture of disbelief. I was selling her a rainbow. Still ... how could she be sure that there wasn't a pot of food at the end of that rainbow?

I held the door for her as we walked out of chambers.

• • •

Carmen ordered the *ensalada de aguacate y cebolla*, and *palomilla* steak with *moros y cristianos*. I said that I'd have whatever the lady was having. There was, indeed, a restaurant across the street. There were even some judges and lawyers having lunch there, to whom I very ostentatiously said hello. A judge, to preserve his aura of omniscience, need only be right occasionally and surprisingly.

Ensalada de aguacate y cebolla is, it turns out, avocado and onion salad in a sort of oil and vinegar dressing. Raw onions upset my stomach, and I really have no taste for oil and vinegar. I did my best to keep up appearances by using pieces of bread to blot slices of avocado and then eating the avocado slices, but I could see that this was upsetting Carmen. She finished her salad with obvious enjoyment, said a few things in Spanish that I didn't understand and probably don't want to, and then switched her plate for mine. While she finished my salad I tried to keep up conversation as if nothing had happened.

It was at about this time that Woody English walked in. He was accompanied by two other young men and a young woman, all probably lawyers. I didn't recognize any of them. If they were from Raul Santos's firm they weren't involved in the Holtzman Museum case. Of course they may simply have been friends of English, perhaps former classmates.

I had been looking around to avoid Carmen's disapproving gaze, but I hadn't really meant to catch Woody's attention. It happened, however; our eyes met. At that point he was obligated to come over and greet me. I was a judge, he was a lowly young lawyer, and he and his supervisors were trying an important case before me.

He walked over with a big smile, pretending to be delighted to see me. "How are you, Judge?" he asked, extending a hand to shake.

I stood. "Just fine. How about you?"

"Fine, thanks. Do you recommend the ...." He looked down at the plate that was before me. It was so empty and clean that it was impossible to imagine what had been on it – Carmen had seen to that. "The ... uh ...."

"Avocado and onion salad. Yes, very much so. Delicious. I only wish I could get Carmen to finish hers. Carmen, you remember Woodrow English, from Raul Santos's firm?"

Carmen looked up from the serious business of eating, but only briefly. She had learned long ago that lawyers had to be nice to a judge's secretary whether they liked it or not, but judges' secretaries had to be nice to lawyers only if they felt like it. For the most part, Carmen was nice to everyone; or at least to everyone who hadn't pissed her off. But Woody English was interrupting lunch.

Woody handled it beautifully. "Please don't let me interrupt your lunch." He said it with obvious sincerity, and Carmen was happy to take him at his word.

I owed him a minute or two of conversation. "You must be quite a wizard on the computer."

He smiled. "I'm almost as good as my twelve-year-old cousin. But how did you ...?"

"Raul mentioned that you were the one who found Herman Bilstein on the internet."

Woody shook his head. "Not me."

"I thought Raul said it was you."

"No, not me."

I glanced across the room. Woody's friends were being seated. "I don't mean to keep you. Enjoy your lunch." I shook his hand again and sat down, giving him permission to go.

"Thanks. Good seeing you, Judge." And he left.

"Say, if it wasn't you ...." But he was gone. I had no right to call him back.

• • •

"Mr. Davis, please call your first witness."

The afternoon session convened on time and uneventfully. The bailiff called for order and actually got it, more or less. Raul Santos, finding himself with no more witnesses to call, announced quickly and quietly that he was resting his case. Zachary Taylor Davis stood slowly, paused as long as he possibly could, and announced, "I call Rabbi Chaim Stein."

I heard again the rustling sound, felt again the sense that the visitors' gallery – already packed to the limit by the press and public – was somehow pulsing against the rails that encompassed it. Rabbi Stein came forward. He affirmed, but would not swear, to tell the truth, the whole truth, and nothing but the truth; and he took the stand.

"Please state your name."

"Rabbi Chaim Stein." His English was excellent, leavened with an all-but-imperceptible accent that gave his speech a professorial quality.

Zachary Davis fixed the rostrum with his death-grip and leaned forward slightly. "Rabbi Stein, please tell us briefly: What is a *bes din*?"

"It is a rabbinic court."

"What, if any, role do you have in the *bes din* on Miami Beach?"

"I am ... what I suppose in English we would call the chief judge."

The briefest of questions and answers had passed between them, and only three such exchanges, but the courtroom had grown wonderfully quiet. They made quite a duet, Zachary Taylor Davis and Rabbi Chaim Stein. Both were large men, both tall and heavy-set. Davis's skin was a rich black and his suit the palest of grays; Rabbi Stein's hair, skin, beard was white, his hat and suit all black. In this tableau of blacks, whites, and grays, the rabbi's luminous blue eyes shined all the brighter. Davis's questions were posed in a voice deep and powerful; the voice in which Stein answered was firm but soft, as if he had an important secret to impart. Neither man gestured when he spoke; but both punctuated their words with animated facial expression.

"Rabbi Stein, you understand, do you not, that a dispute has arisen between Dr. Bernard Gumbiner and the Holtzman Museum?"

"Yes."

Davis straightened his posture. "In fact, I have discussed the nature of the dispute with you, prior to calling you as a witness, haven't I?"

"Yes."

"Did Dr. Gumbiner take part in those discussions?"

"No. I have never actually met Dr. Gumbiner."

Davis nodded. "And based upon our discussions, what is your understanding of the nature of the dispute between Dr. Gumbiner and the Holtzman?"

"Dr. Gumbiner is the owner of a particularly valuable art collection. He would like to loan it to the Holtzman for display. The Holtzman demands that it first be tested in various ways to establish its authenticity. Dr. Gumbiner is unwilling to subject his artwork to such testing and insists, according to a provision in the agreement between himself and the museum, that the matter be resolved by the *bes din*."

There is an expression among trial lawyers: affidavit quality. I was told once that the expression was coined by Edward Bennett Williams, one of the greatest trial lawyers of the American 20th century and a man who must surely have been possessed of affidavit quality. Whether he originated this form of words or not is unimportant. Its meaning is readily understood by all, and its importance is readily understood by lawyers. There are some people whom we just want to believe. It is not so much the content of their words. Perhaps we want to believe them most when the content of their words is most doubtful. It is this effect upon others – this inspiration in the listener of a sense of trustworthiness, of credibility – that is referred to as affidavit quality. The lawyer who has it in good supply has an inestimable advantage. The lawyer who lacks it has a daunting disadvantage. Of all the lawyers I have ever known, Jack Sheridan most unmistakably had affidavit quality.

But affidavit quality is not limited to lawyers. A witness can have affidavit quality. I had never encountered a witness who had it to a greater degree than Rabbi Stein. His summary of the dispute between the parties in this case was as accurate as any lawyer or judge could have made it, but it was not the substance of his answer that engaged the hearer. It was many things separately – the image of Santa Claus, the old-world accent, the bright blue eyes – and it was everything taken together.

Zachary Taylor Davis was lawyer enough to know what he had. He dialed down his own voice, his own personality, and let the spotlight focus on his witness. "Rabbi, is the Miami Beach *bes din* capable of resolving this dispute?"

Raul Santos shifted in his seat. The question might be objectionable on any number of grounds. But Raul was lawyer enough to know that Davis and his witness had a certain momentum, had engaged my attention and that of the audience, and that marginal objections would probably not be sustained. Trials and hearings are not law-school exams; objections are seldom worth making unless they will be sustained or will preserve some vital issue for appellate review. I didn't look at Raul. If I had looked at him, he would have considered himself invited to object. But I didn't look at him, and he didn't object.

"I see no reason why we could not," said the rabbi.

Davis moved slightly to one side, then to the other. His movements appeared slight, but the podium trembled with the force of his grip. He was moving on to a new line of inquiry. "Rabbi, I want to ask a few questions about your background. Are you familiar with a concentration camp operated by the Third Reich prior to and during the Second World War, known as Weeghman?"

"Yes."

"In fact, Rabbi, were you interned at Weeghman?"

"Yes. I was."

"Did you know Ernst Adler?"

The rabbi shook his head. "No. I heard, of course ... there were rumors, constant rumors, that one of the prisoners somewhere was managing somehow to produce works of art, beautiful, inspirational works of art. But I never met him. I never saw what he did."

Zachary Taylor Davis stood at the podium quietly, nodding slowly a few times. He seemed to be in a world of his own, or perhaps one he shared only with Rabbi Chaim Stein. Then he turned his gaze to me. "I have nothing further of this witness, Your Honor."

A judge must not look shocked or surprised. A judge must never look shocked or surprised. But this was a real challenge to my poker face. The testimony that Taylor had elicited from his witness up to this point seemed no more than introductory. I had expected a lengthy recitation on the rabbi's background, his experience serving on the *bes din*, his world-renown scholarship on matters of Jewish religious jurisprudence.

I don't know whether I managed to avoid looking surprised, but I managed to avoid saying anything for a few seconds and that in itself was a small triumph. In those few seconds I had a glimpse of what a really superb lawyer Zachary Taylor Davis was. He had gotten from his witness all that he needed: that the witness had no relationship with Dr. Gumbiner, that the witness was quite confident as to the *bes din*'s ability to resolve the dispute in question, that the witness was not compromised by anything he had learned or seen at Weeghman. Now he would present Raul Santos with two bad choices: Raul could, of course, simply decline to cross-examine Rabbi Stein, on the theory that Stein really hadn't said very much, and that cross-examination might only make matters worse. But that would enable Davis to argue that Raul did not -- or could not -- dispute the rabbi's testimony. If Raul wanted to be able to argue that the *bes din* was not an appropriate forum to resolve the dispute between the Holtzman Museum and Dr. Gumbiner, he would almost certainly have to cross-examine Rabbi Stein. Whether that would help or hurt his case was very much an open question. Cross-examining a saint is almost always a way to look like a sinner. And if Raul thought that he could live with the testimony Stein had given on direct examination, why take the risk of getting killed by the testimony Stein might give on cross-examination?

Davis's decision to place his adversary on the horns of a dilemma was obviously a stratagem he had planned in advance. At the conclusion of his questioning of the rabbi he had not conferred with his cocounsel, had not asked her if there was anything left out. No; he had planned to lay a trap for Raul, and he had laid it. It was damn fine lawyering.

Raul, for his part, saw the trap. But what could he do about it?

"Mr. Santos, do you have any cross-examination of this witness?"

For just a second Raul – smooth, polished, debonair Raul – stared into the middle distance, squinting with concentration and chewing his lower lip. But it was only for a second. Zachary Taylor Davis knew that Raul Santos had to take the dare, and Raul Santos knew that Zachary Taylor Davis knew he had to take the dare. To his credit, Raul made no pretense of conferring with his colleagues. He was senior counsel. The case was his to win or lose. It was his own head that he would place in the lion's mouth, and no matter the outcome he would not say later that he did so on the advice of a junior colleague.

"I have, Your Honor."

"Please proceed."

Raul walked to the podium and placed his pad of notes on it. This could not be a bull-in-a-china-shop cross-examination. To have any chance of succeeding, this cross-examination must be deft, deferential, and above all things careful. Who better than Raul to pull it off?

"Rabbi, you testified that you serve as the chief judge of the *bes din* on Miami Beach?"

"Yes."

"You have done so on many occasions?"

"Yes, I would say so, yes."

"Could you estimate how many times you have participated as a judge in the proceedings of the *bes din*?"

Rabbi Stein pursed his lips. "I would say ... I cannot say exactly. Would it be sufficient to say, perhaps several dozen times?"

Raul gestured; a tut-tut gesture, an obliging expression. "Of course, Rabbi. An approximation is perfectly good enough. Several dozen times, let us say." He paused. "Now, of those several dozen times, on how many occasions was the *bes din* called upon to determine the authenticity of an art collection?"

It was a risk, but only a very slight one; how many times, after all, did such an issue arise? All cross-examination is risk, and not asking the question might have been riskier still.

Raul's trial-lawyer luck was holding. "I do not recall such a matter ever having come before the *bes din*," said the rabbi.

"We have had testimony in these proceedings, Rabbi, that some of the tests by which the Adler collection will be evaluated require a very advanced knowledge of chemistry. Now, permit me to say that I have the highest respect for your very considerable scholarship, but you do not claim to be an expert in advanced chemistry, do you?"

Zachary Taylor Davis stood. He was not obliged to leap to his feet – the very act of his standing drew the attention of all on-lookers – so he stood slowly. "If the Court please, I object. The question is irrelevant. Witnesses may testify to questions of chemistry before the *bes din* just as they may testify before this Court. Your Honor has a very considerable scholarship too, but it does not, so far as we know, extend to advanced chemistry."

It wasn't really an objection. Davis wanted to point out to me the flaw in the reasoning that lay behind Raul's question. But I knew just what to say. "Your objection is overruled, Mr. Davis, except for the part about my having a very considerable scholarship."

That got me some grins from the gallery and a paroxysm of laughter from the assembled lawyers, who were duty-bound to show their enjoyment of the judicial sense of humor. The rabbi, who clearly was a man who liked a joke, laughed too; and I thought – blasphemously, blasphemously – of a line from "The Night Before Christmas:" "And he shook when he laughed like a bowl full of jelly."

"I am not a student of chemistry," said the rabbi, still smiling.

"So far as you know, none of the other rabbis who might serve on the *bes din* are students of chemistry?"

"They are not."

Raul nodded agreeably. "You indicated, sir, that when you endured imprisonment at Weeghman you never saw the paintings or other art objects produced by Ernst Adler?"

"I never saw them."

"You have not made a study of the work of Ernst Adler?"

"I? No."

"You do not hold yourself out as an expert on Adler's artistic style, do you?"

"No, I do not."

"And so far as you know, none of your fellow rabbis, your colleagues on the *bes din*, hold themselves out as experts on Adler's body of artistic work?"

"I am sure they do not."

Raul nodded; but he looked down at his notes, and his lips tightened ever so slightly. This had been the easy part. He had established that the rabbis who made up the *bes din* did not, themselves, claim to be able to evaluate the Adler collection. But that had never been in doubt. As Zachary Davis's objection pointed out, the real question was: why couldn't the *bes din* evaluate the Adler collection in more or less the same way that a secular court would – by calling expert witnesses on art, for example, or reviewing the tests performed by chemists?

Here lay the gamble. If Raul could get the rabbi to say that the *bes din* was not equipped to conduct proceedings that would result in a fair evaluation of the Adler collection, his case was won.

But on direct examination, in response to Davis's question, the rabbi had said just the opposite: that he knew of no reason why the *bes din* couldn't fairly adjudicate the dispute that had arisen over the Adler collection. For Raul to question Chaim Stein on the proceedings of a *bes din* was the cross-examination equivalent of parachuting deep into enemy territory.

"Rabbi ...." Raul wanted to choose his words with the greatest particularity. He extended his right arm toward the visitors' gallery. "Rabbi, you see that these proceedings are open to the public?"

"Yes, certainly."

"It is my understanding – and please correct me if I'm wrong – that the proceedings of a *bes din* are not open to the public. Is that right?"

"In general we do not invite the public."

Raul walked over to the court reporter and stood next to her. "You see, Rabbi, that everything we say in this courtroom is taken down verbatim by the court reporter?"

The stenographer, suddenly the center of attention, sat poised at her machine. "I am aware of that, yes."

"There is, if I understand correctly, no court reporter at the *bes din*?"

"No, there is not."

"So no verbatim record is made of the *bes din* proceedings?"

"Not ... no, no verbatim record."

Back at the podium, Raul posed over his notes. He had demonstrated that a rabbinic court differed in some ways from a secular court. But there was nothing about these differences to suggest that a rabbinic court could not resolve the question of the authenticity of the Adler collection. There was nothing about these differences that would undermine confidence in the *bes din* or its proceedings. Raul needed more. He knew it; but could he get it?

"In the courts of the State of Florida, anyone can testify as a witness. That's not true in rabbinic courts, is it?"

The rabbi paused to frame his answer. I had a sense that perhaps he had been expecting this question, and the line of questions that would follow. "There are limitations on who may testify. Yes."

"For example," asked Raul, "in the *bes din*, women cannot testify, can they?"

Stein took a deep breath and let it out. "It is a very complex matter. There are limitations on the testimony of women."

"With perhaps some rare exceptions, though, women cannot testify in rabbinic courts, can they?"

"I do not mean to be difficult," said the rabbi, and he seemed so very genuinely concerned about not being difficult. "But it is not so simple. It is not a question of yes or no. There is a very elaborate body of rabbinic opinion on this question."

Raul smiled. "I certainly appreciate that, Rabbi Stein. And I apologize if I've phrased my questions in a way to make them unnecessarily difficult to answer. Can we agree to this? That *as a general rule*, women do not testify in rabbinic courts?" Raul, who normally kept his body language to a stark minimum, put a world of body English into "as a general rule."

The rabbi smiled back. "Would it be sufficient to say that, as a general rule, there are limitations and issues that arise when a woman is offered as a witness that do not arise when a man is offered as a witness? Would that be sufficient?"

Raul's smile broadened. He wanted to make it look like he had gotten just exactly the answer he wanted. Was it sufficient? It was goddamn well not sufficient; but it would have to be. "And in the same or a similar sense, sir, would it be fair to say that limitations and issues arise when a Gentile, a non-Jew, is offered as a witness? Limitations and issues that may not arise when a Jew is offered as a witness?"

"Similar," the rabbi nodded. "Yes. Here too I must caution that there is an elaborate body of *responsa*, of rabbinic opinion."

"I certainly understand," said Raul. "I'm sure we all do." He came around the podium, a step or two closer to the witness. "Now Rabbi, suppose that this matter, this controversy between the Holtzman Museum of Judaica and Dr. Gumbiner were to come before the *bes din*. Suppose further that some of the key witnesses, the chemists and art experts, turned out to be Gentiles or women. With respect to those witnesses, there would be ... what was your expression? Limitations and issues?"

"That is possible. Yes."

"Possible." Repeated Raul. "And it is possible that some or all of those Gentile witnesses, or those women witnesses, would not be permitted to testify before the *bes din*? That, too, is possible?"

Stein pursed his lips again. "As I have mentioned, it is difficult to answer in the abstract. But yes, it is certainly possible."

Raul exhaled. The most difficult thing for young lawyers to learn about cross-examination is when to stop. Raul had not gotten everything he wanted, but what he had gotten might well be enough. Trying to make it better could easily make it worse. Raul, I thought, will stop here and now.

But he did not. He stared at his notes very concertedly for a moment and asked, "Rabbi, we are told in the ten commandments, 'Thou shalt not take the name of the Lord thy God in vain.' I realize that's only an English translation, but it's a common translation, isn't it?"

The rabbi appeared inclined to offer an explanation, but settled for, "It is a common translation. Yes."

"Many of us think that means that we shouldn't use swear words. But that isn't the meaning of the commandment, is it?"

"No," agreed the rabbi. "That is a common misimpression."

"Would you be kind enough to explain to us – briefly, now – the proper understanding of that commandment?" Raul was all gentle smiles and slight bows.

"In Biblical times," said the witness, "there were no means of recording and formalizing contracts. If I agreed to buy land from you, for example, we could not record the deed at the ... would it be correct to say, the office of the clerk of court?" Raul offered another gentle smile. "So the process of solemnizing contracts took on great importance. At the time that the sale and purchase was concluded, if you were a worshiper of Ba'al, for example, you might solemnize the transaction by swearing, 'As Ba'al lives, I will honor this agreement.' And as a Jew, I might swear, '*Chai haShem* – as the Almighty God lives – I will honor this agreement.'"

"So this holy commandment teaches us to honor our contracts and promises?" asked Raul.

"Yes. That is correct."

"And not to seek means or excuses to avoid honoring our contracts and promises?"

"No. We must not do that."

It was a perfect endgame, and Raul knew it. He had, apparently, gotten some very good coaching from someone. "I have nothing further of this witness, Your Honor. Thank you very kindly, Rabbi." And he sat down.

I turned to Davis. "Do you have any redirect of this witness?"

By way of answer Zachary Davis took his place at the podium. He brought no notes with him. "Rabbi Stein, Mr. Santos asked you whether the testimony of women was admissible before a *bes din*, and you told him that it was a complex question, is that right?"

"Yes."

"A difficult question to answer with a yes or no?"

The rabbi smiled. "An impossible question to answer with a yes or no, Mr. Davis."

Davis smiled back. "I believe you said that there was a substantial body of rabbinic interpretation on the subject?"

"Yes indeed."

Davis actually let go of the podium. He put his hands in his pants pockets. "Rabbi, please summarize that body of rabbinic doctrine for us in your own words. In as much or little detail as you please."

What followed was the most extraordinary display of intellect and scholarship I have ever beheld. Were it not for the careful notes I try to take during trials and hearings I would be unable to describe it at all. As it is I'm sure my description will be very imperfect. The rabbi, of course, had no notes. His answer ran on for at least ten or 15 minutes, and although he spoke in an unhurried fashion he never had to pause to recollect a name or a date.

He began with the writings of Rambam, known also as Maimonides, a great medieval rabbinic scholar who set down a strict rule against admitting the testimony of women. About a century later, however, other great rabbis acknowledged exceptions to this strict rule. Rashba, like Maimonides a Sephardic rabbi – a member of the Jewish communities in North Africa or the Near East – pointed out that a woman would be permitted for reasons of social policy to testify to the death of a husband. These exceptions remained negligible, or nearly so, within the Sephardic Jewish community, explained Rabbi Stein. Rabbi Jacob ben Asher, who redacted the Arba Turim, Rabbi Aaron ben Yosef haLevy of Barcelona, and even the great Rabbi Joseph Karo in his treatise Shulchan Aruch, generally followed Maimonides's strict exclusion of women witnesses.

There was, however, contrary doctrine. Rabbi Stein then cited the Talmud at tractate *Kiddushin* section 73b for the proposition that a midwife can testify which of two twins was the first-born. Rabbi Mordechai ben Hillel, who lived in Germany during the 13th century, is cited by Rabbis Kolon and Isserles for the view that women may testify to facts arising in situations in which men would typically not be present. The testimony of a midwife as to the first-born of twins was one such example. Rabbi Mordechai identified seven other examples in his teachings; Rabbi Stein listed all of them. This view was expanded upon by Rabbi Israel Isserlein, who lived in Germany from 1390 to 1460. But Isserlein's teachings in this regard were criticized by Rabbi Shlomo Luria in a treatise written by him in Poland during the 16th century. Rabbi Luria took the position that it was clear from what Rabbi Isserlein had said and written that he had not seen certain of Maimonides's writings. Although Ashkenazi rabbis – those who lived in Eastern Europe – continued to liberalize the rules admitting the testimony of women, Sephardic rabbis held to the strict rule of exclusion. This was the teaching of such scholars as Rabbi Uzziel Alhayk, Rabbi Yonah Navon who lived in Jerusalem from 1713 to 1760, and Rabbi Hayim Palache.

But in more recent times, Rabbi Stein explained, the rule admitting the testimony of women had been considerably liberalized, particularly in Jewish communities in the Western world. A very distinguished rabbi in Brooklyn by the name of Klein had ruled that women were competent witnesses in a wide range of matters.

I look at what I have written, and I see a jumble of names, dates, places. Rabbi Stein's testimony was nothing like that. He spoke as if he had been telling this story all his life, as if the rabbis of whom he spoke were his friends, as if the centuries and cities in which they lived were a part of his personal history. At first, he spoke directly to Zachary Davis, but soon the entire courtroom fell silent and Rabbi Stein shared his narrative with everyone present. I saw one of the reporters in the front row stop taking notes, not because he didn't need the rabbi's testimony in his story, but because he just wanted to watch and listen. Zachary Taylor Davis did everything he could to take himself out of the picture, to turn into furniture or become invisible, so as not to detract from the attention being lavished upon the rabbi. Raul Santos probably thought of half-a-dozen objections and dismissed them all, knowing that he dared not interrupt.

Raul had made one very good point on cross-examination: The testimony of certain witnesses, such as women or non-Jews, might be inadmissible or only partly admissible before a *bes din*. Thus if it happened that a really important witness – say, a scientific expert on chemical methods of testing artwork, or an art expert who had important testimony about Adler's body of work – were a Gentile or a woman, his or her testimony might never be received by the *bet din*. And if that were the case, perhaps the methods employed by the *bes din* were insufficiently reliable to resolve so important a dispute. Apart from that, Raul would be correct in believing that I as an American judge would be naturally reluctant to entrust an important arbitration to a forum that engaged in the un-American practice of excluding witnesses based on gender or religion. That was something Raul couldn't come right out and say; but he had gotten his message across.

The question that Zachary Taylor Davis had asked on redirect examination – the question that brought forth Rabbi Stein's wonderful historical dissertation – had a little, but not a lot, to do with Raul's point. When Rabbi Stein was done speaking it was still probably the case that female witnesses would have a harder time getting in the *bes din* door than male witnesses would. But any concern about whether a rabbinic court presided over by

Chaim Stein could be trusted to produce a fair, reliable, accurate result had been dissipated forever.

Affidavit quality. To hear him speak was to believe him.

Zachary Davis asked no more questions, quietly announced that he rested his case, and sat down. "Counsel," I said, speaking as if there were no one in the courtroom but the lawyers and myself, "what's your pleasure? I know that we're all eager to bring this matter to a conclusion, but I don't want to burden you unfairly. If the Court were to take an extended recess – say, thirty minutes – could we then reconvene and proceed to closing arguments? Mr. Santos?"

"I'm sure we could, Your Honor."

"Mr. Davis?"

"I have no objection, Judge."

"So ordered. The court will be in recess for thirty minutes." I looked for the Elgin clock on the back of the courtroom wall, but it was still on the wall of another courtroom across town. Jack sometimes says that there are two places where you never see a clock, Vegas and jail, and for the same reason: they don't want you know how long you've been there.

Carmen was on the phone when I got back into chambers, but she pointed at a stack of telephone messages on her desk. It was a stack several inches high, and Carmen squinted her eyes and tightened her lips as she pointed to it. I picked up the phone messages. More calls from the press: from Florida newspapers, out-of-state newspapers, foreign newspapers; from television reporters, from magazines. They wanted a comment about the murders of Boots Weber and Herman Bilstein. They wanted a comment about the testimony of the revered Rabbi Chaim Stein. I knew that Carmen would never recede from the party line – Judge Addison cannot comment on a matter pending before him – but her patience was obviously wearing thin.

There was one call I could return. Anita answered when I dialed Que Sera Sera's chambers, and after we exchanged pleasantries she put me through to Kay.

"Hello, Clark. How was your visit to federal court?"

It was an annoying waste of time, thanks very much. "Fine, thanks, Kay. I know you went to a lot of trouble to arrange it. I appreciate it."

There was a pause. Had my answer sounded strained to Kay's discerning ear? But "Different world, isn't it?" was all she said.

"Different world. I'm sure Bob Aguilar couldn't make a key lime pie to hold a candle to yours."

She didn't laugh – not loud enough for me to hear – but I could feel her smile. "You didn't try to take a cell phone in, did you?"

A cell phone? "A cell phone?"

"They have rules about that. They have rules about everything. Only federal judges, federal prosecutors, and federal agents can bring their cell phones into the federal courthouse. Defense attorneys, witnesses, jurors, visitors like you and me – you know, the peasant class – can't. The fellow who runs the Umbrella Room will hold your cell phone for a couple of dollars." Outside every courthouse in Miami are two or three hot dog stands on wheels. The heat and mid-day sun being what they are, each of the hot dog vendors has a large beach umbrella set up over his cart, and transacts his business in its shadow. Courthouse regulars pressed for time or cash will grab lunch at the "Umbrella Room."

"I've heard that they have a similar set-up at the Old Bailey in London. There's a bar across the street where you can check your cell phone, or maybe it's your umbrella. The fellow who runs the bar makes more money checking phones than he does selling drinks." The Old Bailey is the central criminal courthouse in

London, the most ancient and storied criminal court in the English-speaking world.

"Is that true?" Kay asked.

"I don't know. I've never been to London. When you're a rich, retired judge, if you want to take some time off from playing with your grandchildren and baking you can visit the Old Bailey and let me know."

"I'll do that. I'll visit you in your fancy chambers in the federal courthouse and let you know."

Maybe. Maybe not. "Sure thing, Kay. Thanks again." Kay was about to hang up when I asked, "How's Floyd's trial going? What's the latest?"

"You haven't heard?"

"Heard what?"

So Kay told me what. The scandal *du jour* didn't involve Sammy the Weasel, or Eleanor Hibbard, or Floyd Kroh Jr. It didn't involve anyone who came to participate in the trial; it involved someone who came to watch the trial. The trial of *State of Florida v. Ivan Vukovich and The Wet Spot* was a matter of general interest, but to certain persons it was a matter of very particular interest. The certain persons, of course, were the strippers who worked at The Wet Spot. Each day, two or three of the girls showed up in court, sitting in the public gallery and observing the trial proceedings. Whether it was Sammy the Weasel's idea that they show up is another entry on the list of things I'll never know, but a trial in America is open to the public, and strippers are members of the public.

It wasn't always the same two or three girls who came to watch each day, with one exception. A very tall, very buxom blond was in attendance each and every day. The word around the courthouse, said Kay, was that this particular girl was Russian, and thus very popular at The Wet Spot. Kay's personal opinion was that the lady was from the part of Russia known as Daytona Beach, but it really didn't matter. Her job didn't require her to speak Russian; in fact it didn't require her to speak at all. She was very tall, very blond, very busty, and apparently, she had a very Russian way of taking off her clothes. All of this made her a favorite with the clientele at The Wet Spot. She has, according to Kay, performed at various times under the names Anna Karenina; or The Molotov Cocktease; or Anna Karenina the Molotov Cocktease.

There are two public entrances to the criminal courthouse. The one in back is opposite the Miami-Dade County Jail, and unless you're a courthouse veteran you won't know that it's there. It's used mostly by lawyers. Members of the public typically use the front entrance, the one facing the parking lot. Visitors pass through metal detectors into the main floor lobby. From there they can take the escalators or the elevators to the floors of their choice.

This morning, like every morning this week, Miss Karenina (or Miss Cocktease; Kay wasn't sure which stage name was currently in use) arrived at the courthouse bright and early. She was wearing something Kay called a *bustier* (I may ask Miriam what that means. Then again, I may not), a very short skirt, a belt with a large metal buckle, and stiletto heels. On her first pass through the magnetometer she set it off. The security people told her to go back, remove her belt buckle, and try again.

Her second trip through the metal detector was no better. The security people told her to go back, remove her shoes, and try again.

When the magnetometer went off the third time, the suspected culprit was the underwires in Miss Karenina's *bustier*. (Kay told me this very matter-of-factly. I'm not entirely sure I know what underwires are, but I didn't interrupt her to ask.) The security people weren't quite certain how to proceed, because they certainly weren't going to ask her to take *that* off. As it turned out, they didn't have to.

Miss Karenina, who after all is a professional when it comes to undressing, concluded that this was not the sort of thing to be left to amateurs. She moved to the center of the lobby and, gyrating furiously to imaginary music, rocked into her routine.

The lobby of the Gerstein Building was, as it always is, teeming with people. Lawyers, cops, bail bondsmen, witnesses, corrections officers, all rushing back and forth, to court and from court, toward the coffee shop or away from it, coming late or leaving early. I would have told you that it would be impossible to stem, even to slow, the torrent of human traffic in the lobby of the Gerstein Building. But today, apparently, I would have been wrong. The sight of a tall, bosomy blond bumping and grinding was all it took to persuade the lawyers, cops, bail bondsmen, witnesses, and corrections officers to put aside their warring interests and focus – intently – on the common interest. Feet froze, jaws dropped, eyes glowed. Three Hialeah cops on the "up" escalator figured out what was happening just in time to do an about-face and sprint down the escalator before it carried them to the second floor and out of the line of sight. An elderly man had been standing at the information kiosk, just about the only piece of furniture in the lobby. He was the sort of old man whose wrinkled skin and too-large clothing gave the impression that once upon a time he had been much larger, but that he had done a lot of shrinking over the years. He seemed the very quiet type of retiree, and indeed he hadn't yet asked anything of the attendant at the information kiosk. But when Anna Karenina unhooked the top hook on her *bustier*, and then the second hook on her *bustier*, and then the third hook on her *bustier*, the old man decided that the least she was entitled to was a little musical accompaniment, and he blared out an *a capella* version of the melody they used to play in movies whenever a stripper was stripping. "You know the one," said Kay. "They used it in a shaving commercial years ago." And she hummed a little: da-da-*da*, da-da-da-*da*. "Pretty soon half the people in the lobby were singing along, and Miss Karenina was whipping her *bustier* back and forth to the rhythm."

"Where was Floyd while all this was going on?"

"Oh, upstairs in chambers, thank goodness. He didn't hear about it till hours later."

"So how did the show end?"

"About how you'd expect," Kay said. I had no idea how I'd expect. "She took it off, took it all off – the *bustier*, I mean – swung it in a big circle a few times as the crowd sang and cheered, and then tossed it to one of the security officers. I think it was the same security guy who was holding her shoes and belt buckle. Then she went back to the magnetometer, went through it one more time, still dancing, naked from the waist up and barefoot, and finally got a passing grade."

"Did she get a big round of applause?"

"Applause? Clark, there were men all over the place trying to hand her money. She must have gotten a hundred dollars in singles and fives, not to mention a dozen lawyers' business cards." Kay sighed. "All in all, just another day at the Richard E. Gerstein Justice Building, Miami's *palais d'justice*." I think Kay had something else to say, but she had to take another call.

And we hung up. At least she hadn't asked me about the Holtzman Museum case.

When I looked up from my phone call there was a face poking into my doorway. The features of the face – the ruddy, tanned complexion, the cleft chin – were the features of a man, but the expression on the face – the look of uncertainty, of questioning – was the expression of a child. The mouth at the bottom of the face spoke, and it said, "Clark! Is this a bad time?"

"Floyd. No ... no, of course not. Please come in." He had left his robe in chambers and his suitcoat in his car. He wore a white dress shirt, loosened at the neck because he was not on the bench, and a dark tie with a simple pattern. In his hands was a large brown cardboard box. I gestured toward a chair.

I would have asked him what brought him here, why he wasn't on the bench at the Gerstein Building, but it would have been pointless. I knew why he was here.

Carefully, he opened the brown cardboard box. Within it was the Elgin clock from my old courtroom, from his new courtroom. He took it out and handed it to me, saying nothing, waiting quietly but eagerly for praise and thanks, a timid kid who brought an apple to the teacher.

It really didn't mean that much to me, but it meant so much to him that it mean something to me. So I tried to sound as effusive as possible. "Floyd. This is very good of you." I cast about for something else to say. "I grew up in Elgin, you know." He nodded enthusiastically; yes, he knew.

I called for Carmen and she came in with notepad and pen in hand. I asked if she would be kind enough to call the Administrative Office of the Courts and have someone come up to affix the clock to the back wall of the courtroom. I told her that Judge Kroh would like to double-check for a particular ashtray belonging to his father that might have been inadvertently left in the area of our chambers, and asked that she be as helpful to him as possible. I even described the ashtray, as best I remembered the description Floyd had given: square, very heavy, about seven inches on a side, rounded corners, with a representation of a mill of some kind in the middle. Floyd paid close attention, nodding again and appearing very concerned. Carmen did an excellent job of pretending to take all this seriously.

Carmen returned to her desk, Floyd was about to commence his scavenger hunt, and I asked a question that perhaps should have gone unasked. "How are things going for you in criminal court?"

Floyd had started to rise. He sat down. "Well ... um ...."

"I heard you've already started a trial."

"Um ... well ...." I took him a minute to find a place to start. More than a minute, perhaps; but he found one. Then it all came pouring out. I heard it from him, and the next time I saw her I heard it from Kay, who had sat in the back of the courtroom for some important portions of the trial. I heard about it, too, from some of the Gerstein Building regulars, lawyers who happened to be present, or made it their business to be present, because the trial of *State versus Ivan Vukovich and The Wet Spot* was just too good to miss. So although I wasn't there, I feel as if I was. It took place, after all, in my courtroom. And I'll bet I know, just about word for word, how it took place.

• • •

"The State of Florida calls Henry Sauer." Eleanor Hibbard did not wait for Judge Kroh to invite her to call her first witness. As far as Eleanor is concerned, judges, criminal defense lawyers, and anyone else who happens to be in the courtroom are just so many speed bumps on the road to conviction. She knows perfectly well when to start calling witnesses, and she doesn't need anyone to tell her. So she hefted herself to her feet, and in a voice that sounds like it should be announcing, "Film at eleven" or "We'll be right back after these important messages," she announced that the State of Florida – not merely the prosecution, but the State of Florida, in all its majesty and power – called Henry Sauer.

A criminal trial does not begin with the calling of witnesses. A criminal trial begins with jury selection, then proceeds to opening statements, and only then moves on to the testimony of witnesses. But Sammy the Weasel's idea of jury selection is name-calling and finger-pointing, and his idea of opening statement is finger-pointing and name-calling, so Floyd Kroh's nerves and his gavel were both pretty worn out by the time the first witness was called. For her part, Eleanor was always eager to get to the evidentiary portion of a trial. She didn't worry much about jury selection because as far as she was concerned one juror was about like another, and any juror who didn't vote to convict should be prosecuted himself.

So Floyd was a little relieved, and Eleanor a little impatient, when the first witness wandered up to the witness stand and took the oath. Henry Sauer appeared to be the sort of fellow who could disappear in a crowd of two. He was average height and average build. His hair was a plain version of brown, his complexion a plain version of whatever we call the skin color that "white people" have. He wore a light blue dress shirt that was not old but not new, and a dark blue tie that was not new but not old. His slacks were a plain beige, and he had no sport coat or suit jacket. He spoke in a quiet, expressionless voice when he took the oath, and Eleanor scarcely waited till he said, "I do" before she began her questioning.

"Please tell the ladies and gentlemen of the jury your name." She gestured expansively, arm extended, toward the jury.

"Henry Sauer."

"And what do you do for a living, Mr. Sauer?"

"I'm a code inspector for the village of Coco Isles Beach." His answers, coming as they did between Eleanor's booming, fully-articulated questions, seemed particularly meek and flat.

"What are your duties as a code inspector for the village of Coco Isles Beach?"

"To visit various businesses within the village and determine whether they are transacting business in conformity with village ordinances."

Some lawyers look for reasons to move around the courtroom when they speak. Perhaps they think it makes the trial more interesting for the jury, or perhaps they do it to establish territorial rights. It may work for some lawyers, but Eleanor knows it would not work for her. She is, by the standards of contemporary fashion, too bulky a woman; and she knows it. So she stands still at the podium when she examines a witness, and moves very little.

In truth she has no need to move, because her voice, her wonderful voice, can do the moving for her. Before her on the podium is a yellow legal pad with handwritten notes, and even the handwriting is large, ornate, full of capital letters, as if it reflected the richness of her voice.

She directed the witness's attention to the late-night hours of a particular date. "Did you have occasion, Mr. Sauer, at that particular date and time, to be at a business in Coco Isles Beach known as The Wet Spot?"

"Yes."

"Where you there in your capacity as a code inspector?"

"Yes."

"Could you explain that, please?"

Sauer nodded, and actually turned slightly toward the jury. "Village Ordinance 350-850 provides at subpart (a) that ...."

Sammy was on his feet. "Objection! The ordinance is a matter of law! Only the court can tell the jury what the law is!" Objections are supposed to be directed to the judge, but Sammy was glaring at Eleanor.

"Fine!" said Eleanor, glaring back at Sammy. "I have the ordinance here." She brandished it, then turned to Floyd. "Will the Court kindly read subpart (a) of Village of Coco Isles Beach Ordinance 350-850 to the jury?" I put a question mark at the end of that sentence, but I'm sure when Eleanor said it there was no doubt in Floyd's mind that he was being told, not asked.

The ordinance made its way from Eleanor to the clerk to Floyd, who cleared his throat and began to read. "Nudity Defined: Nudity is defined to include the exhibition by any female performer or employee of any licensed establishment to any other person of any portion of her breasts falling below the areola, or any simulation thereof, which definition shall include the entire lower portion of the human female breast, as well as ...."

"Fine!" said Eleanor again; and Floyd, relieved, stopped reading. "Now, Mr. Sauer, were you aware of the terms of the ordinance, as just read by Judge Kroh, at the time you went to The Wet Spot?"

"Yes," said the witness. It was about that moment that Kay entered the courtroom quietly and had a seat in the back row of the public gallery.

"By the way, Mr. Sauer, what is meant by the word, 'areola'?"

Floyd was looking down at his fingernails, or perhaps at his wristwatch, knowing what was probably about to happen but hoping it wouldn't happen.

It happened. "Objection!" said Sammy. "Incompetent! No foundation! What makes this witness an expert on the definition of areolas?" Again he glared at Eleanor.

Again she glared back. "Fine! Do you want Judge Kroh to define 'areola' for the record?"

It was then that Judge Floyd Kroh Jr. made one of the most forthright evidentiary rulings of his career. "Overruled," said Floyd, loud and clear. "The witness may answer the question."

"The area around and including the nipple," answered the witness. Some members of the jury appeared to be embarrassed, and others seemed surprised to learn that jury duty was much more interesting than you might think; but for the expressionless Mr. Sauer, defining areolas was just another day, another dollar.

Eleanor turned back to Floyd. "Would Your Honor now read subpart (b) of the village ordinance?"

Floyd, who had been concentrating very hard on becoming invisible, grudgingly picked up the ordinance and began to read. "It shall be unlawful for any person owning or operating a licensed establishment, as defined in section 90-680, to knowingly permit nudity or sexual conduct to occur on the premises of that licensed establishment. It shall further be unlawful for any person, while on the premises of such a licensed establishment, to expose to public view those portions of the human body identified in subsection (a), above."

Eleanor resumed her questioning. "Now, Mr. Sauer, please tell us what you observed at The Wet Spot in your capacity as village code inspector."

"I entered The Wet Spot like any other customer. I didn't identify myself as a code inspector. I sat at a table in the back of the club and observed the performances of the various dancers. At least three of them, the areola was exposed during their performances."

"Were you able to take photographs of this?" asked Eleanor.

"No. Well, not at that time."

"What do you mean?"

"You can't take pictures while the girls are dancing. They make a big announcement about that. If I had tried to take pictures they would have thrown me out. But later, after the show was over, I waited in my car for the girls to leave. I got pictures of them then."

Eleanor fished photographs out of her trial file and handed them to the clerk of court to be marked as exhibits. "I show you what has been marked as Exhibit A," she said, handing the first picture to Sauer. "Do you recognize it?"

"Yeah," said Sauer. He corrected himself: "Yes."

"What do you recognize it as being?"

"It's a picture of the front of The Wet Spot." He pointed. "You can see the sign that says, The Wet Spot."

Eleanor offered it in evidence. Sammy, to Floyd's surprise and relief, stood to announce that he had no objection whatever to the admission of this exhibit, and it was received.

"And who, if anyone, do you recognize in the photo?" There was only one person in the photo.

"The girl. She's one of the dancers I saw that night. She's one of the ones who bared her breast, exposing the entire breast including the areola." Sauer, whatever else he was, was a well-trained witness. He knew what information he had to get across to the jury.

"What time did you take this photo?"

"Sometime after three a.m., when they shut the place down."

Eleanor showed the witness a second photo, Exhibit B. Sauer testified that it was taken a couple of minutes later, that it depicted two girls walking together, that both of them danced at The Wet Spot and that both of them had bared their entire breasts, areola and all. After Exhibit B was received in evidence Eleanor took a minute to check her notes, then announced she had no further questions for this witness.

"What kind of bird seed do you like?" Sammy hadn't waited for Floyd to invite him to cross-examine. He hadn't walked over to the podium. He just popped up from his chair and asked the witness what kind of bird seed he liked. The sound of Sauer's answer – "Huh?" – was lost under Eleanor's thunderous, "Objection."

"He's a stool pigeon, isn't he?" Sammy directed the question to Floyd, who had yet to speak. "You're a stool pigeon, aren't you?" This time it was asked of the witness. "I just want to know what your favorite brand of bird seed is."

"Objection!" repeated Eleanor.

"Judge, it goes to his credibility," said Sammy, who seemed to think he had asked the most natural question in the world, the one that had to be on everyone's mind. "He's a professional stool pigeon, a canary, and we're entitled to know what bird seed they feed him."

Then Floyd made a mistake. "No, no," he sputtered. "How does it, it doesn't, it isn't, no, that doesn't go to credibility."

It was a mistake because it wasn't a ruling. Judges get in trouble when they say anything other than "sustained" or "overruled". When a judge argues with a lawyer, he invites the lawyer to argue back, which of course is just what Sammy the Weasel wants. Floyd had, unintentionally, afforded Sammy a chance to repeat that the witness was a stool pigeon. Eleanor kept objecting and moving to strike, which gave Sammy the opportunity to accuse her of trying to keep the truth from the jury. Nothing pleases Sammy quite so much as accusing a prosecutor of keeping the truth from the jury.

In time – too much time – order was restored. Eleanor's objection was sustained, and Sammy was instructed to ask a proper question.

He walked over to the clerk's desk, picked up Exhibit A, and thrust it toward the witness. "You took this picture?"

"Yes."

"You say you took it some time between three and four o'clock in the morning?"

"Yes."

"What time did you leave The Wet Spot?"

Sauer thought it over for a second or two. "Maybe ... I'd say about 1:30."

"So you sat in your car for two, two and a half hours?"

It was a matter of simple arithmetic. "Yes, something like that."

"Alone?"

"Yes."

"In the dark?"

"Well, yeah. I mean, there were street lights at the intersection, but I ...."

"But you weren't at the intersection, were you?"

"No."

"You were in the middle of the block, across the street from The Wet Spot, in your parked car?"

"Yes."

"Alone in the dark for two hours or more?"

"Yeah ...."

"After spending a couple of hours watching exotic dancers bare their breasts?"

Eleanor saw where this was going, and she wasn't about to sit there waiting for Sammy to ask her witness if he had been passing the time by rubbing his magic lantern. "Objection, Your Honor. This is irrelevant."

Floyd, to avoid having to look at either lawyer, looked straight ahead into the public gallery. There in the back row sat Kay. Ever so slightly she nodded, yes. "Yes. Sustained," said Floyd.

Sammy shook Exhibit A in the witness's face. "Well, this girl, whoever she is. She's fully dressed in the only picture you took of her, isn't she?"

"Yes."

Sammy grabbed Exhibit B from the clerk's desk, waved it around. "These two girls, whoever they are. They're fully dressed in the only picture you took of them, aren't they?"

"Yes."

"No areolas sticking out anywhere?"

"Not in those pictures."

Sammy was practically leaning on the rail of the witness box. "Well, you've already told us you didn't take any pictures inside The Wet Spot, right?"

"I couldn't."

"Oh you *couldn't*," repeated Sammy, rolling his eyes for the jury's benefit. "You couldn't because they make announcements that no photography is permitted, right?"

"Right. Yes."

"If you had taken any photos, it would have been for purposes of enforcing the village ordinances of Coco Isles Beach, isn't that right?"

Eleanor objected; the question was speculative and hypothetical. Floyd stared ahead vaguely, as if considering the matter. Kay moved her head, ever so slightly, from side to side.

"No," said Floyd, quietly. Then, louder, "Overruled."

"If I had taken any pictures, the bouncers would have thrown me out," insisted the witness.

Now Sammy shook his head. "You say you were at The Wet Spot in your capacity as a code enforcement officer, isn't that your story?"

"Yes."

"To gather evidence?"

"Yes."

"Evidence of code violations?"

"Yes."

"Such as dancers exposing their entire breasts, including the a-ree-oh-la?" Sammy was having fun drawing the word out.

"Yes."

"Photographs of the girls exposing their breasts would have been such evidence?"

"Yes."

"Evidence of code violations?"

"Yes."

"The evidence you were there to gather?"

"Yes."

"So once you had the photographs, *it wouldn't have mattered if they threw you out*, would it, Mr. Sauer? You'd already have the evidence you came to get, right?"

The question actually caused Sauer to blink a couple of times. "Well, they ... they could have ...."

"What, Mr. Sauer? They could have what? Are you going to tell us that they would have beaten you up and taken your camera away? Are you?" Sammy, when he wasn't glaring at the witness, was glancing at the jury. He was giving them the eye-roll, the head shake, any everything else he had.

"They might have attempted to seize the camera, yes."

"Mr. Sauer ...." Sammy sense of frustration, real or feigned, made him begin again. "Mr. Sauer, do you have a badge?"

"A ... yes."

"Let's see it."

The witness reached into his back pocket, took out a badge case, handed it to Sammy. Sammy opened it and squinted at the badge. "Look at that," he said with exaggerated admiration. Then he held it close to his mouth, breathed a short, low breath on it, and polished it on his shirt front. Having shined it sufficiently, he held it up and read it. "Village of Coco Isles Beach, Code Inspector." He returned the badge to its owner. "That's what it says, isn't it?"

"Yes."

"And you had that badge in your pocket when you went into The Wet Spot?"

"Yes."

"It's the same badge that the Coco Isles Beach police carry, except that yours says 'Code Inspector' and theirs says 'Detective' or 'Officer', right?" Eleanor objected on grounds of competence and lack of foundation but Floyd, after staring thoughtfully into the distance for a second, overruled.

"Yes."

"So let me see if I've got this right, Mr. Sauer. You were worried if you showed the management at The Wet Spot your badge and explained to them that you were there in your capacity as a code inspector, they'd still beat you up and take away your camera. Is that your story?"

When you put it that way it didn't sound like much of a story, but Sauer was sticking to it. "Yes," was all he said.

Sammy wandered back to the podium to begin another line of questioning. "You said when you were inside The Wet Spot you had a seat at a table in the back, is that right?"

"Yes. I mean, not the very back, but towards the back."

"You weren't up on the stage with the dancers, were you?"

"No, no."

"You weren't sitting at one of the tables up front, near the stage, were you?"

"No. In the back, like I said."

"The distance from the stage to the back of the room is ...." Sammy surveyed his surroundings. "It's farther than from where Judge Kroh is sitting to the back of this courtroom, isn't it?"

Sauer studied the courtroom. "Maybe a little farther."

"Of course this courtroom is very bright, isn't it?"

"I guess so."

"The Wet Spot is dark inside, isn't it?"

"Well, not on stage. There are bright lights focused on the dancers."

Ignoring the answer, Sammy asked, "You understand that the Village of Coco Isles Beach would like to be rid of The Wet Spot, don't you?" Eleanor objected on several different grounds, Kay gave her head a slight but firm shake, and Floyd overruled.

"I know that a lot of people think that The Wet Spot isn't the kind of thing we should have in a nice little town like Coco Isles Beach," said Sauer.

"And knowing that, you've come here to testify that at a distance greater than the length of this courtroom, in a dark nightclub, you saw a woman's areola?"

"Yes. Three areolas. Well, I mean actually six, three women ...." His answer trailed off and Sammy spoke over him.

"And you have no photos to back up your story?"

"No."

"And no one else saw what you saw?"

"Sure they did. Everyone saw it."

"Everyone? Tell me, Mr. Inspector, in the two or three hours when you sat in your car waiting for The Wet Spot to close, did any of the customers leave?"

"Well, yes, ... yes, they left."

"Did you ask to speak to any of them, show them your badge, ask to take a statement from them?"

"Uh ... no."

"So for two or three hours, as you sat in your car doing ... well, whatever you were doing ...." Eleanor started to rise, realized that Sammy was baiting her, and sat down. "You could have tried to interview patrons of The Wet Spot as they were leaving to see if *anyone* – *anyone* – claimed to have seen bare breasts, and you chose to interview no one."

Sauer sat with his lips pressed tight, saying nothing. Sammy waited. Then: "I know what I saw. I saw areolas. I saw naked breasts."

"Do you still see them when you close your eyes?" Floyd didn't need help sustaining the objection triggered by that question.

Sammy sauntered up to the clerk's table and picked up Exhibit A. He held it so that the witness and the jury could see it. "You know this woman, don't you?"

"Not personally."

"Don't you know her name?"

"It's ... Anna Something. It's a Russian name."

"Isn't it a fact that you've tried to get her into bed?"

"Wha ... what? Get her .... No, no."

"Isn't it a fact that you told her that if she didn't have sex with you you'd go to court and tell everyone she exposed her bare breasts during her performance?"

"Objection!" Eleanor's voice bounced off the walls. If Sauer said something no one heard it.

"You're not just a stool pigeon," said Sammy the Weasel, his face a picture of disgust. "You're a pervert. Aren't you a little pervert?"

"Your Honor, I object! I have an objection! Mr. Wea ... Mr. Manheim is making this up! There is no good-faith basis in fact for these questions!"

Eleanor continued to boom her objection while Sammy waggled his finger at the witness, muttering "Pervert. Little pervert." The court reporter, unable to pick and choose among the words and voices, seemed on the edge of tears. Floyd Kroh looked out into the distance, his expression serene, contemplative. But this time it was an empty seat in the visitors' gallery that stared back at him. Kay, as quietly as she had entered, had left. Floyd's expression of contemplation dissolved in horror.

• • •

I was eager to be elsewhere than in chambers while Floyd looked for an ashtray that I knew wasn't there. I sent Bailiff Bud Teachout on an urgent mission to round up the lawyers, and in minutes I was on the bench.

"Are all counsel ready to proceed to closing argument?"

Raul stood, composed and elegant. He held a manila folder in his hand; it could not have contained more than a page or two. To his right his colleagues were arrayed in order of decreasing seniority. With each step down the ladder the aplomb, the composure, dropped. Correspondingly, the pile of papers and files increased. The kid on the end, the junior man, had managed to get his suit jacket on, but no one had bothered to tell him that the collar was sticking up in back and needed to be flipped down. His hair had been combed with an eggbeater and his tie hung at a drunken angle. His appearance mattered little, however, because he was all but invisible behind the boxes, briefcases, and piles of files and documents that surrounded him. This was understandable: urgent assignments, impossible assignments, last-minute assignments, rolled downhill. When they got to him there was no place left for them to roll.

But it made no difference. He would not speak. He would probably not speak in a courtroom for another couple of years. In this courtroom only Raul would speak for the Holtzman Museum; he spoke, and he said, “Ready for plaintiff, the Holtzman Museum of Judaica.”

I turned my gaze to Zachary Taylor Davis, but it was Aimee Arrants who rose. “Ready on behalf of Dr. Gumbiner, Your Honor.”

This was not a jury trial. In such circumstances many judges in civil cases dispense with closing argument entirely. They direct the attorneys to file briefs instead. The judge then reads the briefs, considers everything he has heard in court, and enters a written ruling. In this case, however, I would proceed in the old way. This was my first trial in civil court, and I was not ready to depart from the established choreography. Besides, we had a jury; not a real jury, not a jury that would decide the outcome, but we had an audience. This civil trial was playing to a packed house. This civil trial had attracted more attention from newspapers and television than any criminal trial in memory. Even now the reporters were three rows deep in the visitors’ gallery. Behind them was the mass of observers: Those who had an interest in art, in art of the Holocaust, in the legendary Adler collection; those who had come to hear the testimony of the revered rabbi; those who had come out of a sense of history, to hear about the people who died at Weeghman long ago, and those who came out of a delight in scandal, to whisper about the people who died here yesterday; and those who were just court-watchers, who came for the show and the air-conditioning. Yes, we would have closing arguments.

"Mr. Santos, we are here on your application. Please proceed."

Raul walked up to the lectern, placed his notes on it. "May it please this Honorable Court. It has been said that in the law there is text, and there is context. When was there ever such a context as the one in which this case arises? We have, in the few days it took to conduct this hearing, had a glimpse of the blackest horrors of the Holocaust; and of a defiant expression of the human capacity for art and beauty that even the Holocaust could not extinguish. We have heard testimony from a man whose religious spirit and wisdom are an ornament to this community, and we have been deprived by the finger of death of the testimony of a man who had never before set foot in this community. When was there ever such a context as the one in which this case arises?

"Taken as we are by context, however, we cannot turn away from text. When all is said and done, Your Honor, this is a simple case. It requires the Court to expound the meaning of that driest and most straightforward of legal documents – a contract. It is to the text of that contract that this Court must turn its attention."

The introductory passages of a lawyer's argument were referred to by old-timers as the "exordium." The idea is to engage the listener's attention and frame the terms of the debate. I hadn't expected such rhetorical flourish from Raul, such flowery language, but I understood what he was doing. He didn't want me to be carried away by the historical drama that underlie the facts of this case, by the sympathy due to Dr. Gumbiner as his grandfather's proxy, by the charisma of Rabbi Stein. For him to win, the ball had to be kept between the lines: Here is the contract; here is what it says; make them do what it says.

He held the contract up in his right hand. "This is the document that brings us here, Your Honor. This lawsuit requires you to do no more than to declare its meaning and enforce its terms. That meaning, and those terms, are clear. The parties to the contract intended – and this is not even disputed – that Dr. Gumbiner would loan the Adler collection to the Holtzman Museum, so that this legendary but hitherto-unseen art collection could at last be properly displayed to and enjoyed by the public and the art world. Dr. Gumbiner has dishonored his promise. He has refused to loan the Adler collection to the Holtzman. We appear before you, seeking enforcement of Dr. Gumbiner's contractual promise." Raul directed my attention to two lengthy passages from the contract itself, and read them aloud. Then he set his copy of the contract back down on the lectern.

"It is a rule of law in this and every other American jurisdiction that each party to a contract has a duty to act in good faith," he continued. "I take no pleasure in saying that Dr. Gumbiner has failed in that duty. He has acted in bad faith. His reasons for withholding the Adler collection are arbitrary. They are no reasons at all."

Raul then launched into a detailed analysis of Dr. Gumbiner's testimony. Although Dr. Gumbiner was "a man of science," said Raul, the doctor had been obliged to admit that he had no reason to believe that the examination of the Adler collection would be damaging. Gumbiner had made no inquiries into the nature of the testing procedures. For its part, the Holtzman Museum had every reason and incentive to insure that any tests performed on the Adler collection did no damage at all; the Holtzman was a prestigious art museum, and it hoped to display the Adler collection, not to be sued for damaging it. The doctor's alleged fears about damage to the artwork as a result of examining it were in any event entirely hypocritical, said Raul. Dr. Gumbiner admitted that he would permit the testing to go forward if ordered by the *bes din*. If there were any basis at all to believe that testing of the Adler collection could damage it – and there was none, Raul asserted emphatically, none at all – then Dr. Gumbiner should be objecting to such testing whether or not the *bes din* approved it.

Raul then turned to the arbitration clause of the contract. He read it, word for word. Such provisions, he acknowledged, were standard in modern commercial contracts; it would have been surprising if this contract lacked one. The purpose of an arbitration clause is to enable the parties to resolve factual disputes without invoking the jurisdiction "of this Honorable Court," said Raul. The purpose of arbitration is not to enable the parties to invoke the jurisdiction of another kind of court. Typically, arbitration is performed by lawyers, or retired judges, or professional organizations constituted for just that purpose. Of course the parties to a contract could designate any person or entity they chose to perform the task of arbitration; but they could not, by that designation, change the purpose or meaning of arbitration, or enlarge the power of the arbitrating body. What Dr. Gumbiner proposed to do here was nothing less than a jurisprudential revolution. It was against the intent of the contract, said Raul, and it was against social policy.

He then reviewed the testimony of other witnesses. He spoke at length about the testimony of Morris Arnovitz: how Arnovitz had devoted his life to the study of art of the Holocaust; how Arnovitz was "the principal scholar in the world" on the subject of Ernst Adler and his work; how Arnovitz, and indeed everyone associated with the Holtzman, wanted nothing more than to exhibit, to care for, to study the Adler collection. Was it possible, remotely possible, to believe that such a man would take even the slightest chance of endangering or damaging the precious Adler collection? A man whose whole professional life had built toward the moment when he might unveil the Adler collection to a gasping world? And if the court concluded – "as, we respectfully submit, the Court is bound to conclude" – that the testing of the Adler collection proposed by Arnovitz was routine and not dangerous, why then were we even in court? Why should the Holtzman Museum – and its many supporters, sponsors, visitors here in the Miami area and throughout the art world – be obliged to wait a single moment longer for the display of this marvelous collection?

Raul turned to the testimony of Rabbi Stein. He spent long minutes praising Stein as "a prodigious scholar, a holy man, and a living link to history." But Rabbi Stein was not the issue; a contract was the issue, and the plain written terms of the contract were not altered by the presence in court of even so remarkable a personage. On the contrary; the rabbi himself had testified to God's commandment that we not seek to evade or avoid our contractual obligations. Dr. Gumbiner was seeking to evade or avoid his contractual obligations. The Holtzman Museum sought no more than for this Honorable Court to enforce those contractual obligations.

"Your Honor is no doubt well familiar with the case of ...," said Raul, and he discussed one of the leading appellate opinions on the meaning and purpose of arbitration. I nodded gravely, so as to give the members of the press and public the misimpression that I was familiar with, or had at least heard of, whatever case he was citing. I wrote down the case name and citation, and would make it my business to become well familiar with it before I ruled in this case. "See also ...," said Raul, rattling off a string of additional cases supporting his position. I scribbled them down quickly. He went on for a few more minutes detailing the leading cases and their holdings.

The same classical rhetoricians and old-time lawyers who refer to the beginning of closing argument as the "exordium" will refer to the last paragraph or so of closing argument as the "peroration." Even lawyers who have never heard that term understand that they should, if they possibly can, position themselves and their clients on the moral high ground at the end of their remarks. Raul claimed to be speaking, "for a great museum, a museum that is the crown of this community's cultural raiment," a museum that was seeking no more than the opportunity to display and care for an art collection that would be the jewel in that crown. He claimed to be speaking for "the countless visitors – retirees, working people, and schoolchildren, Miamians and tourists by their thousands" who would derive inspiration and enjoyment from the Adler collection. This, said Raul, was the happy result that the contract between the parties intended to bring about, the result that a petty unwillingness to honor a contractual promise was obstructing, the result that he asked this Honorable Court to compel without further delay. He bowed slightly, thanked me, returned to his seat.

Aimee Arrants came forward to the lectern. She brought with her a three-ring binder notebook, carefully tabbed, and placed it on the lectern. She wore a dark suit, loose-fitting. The skirt came well below her knee. She had dressed to neutralize her youth and gender, to take them out of the courtroom entirely. She wanted neither advantage nor disadvantage from them; she wanted to be judged on her lawyering. A police officer, describing her in cop-speak for a police report, would have written, "African-American female, medium height, no distinguishing features."

"If the Court please," she said, and stood there. She was waiting for me to nod, or to mumble "Proceed, counsel," or words to the like effect. She wanted, and was entitled to, my assurance that she had my attention. So I nodded and mumbled, "Proceed, counsel."

"The contract in question provides that in the event of a dispute between the parties, that dispute will be referred in the first instance to arbitration. The contract further provides that the arbitrating body shall be the *bes din* of Miami Beach. These contractual provisions were not forced upon the Holtzman Museum. They were not smuggled into the contract in the dark of night. These contractual provisions appeared in the contract, in black and white, at the time that the Holtzman and its lawyers" – she extended her right arm toward Raul and his colleagues – "these very lawyers -- entered into the contract.

"Now such disputes have arisen. One of the museum's principal curators, Mr. Arnovitz, himself testified to these disputes." She turned a page in her notebook, but did not look down. "He testified that there are at least three fundamental factual disputes between the parties: whether there is a need for testing of the Adler collection, whether scientific or chemical testing could damage the collection, and whether scientific testing could in any event tell us anything about the authenticity of the collection. In such circumstances the terms of the contract are clear. The disputes must be submitted in the first instance to arbitration."

She turned to the next tab in her notebook. I could see a stack of opinions from the courts of appeals. The one on top, and probably all the others beneath it, had been heavily noted up, highlighted in yellow. She discussed each one in turn, and drew distinctions between the cases she relied upon and those which Raul had cited. She had studied these cases to the point where she knew them almost by heart, and she took her time reviewing each one with me. It was a fine display of legal scholarship but the audience in the visitors' gallery, for the first time since closing arguments had started, lost interest and began to fidget.

At length she concluded her legal dissertation. She closed her notebook and looked at me for a moment without speaking. "Your Honor, Mr. Santos accuses Dr. Gumbiner of breaching the terms of the contract, and of acting in bad faith. But Dr. Gumbiner wants nothing more than the enforcement of the express provisions of the contract. And as for the allegations of bad faith" – she raised her eyebrows, her head, her voice – "Dr. Gumbiner's conduct is and has always been that of a man of faith. He believes with an unbending faith that the same God who inspired his grandfather to produce art in the hell-hole that was Weeghman will inspire the holy men of the *bes din* to produce justice in this cause. That is his faith, Your Honor. And his faith is very good."

Someone lost in the pack of the gallery started to applaud, realized he was making a damn fool of himself, and stopped before Bailiff Teachout could descend upon him. Ms. Arrants returned to her seat. Raul was entitled to a rebuttal argument, but he didn't tell me anything I hadn't heard already.

• • •

Floyd Kroh was standing in the middle of my office, looking lost. It would be impossible to be lost in so small an office, but Floyd stood in the middle of it, staring at no particular thing, swaying a bit, going nowhere. There is no tooth fairy, Elvis is dead, and he won't be coming back, and Floyd's father's ashtray was nowhere to be found.

Floyd had looked. My God, how he had looked. Carmen described the process to me later. Floyd had looked in a box of paper clips for an ashtray seven inches on a side. He had gone through my desk and Carmen's desk, being thoughtful enough afterward to put everything back where he had found it. He had gone through my wastebasket, and picked up the cushions on my couch. He had moved Carmen's credenza away from the wall to look behind it for a lost ashtray, and he had moved it back when he didn't find one. He wandered up and down the hallway; Carmen thought he might try calling for his ashtray like a runaway dog: "Here, Lassie! Come on home, Lassie!"

I did the best I could to seem sympathetic. I assured him that his ashtray would turn up in the fullness of time, as such things always do. And I squired him out of my chambers, so I could, at long last, actually get some work done.

CHAPTER SIX

THURSDAY

The *Miami Herald* will be tossed onto my front walkway sometime between 5:45 and 6:00. If I listen carefully I can hear the flop, the noise that it makes as it lands. If the flop of the newspaper comes at the same moment as the last gurgle of the coffee machine, the day has begun in perfect synchronization. The whole thing is timing the coffee.

So it was a good sign that on that particular morning the coffee machine had ceased to coo and gurgle at the very moment that I heard the flop of plastic-wrapped newspaper on Chattahoochee stone paver. I retrieved the paper, poured the coffee, and sat at the kitchen table.

Perhaps it was a slow news day. Fidel Castro had not died, and Sandy Koufax had not come out of retirement to sign with the Marlins. Whatever the reason, the entire paper seemed to be given over to the coverage of *Holtzman Museum of Judaica v. Gumbiner.* There was an article on the front page detailing the progress of the case, and another devoted to the Adler collection itself. The second article -- the one that discussed the Adler collection -- included an extended interview with a professor in New York City, an art history expert who had written various books and articles taking the position that the Adler collection was a myth. "Like the philosopher's stone that turns baser metals into gold, the Adler collection is a beautiful dream, but nothing more than a dream," said the professor. "However much comfort and vindication we may derive from pretending that someone immured in a Nazi concentration camp managed to produce a body of artwork, the fact of the matter is that it would have been physically, logistically impossible." Then there were quotes from other experts, saying in cautiously worded ways that the professor was ... well, as Billy would have said, full of canal juice. Raul Santos, who was good at dealing with the press, managed to sound hopeful and positive; Zachary Davis, who was even better at dealing with the press, managed to sound very hopeful and very positive. "Judge Addison, who continues to decline comment, is expected to announce his ruling tomorrow morning from the bench," the *Herald* concluded.

It must have been a slow news day yesterday, because it had been the same yesterday. It must have been a slow news week, because it had been the same all week. Tuesday's paper, of course, was devoted in substantial part to the murders of Boots Weber and Herman Bilstein. The Police Information Office had released a very brief statement, concluding that the matter was under investigation and that more detailed information would be forthcoming at an appropriate time. Someone at the *Herald* had called Israel and scrounged up some biographical data about Bilstein: born in Vienna, had studied journalism and sociology, had lived in Austria and France before the war, never fully recovered his health from the ordeal of Weeghman, had lived quietly in Israel since the war. Mention was made of his involvement in various organizations of Holocaust survivors, and of how he had participated as an observer or witness at trials of camp guards, trials held in Europe decades ago. There was, of course, no difficulty finding friends and co-workers of Bootsie Weber, all of whom were willing to share with the *Herald* their remembrances of her, and their sense of shock and loss.

A couple of days ago the paper included a sidebar on Dr. Gumbiner. A number of fellow-physicians were quoted regarding his professional skill and stature. All were familiar with the legend of the Adler collection. None claimed to have seen it. According to the *Herald* it was Gumbiner who had suggested that the Miami Beach *bes din* be designated as the mediating body in the event of a dispute under the contract; but just because the *Herald* said it didn't make it so. The sidebar included a photo, probably obtained from a hospital at which Gumbiner had privileges.

Today's sidebar was Rabbi Stein. There was a photo of him standing with Ronald Reagan and the Pope when, during the Reagan presidency, the Pontiff had visited briefly in Miami. Other rabbis and Miami Beach civic leaders were quoted at length extolling Chaim Stein's scholarship, wisdom, godliness. Someone whose name I didn't recognize, but who claimed to have been present in the courtroom yesterday, said that watching and listening to Rabbi Stein's testimony had been the most religious experience of his life.

Bagel wandered into the kitchen, found his way to his water bowl, lapped the water till the bowl was dry. He then looked up at me with a look that said, "You wouldn't happen to have a couple of aspirin, would you?"

We were alone in the kitchen, just the two of us, so I asked him, "You don't have a doggy hang-over, do you?"

He didn't find that particularly amusing, but then Bagel has never really liked my sense of humor. I picked up his water bowl, filled it at the kitchen tap, and put it back. He looked at it for a second and then looked back at me. Aspirin, said his look. Not more water; aspirin. Don't you understand the difference?

I was going to ask him if today was the day when he finally planned to go out and get a job, but he walked away. I finished the paper and left it on the kitchen table for Miriam.

By the time I had showered, shaved, dressed, it was time for Miriam to get up. I sat on the bed next to her. "Good morning, Mary Sunshine."

"Mmmph." That may not be an exact quote.

"I'm leaving. Have a nice day. Love you."

"Mmmph."

"Yes, I know," I thought; but I didn't say it.

I pulled out of my driveway about the time that my across-the-street neighbor plodded out in his bathrobe to pick up his newspaper. When he saw me, he flagged me down. I stopped and rolled my window down.

"Clark, I'm glad I caught you. I got a jury summons in the mail. What should I do about it?"

Felipe and Consuelo have lived on our block longer than anyone else. We have always been friendly but never really been friends. I know, because he has told me, that he owns a factory of some kind in Hialeah, but I can never remember what exactly it is that he manufactures. He is a large man, with a large and mostly bald head. His nose and ears suggest that their owner boxed or played football in his youth. He retrieves his newspaper in a bathrobe that makes me proud of mine.

"You should go to court and serve on a jury, Phil. You'd make an excellent juror."

This was the civics-class answer, but it was not what Felipe had been looking for. He was leaning up against the driver's side of my car, and he shifted his weight once or twice before saying what was on his mind. "Look, you can get me off the hook for this.

It's our busy season at the factory. I just don't have time for this now."

"Phil, honestly, I can't. Judges can't get people off jury duty. If we could, we'd have full-time jobs doing nothing else." He shifted his weight a couple of times again, fiddled with the plastic wrapper around the newspaper, muttered something under his breath. Then he nodded in my general direction and turned to walk back inside his house. "Sorry, Phil. Have a nice day."

Terrific. Next election even my across-the-street neighbors won't vote for me.

A few streets of local traffic and I was turning onto U.S. 1, which would take me downtown at speeds sometimes exceeding ten or even 12 miles an hour.

Every two weeks the clerk of court issues hundreds, maybe thousands, of jury summonses. The summonses go out by regular mail, so there is no way to know who got his and who never did. If Phil simply chose to throw his summons in the waste basket there would be nothing anyone could or would do about it. If Phil simply chose to throw his summons in the waste basket he would be doing what about three-quarters of summons recipients do. Whether a judge could get someone off jury duty is something I'm better off not knowing.

When I was a young prosecutor I frequently appeared before Judge Ogden Galena. I never met anyone, ever, who remembered a time before Judge Galena was a judge. He wasn't a particularly nice man, and he wasn't particularly popular, but I suppose I have to admit that he made lawyers out of the young prosecutors and public defenders who appeared regularly in his courtroom. Depending on how I drove downtown from my house, and particularly if I went in on a weekend, I used to see him in his front yard, standing there patiently while his ugly dog fertilized the flowers. Most of the other judges of his generation had died or moved away and he had no real friends. That was by design. He told me many times that a judge should have no friends in the legal profession but other judges. You never really knew another man, Judge Galena used to say; you never really knew what went on under his roof or in his heart. Having friends other than judges exposed a judge to a thousand unknown dangers, he said. And a judge, like Caesar's wife, must be above suspicion. Then he'd recite one of his dirty limericks, like the one that began, "There once was a milkman named Schwartz."

I suppose it was the truth, but it was a hard truth. The litigants who come before me, the litigants whose cases and fates I must decide, will not be judges. They will be people like my neighbor Phil. Restricting my circle of friends to other judges would not necessarily make me a better judge of the Phils of this world. Hearing Phil talk about his widget factory in Hialeah isn't much, but it beats hearing Bob Aguilar talk about Bob Aguilar.

Inching along U.S. 1 I thought about the order and opinion in the Holtzman Museum case that I would spend today writing. Strictly speaking, of course, I was not obliged to write anything. I could walk into court, grant judgment in favor of one party or the other, and that would be the end of it. I didn't even have to walk into court; I could have Carmen type an order granting judgment for one side or the other, file it with the clerk's office, and let them distribute copies to the interested parties. But I wasn't going to be doing it that way. This was my first civil case, and it just happened to be the biggest case in town. If I wrote a thorough and scholarly opinion it would be cited in newspapers around the country, perhaps around the world. I had agreed to move from criminal court to civil court in order to get the exposure and experience I needed to apply for a federal judgeship. Here was the exposure, if I handled it right.

So I planned to spend most of today in my chambers writing an opinion that would follow the law, bring about justice, and show off my judicial skill and scholarship. Carmen had mentioned pointedly yesterday that other cases were backing up – the Holtzman Museum case had been scheduled to take a day, not a week – but I told her that having waited this long, those other cases could wait another day or two. I had everything spread out on my desk just the way I wanted it, and I should have been able to start writing. I should have. It just wasn't working out that way.

First the bailiff, Bud Teachout, wandered into my office. He knocked, of course, and was apologetic for interrupting, but he clearly wanted a moment of my time and I felt that I ought to oblige him. I offered him a seat. He started to decline, feeling perhaps that he ought to stand; then did the sensible thing and sat down.

There is an unwritten rule somewhere that all the bailiffs in all the courtrooms in Miami must be retired cops from New York or New Jersey. Al Guerrero, who was born in New York City himself, likes to joke that if you're born in New York you have two choices: you can stay there and spend your life complaining about what a miserable place to live it is, or you can move to Miami and spend your life complaining about how much you miss New York. Al says that we get three kinds of natural disasters in Miami: hurricanes, citrus canker, and New Yorkers, but that at least the hurricanes and the citrus canker don't complain about how things were better where they came from. If a cop, retired from New York and living in Miami, finds himself with too much time on his hands, or if his wife says he's getting on her nerves, he gets himself a job as a bailiff. The pay is lousy, but it's an easy job, and it gets him out of the house and back into court. He can meet the local cops and tell them, for as long as they'll listen, how much tougher it was to be a cop in New York.

It turns out that Bud Teachout was a cop in New York, or somewhere thereabouts. His fine bass voice, tailor-made for crying "All rise!", drops r's from some words ("It was *hahdah* to be a cop in my day") and grafts them onto others. Physically he is a nondescript man: average height, neither fat nor thin, nothing distinctive or noticeable about his appearance. He must be well into his 60's but his hair is still full and wavy. The hair is black, but too black, the sort of black that comes from cheap hair polish. He wore a pair of old bifocals, and of course the only outfit in which I had seen him was the bailiff's uniform he was required to wear. I had never seen him smoking – the courthouses are all non-smoking buildings by law – but he smelled perpetually of cigarette smoke, and a pack of cigarettes bulged in his shirt pocket.

To the extent we talked about anything – I think all he really wanted was to get better acquainted – we talked about the two homicides. Hell of a thing. New York was a tough town, but you never saw this kind of thing in New York, not right in the courthouse, no sir.

I asked him what family he had here in Miami, what part of town he lived in, that sort of thing. He showed me a couple of cellphone photos of the grandchildren. As he was putting his phone away I said, for no reason I could think of, "Come on, Bud, take a walk with me." He followed me out of chambers, down the corridor, and into the stairwell.

We stood on the stairwell landing, a Miami prosecutor turned judge and a New York cop turned bailiff. The stairwell was as it always was: empty and silent.

"Whadaya looking for, Judge?" Bud asked.

What was there to look for? What was there to see? "You tell me." He shrugged, shook his head. "Bud, you ever sneak in here to smoke?"

"Not me, Judge. I go outside, on the front courthouse steps. There's a bunch of us bailiffs who meet on the courthouse steps to grab a smoke and visit for a minute. You know, most of us are ex-badges from the city."

"Is that right?"

"Yeah. Small world."

I patted him on the shoulder and sent him on his way, if he had a way. I went back to chambers, intending to get to work on writing an opinion.

I didn't want to be disturbed and asked Carmen to hold all non-urgent calls. That worked well enough for half an hour or so; then Carmen told me that Jack was on the phone, saying that he needed to talk to me and it would only take a minute. So I picked up the phone.

"Hello, Jack."

"Clark, I know you're busy, so I'll make this quick. Lu Warneke's in town. You've heard me talk about her a hundred times, but you've never met her. We're having lunch at that place off Eighth Street, the one that you and Ed and I used to go to on Saturday mornings. Can you join us?"

"I doubt it, Jack. Thanks for asking, but I'll probably work through lunch today."

"Look, don't give me an answer. We'll get there about 12:30. If you can stop by, even for a few minutes, please do. Quite a girl, is our Lu." I told him I'd think about it but not to expect me, and we got off the phone.

I looked at my watch. If I could get most of a first draft of my ruling written by lunchtime, maybe I'd meet Jack for a minute.

It occurred to me that there were any number of reasons why a state judge who wanted to be a federal judge shouldn't be seen having lunch with the most notorious federal drug informant in Miami. Still, by the time noon rolled around I found myself looking at my wristwatch every couple of minutes, and at about 12:15 I gave up and told Carmen I was going out to lunch.

The coffee shop was where I had left it almost three years ago. It had never really had a name, and that was the only change I noticed on the outside: a small sign, hand-painted, that read, "*Los Delfines*," the dolphins. To the right of the sign, on the side of the place facing the street, was an open window and outdoor counter, at which a passerby might stop in the morning for a *pastelito* and *café*, or at lunch for a *medianoche* to go. Inside everything was just as it had been. The seating area was tiny. It accommodated seven or eight tables, mostly two-tops and a couple of four-tops. The tables were packed close together, and no two chairs seemed to be exactly alike. There was a lunch counter, like a bar, with half-a-dozen stools, but when I arrived there were only two people at the counter, one eating and the other, several bar-stools away, staring off into the middle distance. On a shelf on the wall behind the lunch counter, between stacks of cups and saucers, an old radio was tuned to one of the Spanish-language talk-show programs. There were ceiling fans at opposite ends of the place, but neither was rotating except when the door opened and a draft of air gave the paddles a push.

Against the far wall, at a table with paper place-mats featuring a map of the state of Florida, Jack sat with a woman who must have been Lu Warneke. I had expected to see a modern-day Mata Hari, an exotic vamp. What I saw was very different. Lu Warneke was a small woman, blond, with her hair cut short and combed carelessly away from her face, almost a man's haircut. Her features were regular, but her face was long and thin, and the effect was anything but exotic or seductive. She wore a long-sleeve cotton shirt, very loose-fitting and not ironed, and she had her sleeves rolled up to her elbows. Instead of a short skirt and stiletto heels, or whatever I had expected to see, she had on cotton pants and sneakers. She appeared to have no make-up on, although I can never really tell whether a woman is wearing make-up. If I had been told that she was a professor of Latin American studies at a small New England liberal arts college – and, come to think of it, I had been told that, or something like it – I would have believed it.

Jack waved as I walked over and stood to shake hands. There is a very short list of people with whom Blackjack Sheridan is genuinely impressed, but Lu Warneke was clearly near the top of that list. He was beaming, almost blushing, as he introduced me to her, as if he were presenting me to a rock star. She leaned forward, shook my hand, said that it was a pleasure to meet me, then slumped back in her chair.

A waiter appeared. He was a small, thin man, very dark complected. His hair was short, his eyes were slits, and his entire face was a life support system for a large nose, a hooked nose with cavernous nostrils. He placed four glass of ice water on the table because he had brought four glasses of ice water with him. Then he asked a question, but it was mumbled in such a way that I wasn't even sure if he had spoken English or Spanish. Lu responded in Spanish, and a short conversation between the two of them followed. I had no idea what they said, but she appeared to have told him to go away and come back later. He went away. She squinted to read a blackboard on the wall closest to us, on which today's menu had been written in faint chalk marks.

"Salvadoran," she said, still looking at the blackboard. "I saw at once that he was Central American, but I had to endure a few of his malapropisms to place him specifically. Salvadoran."

"Lu can do that," said Jack, delighted. "She can tell you if somebody's from Spain, Colombia, Argentina, any of those places. Hell, she can convince them that *she's* from any of those places."

I felt like I was supposed to say something, so I said, "That must be quite an accomplishment. You don't appear ... uh." I cut myself off, not liking the sound of what I was about to say.

"Funny, you don't look Hispanic?" Lu asked. Yes, dammit, that was the foolish thing I was about to say, so I said nothing. "And of course the name Warneke doesn't sound Spanish either, does it?"

It was Jack who responded. "I always figured you used half-a-dozen made up names in your line of work."

"Not at all," she said. "Most of my contacts in Latin America don't even bother to wonder about the incongruity between my appearance and my speech – the natural hebetude of the Hispanic mind, I suppose. And for those who do, I hint darkly about my family having fled Germany at the close of World War II and settled quietly in Uruguay or Argentina. They always love that story. A young sans-culotte in the FARC – the Colombian Revolutionary Armed Forces, the guerillas – told me very confidentially that he knew that I was the illegitimate daughter of Goering, or Himmler, someone like that, but that I could trust him to guard my secret with his life." She spoke quietly and with little expression, as if the story and those about whom it was told were a bore and a bother.

My poker face, carefully cultivated during two terms as a judge, must have failed me when she made reference to the "natural hebetude of the Hispanic mind." Lu Warneke was the last person I would have expected to speak in a derogatory fashion about Hispanics. For the second time in a short conversation she saw through my thought. "Have I given offense, Judge? You take umbrage at my observation about the ... what was the locution I used? 'the hebetude of the Hispanic mentality?"'

"Well, ..."

She cut me off. "It was an observation directed to culture, not to race." That, apparently, was as close to an apology as she would be going.

The waiter came over. I ordered *pan cubano* and *café con leche*. *Pan cubano* is French bread, buttered and toasted in a press more or less the same way that Americans make a grilled cheese sandwich. *Café con leche* is coffee with warm milk and sugar. It was a breakfast-type meal, not really something anyone would order for lunch, but it was what Ed and Jack and I sometimes ordered when we used to meet here for breakfast on Saturday mornings. Jack looked at me for a minute, realized what I was doing, and told the waiter he'd have the same. Lu ordered in Spanish.

"So," Jack said, smiling at Lu, "how long will you be in town?"

"Just a few days. I'm in the midst of some very delicate negotiations in Colombia, and I must get back to them." She turned to me. "I'm afraid, Judge, that this must be a business meeting. Will that be a problem for you?"

"I'm Lu's lawyer," Jack explained. He seemed very proud to say so.

"I'm sure I won't be staying very long. I have some important work on my desk to get back to. I'll afford you and" – I turned to Jack – "your lawyer" – back to Lu – "plenty of time to talk."

"Lu's having some trouble with her handlers," Jack explained. A civilian informant is supposed to act under the supervision of law enforcement officers to whom he (or in this case she) reports. These supervising agents are referred to as the informant's "handlers."

"The usual thing," said Lu. She blinked slowly. Her handlers, like our waiter and the Hispanic mentality, seemed very boring and needlessly annoying. "They report to their higher-ups that I insist on being paid in cash. It's rubbish, of course – *they* insist that I be paid in cash. The cash is issued to them, to be delivered to me. At the time they deliver it, they ask me if I wouldn't mind 'loaning' them a thousand or two, just to get them to their next paychecks. Of course I have no choice but to accede to their demands."

I looked at Jack. "Why? If the agents are shaking her down ...."

Lu gave Jack a look that asked without words whether all his friends still believed in Santa and the tooth fairy. Jack was obviously embarrassed. "Clark, if Lu complains to higher-ups within the DEA, her handlers will swear that she's lying and making the whole thing up. Given a choice between believing their badge-carrying brethren or a paid informant, the higher-ups will conclude that Lu is trying to deceive them, just as she deceives dopers for a living. Her relationship with DEA will be strained, and of course her handlers will find little ways to punish her for ratting them out."

The waiter arrived with my order and Jack's. Whatever Lu had ordered would take a little longer.

"So what can you do?" I asked.

Jack smiled, the good Blackjack smile. "That's what Lu and I will talk about after you're gone."

"In all likelihood, nothing," said Lu. "I'll be forced to endure the petty thievery of those wicked witlings for the foreseeable future. The shelf-life of an informant is brief. I'll be out of the business in a couple of years. In the meantime I will probably be obliged to possess my soul in silence."

That left nothing much to say. With none of us talking, the Spanish-language program emanating from the radio across the room was suddenly audible. Lu seemed strangely amused by whatever was being said.

"You're quite a celebrity, Judge," she remarked.

"I am?"

She nodded in the direction of the radio. "That trial over which you're presiding. One can't turn on the radio without hearing about it."

"What are they saying?"

"Oh ... the same sorts of things that have been in the newspapers all week. The mysterious, mythopoeic art collection. The suffering of the artist. The yearnings of the museum, indeed of the entire art world. Rabbi Stein, the *eminence grise* of Jewish theology. And the imminent resolution of all questions by Judge *Ah-dee-son*." Lu wasn't a laugh-out-loud kind of girl as far as I could tell, but she seemed to find the radio news coverage – or at least her rendition of it – hugely entertaining. "Far be it from me to interject myself into the adjudicative process, Judge, but if I were you I'd be careful of ruling against Rabbi Stein and his black-hatted colleagues. You wouldn't want to end up excommunicated for your views, like Spinoza."

That didn't leave much to say either. I don't speak Spanish, but I didn't believe that Lu's translation of the news broadcast was a very literal one. I didn't believe that Lu Warneke was particularly concerned about the prospect of my excommunication, either. I remembered that someone – maybe it was Jack; probably not – had once warned me that Lu Warneke is so bigoted she's probably lactose intolerant.

The waiter brought Lu's lunch, a rice casserole dish that I had seen in Cuban restaurants but the name of which I could never remember. She gave her attention to eating, and we all fell silent for few minutes. I dunked a small piece of my bread into my cup, letting it soak up the warm, sweet coffee-milk.

"Ed used to do that." Jack had spoken.

I nodded. "I remember." The piece of bread, engorged with the liquid, crumbled into the cup.

"Ed did it better," Jack said.

I smiled, nodded again. "Yeah," I said. "I remember that too." I turned to Lu. "Then what?"

She looked up from her meal, surprised by my question. "Pardon me?"

"Then what. After you retire from the informant business in a couple of years. I don't mean to pry, but curiosity has the better of me. May I ask what you plan to do then?"

She gave me that bored, droopy-eyed look again. "I plan to return to Brown. I plan to return to teaching." No doubt I was a witling for having asked. "I enjoyed being a college professor. I disliked being an impoverished college professor. I will relish being a very rich college professor."

We were seated so that Jack was across from me to my left, and Lu across from me to my right. As we were speaking a figure came from somewhere on my left, managed to pass behind Jack, and stood on the side of the table directly opposite me. I looked up from my coffee to see a very big man dressed in a black overshirt and black jeans. The half-sleeves of the overshirt were stretched tight by the bulk of his upper arms. He wore large sunglasses, beneath which his fleshy face was pock-marked with acne scars. He positioned himself with his back to Jack, his right side to me; he was facing Lu. He put his left hand on the back of her chair and spread his legs wide, so he could bend forward and put his face almost up against the side of hers. He spoke to her: low, angry, hard.

Although his lips were almost touching her right ear and cheek, Lu continued to look forward, or down at her plate. She even continued to eat. I couldn't make out his words, but I was sure that she could. And even without speaking Spanish, I got his message. I was sure that she did.

I was trying to think of something to say or do when, abruptly, the man's head snapped up; a movement so sudden that his sunglasses were dislodged. They didn't fall, but they were tilting off his face at so bizarre an angle that he looked like a drunk, or a figure in a Picasso painting. Behind the sunglasses his eyes were squeezed tight in agony, and his mouth gaped. Instead of words an animal sound of pain emerged. His knees started to give way, he began to sink slowly, and I thought for an instant that he was having a heart attack. Then I saw Jack's outstretched left arm. The big man had stood with his back to Jack and his legs spread wide; Jack had simply extended his arm, grabbed the man's scrotum, and was squeezing for all he was worth. Years of hanging on tight to glasses and bottles had given Jack a good, strong grip.

The man's legs gave way beneath him, but gradually, so that it appeared for a few seconds as if he were somehow suspended, defying gravity. Then Jack let go, and the big man collapsed heavily, his bulk hitting the floor with an impact I could hear and feel. Jack leaned over him and spoke: low, angry, hard. "Your balls are leaving the building," he said. "If you hurry, you can just catch them." The man turned on his front and clawed at the floor furiously, moving himself, crab-like, toward the door. He was in an obvious agony that his crawling, scuttling motion only made worse; but he moved as fast as he could, as if in actual pursuit of fugitive testicles.

Lu put her fork down, picked up her napkin and wiped her lips. Then she turned to Jack and said simply, "Thank you."

Jack smiled a smile of pure delight. When he spoke, his words were buoyed along on a southern drawl running at flood tide. "All part of our full service at the Law Offices of John Wentworth Sheridan IV, your full-service law firm."

She turned to me. "As I say, the shelf-life of an informant is brief. I look forward to returning to the groves of academe." She paused; then, feeling perhaps that she owed me some small talk, asked, "If you hadn't become a lawyer or judge, Judge, what would you have become?"

I didn't have a ready answer, but Jack did. "If Clark weren't a lawyer or a judge, he wouldn't exist at all." He was still smiling. I couldn't improve upon his answer, and I didn't try.

I finished my coffee, we chatted for a moment or two, and I left.

• • •

There were no calls that afternoon, and I was able to complete what I considered to be a good semi-final draft of my opinion. I sketched out each party's position in turn, trying to make the best case for it that I could. The Holtzman Museum had initiated the lawsuit, seeking an order compelling Dr. Gumbiner to turn over the Adler collection. On the face of it, the Holtzman's demand was reasonable. Dr. Gumbiner, having been carefully advised by excellent lawyers, had entered into a contract the purpose of which was the display of his legendary art collection at a museum eminently qualified to receive, care for, and exhibit that collection. The contract included a clause that all agreed was standard in such cases: a clause authorizing and obliging the Holtzman to examine the various art objects and confirm their authenticity. The museum, the art world, and the public that would flock to see the Adler collection, all deserved to know that the Adler collection was what it was believed to be. The Holtzman was eager to do what it had contracted to do. The balance of equities, that immeasurable measure of fairness, seemed to favor the museum. And the public interest, always to be considered in cases such as this one, was clearly on the side of compelling Dr. Gumbiner to deliver his art collection to the Holtzman without further delay.

In the course of implementing contracts, disputes will inevitably arise. To provide for such disputes in a relatively inexpensive and time-saving way, most modern contracts include arbitration provisions. Disputes had arisen in the implementation of this contract, and there was an arbitration provision. But what an arbitration provision!

Of course the parties to a contract can choose any arbitrators that they please. There are firms of professional arbitrators, many of them made up of lawyers or retired judges, who do this sort of thing all day long. The parties could have named such professional arbitrators in the contract. Instead, they named a religious court.

From my standpoint, however, it made no difference whether their choice was wise or foolish, sensible or crazy. Both parties had agreed in the contract that in the event of a dispute, that dispute would be referred to the *bes din*. The *Miami Herald* said that it was Dr. Gumbiner's idea in the first place, but the *Miami Herald* is not evidence in my courtroom and in any event, it makes no difference whose idea it was as long as both parties go along with the idea. Both parties had gone along with it. Dr. Gumbiner claimed that there was a dispute, several disputes, harsh disputes, between the parties; and that in the event of disputes, the terms of the contract are clear.

That was about as far as I had gotten when Carmen left on schedule at five o'clock. Twenty or thirty minutes later there was a knock at the outer chambers door.

I hadn't actually seen Lt. Cabrera in two or three years. He is a tall man, a six-footer, and his hair is still thick and black as tar, combed straight back. But I noticed that the skin of his face fit him a little looser than I remembered it, particularly around the eyes. Detectives seldom wear the police uniform; Cabrera had on a short-sleeve sport shirt, khaki slacks, and boat shoes. Judging by his wardrobe he could have been a tour guide, or maybe the social director at one of the Miami Beach hotels. But tour guides and social directors smile a lot and have animated expressions. The face of a homicide cop is not animated. His face is simply the side of his head that happens to be on the front. He has learned long ago that if he does not bury his feelings they will bury him. My friend Ed Barber was a homicide cop who forgot that lesson.

I invited Cabrera in, and when we were seated he handed me a manila mailing envelope. Inside were the police reports that had been done to date on the Bilstein and Weber homicides. Of course they were just preliminary, but they were extensive: names of potential witnesses who had been interviewed, summaries of what they had to say, detailing of the investigative steps taken by the officers involved. I leafed through them; I would read them carefully later, when Cabrera was gone.

"Are these my copies, Detective? May I keep them?"

"As long as no one else sees them." Which, of course, was why he brought them to me himself.

"I promise. It was kind of you to bring them over yourself."

He almost smiled. "I didn't. In fact, I don't know where you got them."

I smiled back. "Got what?"

He nodded, started to get up, but I had a couple of questions. There had been no arrests. Were there any prospects for an arrest?

"The investigation is ongoing." It was the answer right out of the manual. But it meant: We've got nothing.

"There's no possibility that they killed each other?"

He shook his head. If I weren't a judge, he might even have rolled his eyes. "They never knew each other, so there's no motive. No murder weapon was found at the scene. And he was in no condition to kill anyone, much less a healthy, heavy-set girl like her." He was right, of course. It was a stupid question.

"I suppose it's possible that someone was killing one of them, and then the other just happened along and had to be killed to be silenced?"

He didn't shake his head this time, but he didn't have to. "Sure it's possible. Now all we have to figure out is which one was being killed first, and why, and by whom, and with what, and why the other one happened along just at that moment."

I tried to make a joke of my own foolishness. "Glad I could be of so much help, Lieutenant. If there's anything else you need to know ...."

He wasn't angry at me. He wasn't even disappointed; he'd been asked stupid questions by judges and lawyers and police supervisors all his life. He was frustrated because he had a double-homicide on his hands, a horrible, tragic, seemingly-pointless double death on his hands, and no real prospect of solving it. Yes, the investigation was ongoing, just like the manual says; but homicide investigations do not get better as they get older. The best time to solve a homicide is now, and the next-best time is soon.

Cabrera pointed at the materials he had given me. "There are a couple of reports we haven't finished. We wanted to interview the ... uh ..." he made some gestures that were, I suppose, intended to describe a large hat and then a beard, "you know, the rabbis or whatever they are, but they weren't cooperative. They seemed to think we were accusing them of something, no matter how many times we explained that field interviews are just part of procedure. Anyway, the head rabbi, the old one, let us interview him and told the rest of them to do the same, so we finally got statements from them. But they haven't all been written up yet."

"Thank you for telling me."

He nodded. "And we haven't found one."

"Found one what?'

"One of the ... are they all rabbis?"

"I don't know."

"Well, one of them. Mordechai Braun." Cabrera gave a quick physical description, from which I took it that Braun had been one of the younger men sitting in court with Rabbi Stein. "No one seems to know where he is. But he'll turn up." Cabrera didn't seem unduly worried.

"You don't think his disappearance has anything to do with ...?"

Cabrera was already shaking his head. "We checked every angle. There's absolutely nothing to tie him with these homicides in any way."

"No, I'm sure there isn't." I thanked him for his time and trouble and walked him out of chambers.

After Cabrera left I started packing up my briefcase; I would finish working at home, after dinner. I packed up my semi-final draft of my opinion in *Holtzman Museum v. Gumbiner*, and the police reports and autopsy protocols in the investigations of the deaths of Herman Bilstein and Boots Weber. Then I looked at my briefcase and almost said to it, Briefcase, you must be what people mean when they talk about a mixed bag: an opinion on a contracts case and the investigative reports in a homicide case. Whoever mixed those things up together in one briefcase, Briefcase?

I left chambers, headed one floor up. I thought for a moment about taking the stairs, but I had seen enough of the stairwell. I pressed the "up" elevator button and waited patiently for the tired old elevator.

When I got to the next floor I knocked on the door marked "Chambers of Hon. Judith Waller." I had to knock twice – it occurred to me that Judith might have gone home already – but the door opened and there she was, mumbling what might have been, "Hello, Clark."

The first thing you see when you see Judith is her complexion. Judging is what Judith does when she and her husband (whose name escapes me just this minute) are not on their boat, and her face is as lined and weather-beaten as that of any old sea-salt. In between the lines she is tanned in some places, burned in others, peeling slightly around the burns. Her hair is a dark blond, but there is always a margin of gray roots visible where she parts it. It is only fair that her eyes are the same shade of green as the sea at which they love to gaze. She is tall for a woman, neither fat nor thin. She was wearing a loose-fitting gray blouse and a dark skirt. In the doorway she stood quietly for a minute, then mumbled something and turned to head toward her private office. I suppose she had invited me in, and I went.

Her office layout was the same as mine; the same, I suppose, as every judicial office in the building. As we were seated she gestured carelessly with a sweep of her arm. "Ignore the mess. The Administrative Office of the Court says I'll get a new secretary, at least a temporary, tomorrow." Files and office supplies were piled everywhere.

We chatted uneasily about the old days, about when I had been a prosecutor and had tried a few cases before Judith in criminal court. It wasn't much of a conversation. Silence set in, awkward for me if not for Judith. I had come to express my condolences, so I did. She nodded, said nothing.

There were a few paperclips on her desk. I reached for them, scooped them up, started connecting one to the next. Then I looked up and asked, "Do we know why Bootsie was in the stairwell?"

She shook her head, and I thought she meant no, we don't know. But that's not what she meant. "You know, she was a ... always a chubby girl. And she was always on some kind of diet or another. She said that ... she said that some people want to see Paris before they die, but she just wanted to see her cheekbones." Judith tried to smile at Boots's joke. "She had just gotten one of those little things" – she tried to indicate, with thumb and forefinger, the size and shape of a little thing – "that you put on your belt or your shoe, and it tells you how far you've walked today. So as part of her latest weight-loss plan she was going to walk up and down the stairs, instead of taking the elevator. She had just gone down to the clerk's office on the first floor to drop off some files. She made it down there. They saw her in the clerk's office, they took the files she was returning. But she never made it back." Judith took a deep breath. "She was doing it for her health. Isn't that something? For her health." Her voice dropped off. Mumble-mumble-mumble. "And you remember, she was never sick a day in her life. She thought that she was fat. Well, she was fat. But full of energy, happy, energetic, you remember." Mutter-mutter-mutter.

It was true. Bootsie was as healthy and full of life as Herman Bilstein had been ill and frangible. She was relatively young, and he was very old. She was a Jamaican-American woman and he was a Jewish man. She was known and liked by everyone in the legal community in Miami, and no one had any reason to kill her. He was known by no one in the legal community in Miami, so no one had any reason to kill him. They had nothing in common but the time, and the place, and the circumstance of their deaths.

We sat there for ... oh, I don't know how long. Probably not as long as it seemed. Judith had nothing to say, and neither had I. But it was my week for stupid questions, so before I thought carefully I said, "Judith, you were on one of those Florida Bar ethics committees for a while. What would you do if you knew that someone had committed a crime? Hypothetically speaking." She said nothing, and then she mumbled something. I didn't catch it. "What was that?"

"I said I guess I'd flag down a hypothetical cop and tell him about it," she answered. She didn't seem much in the mood for hypothetical questions. I couldn't blame her. I felt bad for asking; but apparently she felt bad for answering the way she had, because she went on, "As a general rule there is no legal duty to report a crime. Of course it's a duty of citizenship, a moral duty, but that's different."

"Even for us? Even for a judge who knows about a crime, there is no general legal obligation to report it to the authorities?"

"It depends on the crime. A judge could be punished for failing to report a crime, or even misconduct not rising to the level of crime, if the crime or misconduct undermines the legal system. So if you hypothetically saw a mugging and didn't call 9-1-1, Clark, the only thing you'll have to worry about is the *Miami Herald* finding out. But if you hypothetically saw something that undermines the fair and orderly administration of justice, ..." Her voice dropped off and I didn't hear the end of the sentence.

The fair and orderly administration of justice. It was a phrase with a certain majesty to it. I, a judge, must not sit idly by while someone, anyone, engages in conduct inconsistent with the fair and orderly administration of justice. I can stand on the street corner and watch while a bank is robbed, or while drugs change hands, or while a child is beaten black and blue, and if I do nothing, don't intervene, don't call for a cop, don't call 9-1-1, my worst worry in the world will be a headline in the *Miami Herald* a couple of months before election time. But I must act promptly, forthrightly, to defend the fair and orderly administration of justice.

"What would you do, Judith?"

She was looking down, and for a second, I thought that she hadn't heard me, but she had. "Depends on the hypothetical crime, I guess." Her hands were folded on the desk before her, her nails polished but cut very short. Long nails have no place on a boat. She looked up. "I understand what orderly administration is, Clark. You and I are in the orderly administration business. We administer the thousands of laws to be found in thousands of law books, and we try to do so in an orderly way. But I never did figure out the part about justice. I became a judge looking for it, and after years as a judge I realized that I wasn't supposed to find it. I'm not sure it's there to be found, and I'm not sure I'd know it if I saw it. So I stick to fair and orderly administration, and I let justice take care of itself." She said something else, but I didn't catch it.

We sat there in silence for a long minute, and then I told her how very sorry I was for her loss. She nodded a little, but said nothing; she didn't even bother to mumble. I reached out and patted her hand slightly, and I left.

• • •

For lack of anything else to do as I inched homeward in Miami traffic, I made a few phone calls. I had heard enough about the progress of the trial of *State v. Ivan Vukovich and The Wet Spot* to know that I wanted to hear more. Say what you like about the imperfections of our system of criminal justice, but it's a grand source of entertainment.

The prosecution had rested its case late yesterday, and now Sammy the Weasel was presenting the case for the defense. The public gallery was packed; a rumor, based on nothing more than wishful thinking, had gone around that "Anna Karenina" would be testifying and that she might reproduce the performance she had given in the courthouse lobby. Male onlookers must have been particularly disappointed when Sammy the Weasel announced that his first witness would be Jon Holland.

Apparently, Jon testified that he carefully instructed all the dancers at The Wet on the law applicable to their art: how they must not, during the course of their performances, permit any part of the areola or the lower portion of the breast to become exposed. Jon also testified, probably in the same tone of voice that he would use to give you driving directions to the public library, that from time to time he personally inspected the dancers' attire to determine that it fit snugly in the requisite areas. Sammy found this testimony fascinating. Jon managed somehow to get in the facts that prior to becoming a lawyer he had attended Andover Academy for prep school and Swarthmore College, and that he spoke fluent French. Sammy found this testimony not fascinating. In my mind's eye I picture Eleanor Hibbard cross-examining Jon, her voice filing the courtroom, about how he personally inspects the dancers' attire.

While Eleanor is taking her seat and Jon Holland is leaving the witness box, I should tell you that a criminal jury in Florida consists of six, not 12, jurors. The exception is a capital case, a case in which the defendant could get the death penalty; then there are 12 jurors. But in every ordinary criminal trial a jury is made up of only six members. The theory, as far as I can tell, is that we have twice as many criminal trials in Miami as they have anywhere else, so if we have 12 jurors we'd better get two trials out of them.

I mention this, so you'll understand why there were only four men on the jury in the case of *State v. Ivan Vukovich and The Wet Spot*. It was a six-person jury, you see; four men and two women. I suppose that each of the four men went home to his wife or girlfriend at the end of the day and told her that he was a juror on a case involving a stick-up of a gas station, and that it was boring and a waste of the taxpayer's money, and that he couldn't wait till it was over and he could get back to the office or the factory or wherever he was supposed to be. I don't suppose that any of the four of them told his wife or his girlfriend what happened that Thursday. They may have told their buddies later, under promises of secrecy sworn in blood; but I don't suppose they told their wives or girlfriends.

Because what happened next was not to be forgotten. Sammy the Weasel, rubbing his hands together in a very weasel-y way, announced that his next witness would be DeeDee Fondy. DeeDee Fondy, it turned out, was Anna Karenina; except that she wasn't.

DeeDee Fondy's blonde hair was pulled straight back and gathered in a bun behind her head. She wore a dark blue shirt, a long-sleeve shirt with a high collar; a blue plaid skirt, pleated, that came far below her knees; and flat shoes. Sammy was going to pass the Molotov Cocktease off as a choir girl. At least he was going to try.

"Please state your name."

"DeeDee Fondy."

"Where are you from, Miss Fondy?"

"Ormond Beach, originally. But I live here in Miami now." Ormond Beach is suburban Daytona. Kay was always a good guesser.

"And what do you do for a living?" Sammy had never been so deferential to, so supportive of, a witness. He was going to give the members of a jury every opportunity to warm up to Miss Fondy. Sammy was feeling pretty warm himself.

"I'm a dancer." She spoke very matter-of-factly. Odds are she didn't have a master's degree from the Sorbonne, but she had no difficulty speaking up for herself and she didn't come across in the sort of breathless, ditzy way people do when they tell "dumb blonde" jokes.

"Where do you perform?" Sammy was keeping the questions short and simple, although that may have been for his own benefit – to keep his mind from wandering – as much as for the witness's.

"At The Wet Spot."

"Who choreographs your dance routines?" It wasn't the question Sammy most wanted to ask – it wasn't even in the top 50 – but it was the one he needed to ask to get where he needed to go.

"I do."

"By yourself?"

"Well, sometimes I try things out with the other dancers, but yes, mostly by myself."

The thought of her trying things out with the other dancers caused Sammy's mind to veer wildly off course, but he forced himself back to his notes. "And how do you decide what moves to put in your routines, and what moves to leave out?"

"Well, my own sense of artistic expression, of course." Of course, thought Sammy. Of course. "And things that the audience has liked in the past." She paused. "And what Mr. Holland, the lawyer, has told us about what we can and can't do."

"What has Mr. Holland told you?"

Eleanor objected on grounds of hearsay, but not too energetically; and her objection was overruled. "He told us that our dance routines, we can't let the audience see our" – she stopped in mid-sentence; what was the nice word for nipples, again? – "areolas, or the lower half of our breast. Not even by accident."

"Not even by accident." Sammy seemed so genuinely disappointed.

She shook her head from side to side, no. Sammy was about to instruct her that she had to answer aloud, but she was licking her lips and he wanted to wait till she was finished.

"Please answer alick ... aloud," said Sammy.

"No, not even by accident."

Sammy directed the witness's attention to the date and time in question. "Did you perform that night?"

"Yes."

"Did you, at any time, bare your breasts?"

"No. Not at all."

"Were you wearing a top during your dance routine?"

"Yes."

Sammy forced himself to keep the pace of his questioning slow. It wasn't easy. "I understand that you have a custom-designed top that you wear during your performances?"

"Yes."

"Did you have that top on at all times on" – he gave the date again.

"Yes." Sammy may have been lathered up, but at least his witness was taking all this in stride.

"Does it fully cover your areolas and the lower portions of your breasts?"

"Yes, it does."

Slow and easy, now, Sammy told himself. "And did you, at my request, wear that top to court today?"

"Yes. I have it on under my shirt."

"Would you please stand up?"

The realization of what was about to happen evoked a variety of sounds from the public gallery; and juror number five, a Cuban-American lad in the full bloom and vigor of youth, emitted a low moan which he immediately stifled. Eleanor, not entirely ready to believe that even Sammy the Weasel, even Sammy the Weasel, would try such a thing, rose slowly to her feet as the witness did. "Your Honor, perhaps we should approach the bench ...."

It was Sammy's moment, and he seized it. "Miss Fondy," he said quickly, loudly, "please remove your shirt."

"Objection! I object!" bellowed Eleanor.

"Remove your shirt!" bellowed Sammy. And the witness proceeded to comply.

There was no music. She didn't dance. She didn't even throw in any of her sense of artistic expression. But she did start unbuttoning buttons.

And there was Floyd. Poor Floyd. Marooned on the bench with Eleanor Hibbard's angry voice demanding that he do some judge thing, a tall blond about to show her foundation garments and all they contained to an eager jury and courtroom (well, at least four of the jurors were pretty eager), and Sammy the Weasel grinning devilishly as he egged the whole thing on.

Oh, thought Floyd. Hmm, thought Floyd. It was never like this in civil court, thought Floyd.

• • •

A lot of people who don't know any better think that Miami is full of retirees. It was that way once upon a time, of course; but once upon a time Notre Dame always won the college football championship and the Yankees always won the World Series.

Nowadays the retirees from the east, from New York and New Jersey, settle in Broward or Palm Beach Counties, and the retirees from the Midwest settle in Sarasota or Naples. The University of Miami is as likely to win the college football championship as Notre Dame is, and the Marlins are as likely to win the World Series as the Yankees. Times change, towns change with them.

Which isn't to say that Miami has no retired people. People come here from all around the world. They come here from New York and they come here from Cuba and they work and raise kids and when it's time to retire ... well, it's too cold to go back to New York and they can't go back to Cuba. So Miami has its retirees.

I've mentioned Coco Isles Beach in connection with the case that Floyd Kroh is trying this week. Like a lot of communities in Miami-Dade County, Coco Isles Beach has a little of this and a little of that. Once upon a time it was a resort community, with a string of tacky motels lined up along the beach like cars in heavy traffic. Most of that's gone now, pushed out by luxury condo developments, big money deals. For a while Coco Isles Beach was a nice little residential community in which you could get a nice little free-standing single-family home for what, by Miami-area real estate prices, was considered very reasonable. It wouldn't be on the beach, of course, but you could take the bus to the beach. Most of those homes are still there, still occupied by people who worked in them and raised kids in them and now are retired in them. The Russian mob guys brought money to town, but they also brought strip clubs and a couple of low-end motels that rent rooms by the hour, extra charge for sheets, pillow-cases, trapezes, and so on. A little of this and a little of that; that's Coco Isles Beach.

I didn't know it at the time, but when Lt. Cabrera left my chambers he was headed to Coco Isles Beach. I got all the details later. Cabrera is a good detail man.

Cabrera's travels hadn't taken him to Coco Isles Beach in a long time. When he was a kid growing up in Hialeah – this was back in the days when Coco Isles Beach was motel row – every once in a while, a car with a family of tourists lost as hell would pull over on the street where he was playing baseball with his pals and ask, "Can any of you kids tell us how to get to Coco Isles Beach?" Then Cabrera and his buddies would mutter "Cuckoo Eyes Bitch?" or some other doubletalk, sure, no problem, and send the tourists off with directions that would get them to Homestead. That kind of thing was great fun when he and his buddies were nine or ten.

Cabrera was headed to the home of one Isidore Katznelson. Katznelson and his wife were retirees, living in the same home they had bought shortly after World War II, shortly after they came to America. Katznelson had called the police department claiming to have something to say about the death of Herman Bilstein. Cabrera knew that in all likelihood Katznelson had nothing to say about the death of Herman Bilstein, or in any event nothing that would help Cabrera make an arrest in connection with the death of Herman Bilstein. But Cabrera knew, too, that his investigation was stuck in the middle of nowhere. So if Isidore Katznelson wanted to be interviewed about the death of Herman Bilstein, Cabrera would interview him.

Cabrera was considered an excellent interviewer and report-writer. These skills, of course, were appreciated only by the higher-ups, never by the young cops. Young cops in Miami, like young cops in a lot of places, became cops so they could hit people and drive fast. When he was a young cop Cabrera liked to hit people and drive fast. But hitting people and driving fast didn't close out cases, and cops who didn't close out cases didn't move up the ladder. Cabrera didn't want to end up an old cop with nothing to show for his years with the department but hitting people and driving fast, working under a sergeant who had once been his rookie trainee. So as time passed he cut back on the hitting and the fast driving and taught himself to be a good witness interviewer and report writer.

Over the years he had decided that there are three important rules for witness interviewing. There are other rules, of course, many rules, but three important ones. First, don't take notes. Too many cops take notes while they interview the witness. If you take notes the witness starts talking to your notes, not to you. Look at the witness. Watch his face and eyes, his expressions and gestures. A lot of cops new to detective work worry that if they don't take notes they won't remember what they heard, but they're wrong. Force yourself to pay attention, to listen, to remember, Cabrera told them. You can write your notes later, in the car or back at the station.

Rule number two is the tough one for cops, because it requires patience and cops have no patience: Don't interrupt the witness. It drives a detective nuts when he asks the witness how many gunshots he heard, and the witness launches into some long cock-and-bull story about why ice floats, shouldn't it sink to the bottom of the glass? But let the witness talk himself out. He may, without even intending it, tell you something about the case, or about himself. When he stops to draw breath you can ask your question again, or ask another question, drawing him slowly but surely back to the number of gunshots that were fired. Don't interrupt the witness.

Of the three rules Cabrera considered the third to be the most important. If the witness claims to be an eyewitness – if he claims actually to have seen the crime, or some part of the crime – interview him at the place where he saw it. If he says the shooting took place on Biscayne Boulevard in front of the Freedom Tower, take him there and interview him there. If he says it took place at three in the morning on a Tuesday, take him there at three in the morning on a Tuesday and interview him then. Tell him to stand where he was standing, look where he was looking; that's how to interview him.

Most cops don't want to be bothered, of course. It's hot in Miami, even at three in the morning on a Tuesday. Much more comfortable to tell the guy to come to the police station, interview him there, show him the mug book while you sit at a desk with your coffee. But you never get quite the same interview that way.

Cabrera felt strongly about Rule Number Three, but it didn't apply in this case. Isidore Katznelson, whoever he was, whatever he saw, wasn't an eyewitness. He certainly hadn't been standing in the stairwell when Herman Bilstein and Boots Weber were murdered, so he wasn't an eyewitness. But he had called the police department, claiming that he had something to say about Bilstein's case. Cabrera didn't have any other witnesses to talk to, so he would take the long drive up to Coco Isles Beach and talk to Isidore Katznelson.

The streets in the residential section of Coco Isles Beach are named after tropical trees and flowers. They're Clematis and Hibiscus and Tabebuia, not First Street and Second Street and Third Street, so it took Cabrera a little longer to pull up in front of the Katznelson house. It was a small house, done in the old style with Bahama shutters in front and a screened-in Florida room in back. But it was nicely kept-up, and there was a birdbath in the tiny front lawn, and a bird-feeder affixed to a tree.

He took out his badge case as he rang the bell and held it open, badge above the fold and ID below. The woman who opened the door glanced at it, but she had clearly been expecting him and knew who he must be. She was already smiling and nodding as he said, "Mrs. Katznelson? I'm Lt. Cabrera, Metro-Dade Homicide."

She was, of course, a very elderly woman. She was thin, and her thinness was such that Cabrera wondered if maybe she was sick. Of course you don't have to be sick to be thin; but her face was drawn, and she was clearly very old, and Cabrera wondered if maybe she was sick. She had a little sweater on, although it seemed more than warm enough for Cabrera.

Still, she was smiling, not a token smile but one that seemed as if she were genuinely happy. "Yes, my husband has been looking forward to talking to you, Lieutenant. Please come in. He'll be out in just a minute, he was just resting." They were in a small hallway, its walls lined with photographs old and new. He followed her into a small living room. There was a sofa on one side of a coffee table, and a love seat on the other. The back wall was a sliding glass door that opened onto the Florida room, a sort of screened-in patio with elaborately tiled floor; the opposite wall was taken up with a breakfront that held a television, an old-fashioned stereo for playing phonograph records, and shelves filled with books. "Can I get you something, Lieutenant? Some coffee maybe?"

It was another of Cabrera's rules of witness interviewing that when the interview was conducted in the home of the witness, Cabrera would accept something like coffee from the witness; in fact if it wasn't offered, Cabrera would ask for it. He never asked for anything unusual or elaborate, just the sort of thing a host routinely offers a guest: coffee, if it was available; water, if it wasn't. He would accept it even if he didn't want it. He couldn't explain why this was a good idea, couldn't express the psychological or social dynamics it involved, but he knew it was a good idea and he made it one of his rules.

"Yes, ma'am. I'd like some coffee, thank you."

She smiled again and turned to go, took a step, stopped and turned again to face him. Her smile was gone. "Lieutenant, if my husband comes while I'm getting the coffee, please remember: He shouldn't get excited. Talking about this always makes him excited, but the doctors say he shouldn't get too excited. Please."

He nodded. "Yes, ma'am." She nodded back, then disappeared toward what he assumed was the kitchen. He really had no idea what she was referring to. Talking about what always made Isidore Katznelson excited? How often did he talk about the murder of Herman Bilstein?

He had noticed that Mrs. Katznelson had a pretty thick accent. Of course a Miami cop gets used to accents. Many of the witnesses to whom Cabrera spoke – maybe half, maybe more; he never bothered to count – spoke to him in Spanish. That was fine with him, Spanish was his first language. But among Spanish speakers as among English speakers there were different accents to contend with. His Spanish was Cuban Spanish, a very different thing from what was spoken by Guatemalans or by Nicaraguans or by Venezuelans or by Colombians. And then there were Haitians and Jamaicans who claimed that they were speaking to him in English but as far as he could tell might have been speaking to him in Martian. He once had a case in which a tourist from a small town in Maine had the bad fortune to witness a multiple shooting in a shopping mall. Two minutes into the interview Cabrera was wondering if Maine had an embassy in Miami, and if the embassy could send over an interpreter.

Mrs. Katznelson's accent was one with which he was not entirely familiar. He assumed it was an Eastern European Jewish accent; he had heard those once in a while in this part of town, although not much recently because the old Jews had died or moved up to Boynton Beach. The letter W, for example, was pronounced as a V (her husband had been looking "forvard" to meeting him; he "vas" just resting), and the TH diphthong was sounded as a T (can I get you "someting"). It was important that he be able to filter out the accent, to prevent it from becoming a distraction, so that he could concentrate on what the witness had to say. He assumed that Mr. Katznelson would speak with the same accent as his wife.

She was back quickly with coffee in a beautiful cup and saucer. He knew nothing about cups and saucers, but these were too elaborately designed for his eye to miss them. There were ornate flowers, pink and red, and green leaves. Around the outer edge of the saucer and the lip of the cup was gold trim. If he had to guess he would have guessed that Mrs. Katznelson collected cups and saucers, so he made a point of telling her how lovely the cup and saucer were, and she seemed very flattered. She had also brought a plate – it didn't match the cup and saucer – with an assortment of cookies. "These," she pointed "I made myself. These" indicating the other side of the plate "are only from the store." He didn't want cookies any more than he wanted coffee, but he would make a point of eating one of the cookies she made herself, just as he would take a few sips of coffee; and he would tell her how good it all was.

It was then that Isidore Katznelson came into the room. When Cabrera had first seen Mrs. Katznelson he had had an unparticularized sense that her health was failing; but with Mr. Katznelson there could be no doubt. He was wrinkled and liver-spotted and his face bore the expression of someone who is never entirely at ease and free from pain. He was dressed very casually – he had his house slippers on – and there was a shuffle to his walking gait. He sat gingerly in the love seat across from Cabrera, and there was a slight groan when he finally reached the sitting position. He did not extend his hand, but looked up and, with the same pinched expression of discomfort, said, "I am Isidore Katznelson."

"How do you do, Mr. Katznelson." Cabrera handed him a business card. Detectives get business cards.

"My wife has been" – here he used a foreign language expression; it sounded to Cabrera like he said something about China – "about our grandchildren?"

Mrs. Katznelson, standing next to the love seat, brightened up. "Our grandson is a dentist in Boca. First in his class in dental school. You have children, maybe, Detective?"

Cabrera was spared from answering – it was another interviewing rule that he tried not to be put in the position of answering questions rather than asking them – when Mr. Katznelson spoke to his wife in a foreign language. She answered in the same language; then, as far as Cabrera could tell, asked some kind of question.

"No. Tea," said Mr. Katznelson; and his wife left the room.

Cabrera wanted to pose a question right away. He didn't want Katznelson to set the direction of the interview. So he asked, "Did you know Herman Bilstein?"

Katznelson blinked, as if he hadn't understood the question. "Bilstein?"

"Herman Bilstein. The man who was murdered in the courthouse stairwell. Did you know him personally?"

"No. How should I know him?"

Mrs. Katznelson returned. The cup and saucer she brought for her husband were not identical to the one she had given Cabrera, but they were equally ornate, beautiful in an old-fashioned kind of way. The cup contained hot water; the saucer held a tea bag, a spoon, and two sugar cubes. Cabrera watched to see if Mrs. Katznelson, having delivered her husband's tea, would stay or go. He preferred to conduct interviews with no one else present. Other people invariably interfered with the witness, suggested or corrected answers, offered distractions. But he was hardly in a position to tell Mrs. Katznelson to leave her own living room, and she gave no sign of doing so. She made herself as comfortable as she could on the arm of the love seat.

He began the interview again. "Mr. Katznelson, you telephoned the police department claiming to have something to say about the death of Herman Bilstein?"

He nodded, dunking the tea bag slowly into the water. "He was in Weeghman?"

Cabrera watched the old man hold the spoon over the cup, place the tea bag in the spoon, wrap the string of the bag once around the bag, then squeeze, so that the last dark drops of tea drained off the side of the spoon into the cup.

"Yes."

Katznelson unwrapped the now-drained tea bag and set bag and spoon on the saucer. Then he picked up one of the sugar cubes and, rather than dropping it into the cup, put it in his mouth. He appeared to be holding it in his cheek, almost as if it were a piece of chewing tobacco. He sipped his tea. "I was not. I was in

...." He gave a name; a multi-syllabic, German- or Slavic-sounding name. Cabrera had a sense of having heard the name before.

The old man paused, sipped his tea again. Then he launched into a long story. The story presented a challenge to Rules One and Two. Rule One was not to take notes, but Mr. Katznelson spoke rapidly, his accent thick at some points, and he freely made reference to places and things that had what Cabrera took to be German or Polish names. Without notes Cabrera would never be able to reproduce this narrative.

The greater challenge was to Rule Two. Cabrera realized early on that it would make little difference if he could reproduce Katznelson's narrative. It was unlikely in the extreme that anything the old man was telling him had anything to do with the death of Herman Bilstein. Cabrera would, if he observed Rule Two strictly, end up listening to an unbearably lengthy and utterly useless story. The old man grew angry as he told his tale, pausing at several junctures as if he expected Cabrera to interrupt him to exclaim, "That's terrible!" or "What an outrage!". At one point he rolled up his sleeve to show the numbers that had been branded into his forearm.

From time to time Mrs. Katznelson would attempt to interrupt, reminding her husband that he was not to excite himself, the doctors didn't want him to excite himself. At each such interruption Katznelson would take a sip of tea and a deep breath, and promise his wife that no, no, he wouldn't excite himself. But Mrs. Katznelson's calming influence was never very long-lived.

The old man's anger was his only source of strength. He was short of breath, weak, and he grew tired. Cabrera hated to take advantage of the ill-health of a Holocaust survivor, but the interview had to have some direction. As Katznelson became more and more winded, Cabrera had chances to ask pointed questions: You never spoke to Herman Bilstein? You never knew of him, for example through any organization of Holocaust survivors? Do you know anyone who knew him? Who was in Weeghman with him?

Each question brought a response; but none brought an answer. Isidore Katznelson, after all, had not called the police department claiming that he knew who murdered Herman Bilstein, or that he could help the police find the murderer of Herman Bilstein. He had called the police department claiming to have something to say about the death of Herman Bilstein, and in a sense that was true. He had something to say. He wanted to say how angry he was, across the gulf of more than half a century, how very angry he was about what was done to him, and to Herman Bilstein whom he never met, and to six million others. He wanted to say it to anyone who could be got to listen. He wanted to say it so it would not be forgotten, so the sense of outrage would not pass, so the evil would never be permitted to be repeated.

When he had said it – when he was done saying it – he sank back in the love seat, very tired. Cabrera got up to leave. Mrs. Katznelson was commuting to and from the kitchen, tidying up, and Cabrera would not go until he had had a chance to thank her.

But Isidore Katznelson, staring up at Cabrera, had one more thing to say. "They buried it. Weeghman."

"Pardon me?"

"I see in the paper something, that the anniversary of the liberation of Weeghman is coming up?" Katznelson had, apparently, been following the trial with great care. "That's ...." He used a foreign word, a very guttural word. "How was there a liberation? What kind liberation? They buried Weeghman."

Cabrera sat down. He had come to understand Katznelson's accent (How "vas dere" a liberation. "Vat" kind liberation. "Dey" buried "Veeghmahn"), but now he did not understand the meaning, the content of the old man's remark.

So he asked. That, too, was a rule of witness interviewing. If you don't understand, make them explain it to you. "I don't understand."

The old man sagged in the love seat, exhaustion having overtaken anger. He took a deep breath and let it out. "The Nazis. *Amalek*. When they saw that the war was ending. They knocked down all the buildings at Weeghman. They removed the wood, the wire, everything. What they couldn't remove they plowed under. Also the bodies, they buried the dead and the dying. The ones who were well enough to walk were given civilian clothing, told to take what possessions they had and go. They were told that if they were seen within ten kilometers of Weeghman they would be shot.

"The Nazis planted grass, even wildflowers. You wouldn't know the camp ever existed. There was nothing to see, nothing to tell you. Even the roads leading to the camp they re-routed." Katznelson stared away for a moment, silent. Then he looked up at Cabrera, and a flicker of the old anger appeared in his eyes. "For months the allies couldn't find it. They wanted to stop looking. Who had time to look for a death camp that had disappeared, that maybe never really existed at all? Months, for months they couldn't find it. So when they found it, what then? They put up a ... what do you call, a plaque? A plaque?" Cabrera nodded. Yes, plaque was the word. "Liberation means 'to set free,' no? Isn't that what 'liberation' means? So who did they set free?" The old man shook, and tears came to his eyes. "Who did they set free?"

Mrs. Katznelson stroked her husband's shoulder and made a shushing noise. "Izzy, please, remember what the doctors said." The old man nodded, leaned back in the love seat. His wife spoke again, this time to Cabrera. "He should rest."

Cabrera stood again, shook hands, thanked them. Back in his car he had no sooner pulled away from the curb than he called me.

I was surprised to hear from him. I hadn't exactly covered myself with glory when we discussed the case in my chambers.

Perhaps he believed that because Katznelson was Jewish and I was Jewish I could provide some insight into the old man's story, or at least help with the spelling of the foreign names and places. Perhaps because I'm a judge he felt a policeman's obligation to cater to me, to make me feel involved and useful. Whatever his reason for calling, I doubt that I was of much help to him. He gave me a very detailed description, an almost verbatim description, of what he had heard. I think I managed to spell some of the European place-names.

• • •

I bring work home with me most evenings. I've told Miriam many times that I think it's a good thing for kids to see one or both of their parents doing "homework" after dinner. My message is that homework is responsibility, but it's not a punishment or burden for which children are singled out. Miriam says that she understands and agrees. She probably says so because she knows I'd bring work home anyway, but she says so.

I do my homework at the kitchen table. When the kids were little they did too. Now they do their homework on their computers, so I have the kitchen table to myself. I can concentrate on what I'm doing without being interrupted to spell "dilemma" (one l, two m's) or to name the capital of Iowa (Des Moines). I miss those interruptions very much, but you can't fight progress.

At some point during the evening I became aware that Bagel was standing just inside the patio door, making the whimpering noises that are dog-talk for, "I have to go to the bathroom." I started to ask one of the kids to take him outside, but when I looked up I realized that the only lights on in the house were in the kitchen and that everyone had probably gone to sleep. I let the dog out and waited the couple of minutes that he needed; Bagel is very efficient about this sort of thing, because he doesn't like to be outside.

Back at the kitchen table I penciled in the last changes to the last re-draft of my ruling in

Holtzman Museum v. Gumbiner. Joel, the quiet child, came silently into the kitchen. He had almost seated himself opposite me at the kitchen table before I realized he was there.

Joel is Miriam's son. It's not so much a matter of appearance; Miriam and I actually look very much alike, with our curly dark hair, our large dark eyes, our pale complexions. Somewhere in Miriam's family tree are tall relatives, or at least less short relatives, so there was always hope that Joel would someday grow past me. But Joel is Miriam's son because he has inherited her soul. He has her inner calm, her unarticulated belief that good things will come to good people and that most people are good. In the spring he will try out for the school baseball team, and he will play with enthusiasm; but if he ends up on the bench he will try out with the same enthusiasm next year. He has none of my vices, is not plagued with secret doubts that can never be resolved or secret ambitions that can never be satiated. He is Miriam's son, which is why – try as I do not to show it – I love him the best of my children.

"I thought you went to bed."

He shrugged a little. "Not sleepy."

"Are the kids asleep?" Joel, the eldest, is pleased when "the kids" refers to his siblings but not to him.

"Uh-huh."

"How about Mom?"

He shrugged again. "I don't know. I guess so. The lights are out in your bedroom. You know Mom." Miriam falls asleep easily and sleeps soundly. I hope that this, too, is something Joel has inherited from her.

As is my way, I had spread my notes all over the kitchen table. The papers nearest me were those on which I was presently working: the draft of my opinion in the Holtzman case, and copies of appellate opinions that would guide my decision. Across the table, near Joel, the autopsy protocol for Herman Bilstein lay on top of my briefcase. Joel glanced at it; then picked it up and read it with care, read it through twice. Of course I hadn't intended that my children read autopsy protocols, but I had left this one lying around, and I didn't want to precipitate a pointless argument with my teenage son by telling him not to read it.

He said nothing after he read it. I continued working, and in a few minutes, he stood and started to walk away. When he got to the far side of the kitchen he turned to me and said, "Dad, that Bilstein guy ... it said he walked with a cane, right?"

"Yes. A special one, what they call a walker."

"So he probably couldn't walk up and down stairs, could he?"

"I doubt it. Probably not."

"So ... why did he go out to the stairwell? I mean, if he couldn't walk up and down stairs?"

I shook my head. "I don't know, Joel. Maybe he was looking for the men's room and got lost. Maybe he just needed to get away from the crowd and the noise in the courtroom and find someplace quiet. Maybe ...." I shook my head again, turned my palms up. "I don't know, son. Maybe we'll never know."

Joel stood there in the doorway, silent for a moment. Then he said, "But if we never know what happened, it's not ... I mean, anyway, it's not *your* ...." He fished for the word he wanted.

I tried to supply it. "It's no reflection on me, son. It's a tragedy, of course, but no one thinks less of your old dad because it happened in the middle of a hearing over which I was presiding." It would be just like Joel to be concerned about me and how it would all affect me. "Right now it's the police's problem. If they arrest someone, it will be his problem, and his lawyer's problem, and a problem for whatever criminal-court judge the case comes before. But it won't be me, because I'm a fancy downtown civil-court judge." I smiled, to try to make sure that my teenage son understood. I looked at the clock on the kitchen wall, and Joel saw me looking. "It's late. Try to get some sleep."

He nodded, turned to go. "G'night, Dad."

"Goodnight, Joel." I watched him walk down the hallway to his room, saw him enter it and close the door, saw light seeping out from under the doorway. He would probably read, or listen to music, or both, before he could fall asleep.

Good night, my son. I love you, and I'm very proud of you. Thank you for your concern for me. Thank you for asking, and wondering, and thinking, about the events around you, even the horrible events. Thank you for posing questions I can answer, and for posing questions I cannot answer. Yes, you're right, Herman Bilstein walked with a cane. Yes, you're right, Herman Bilstein probably couldn't walk up or down stairs. Yes, you're right to wonder why he went into the stairwell in the first place.

But in one respect, my son, you're wrong.

Because I do know who murdered Herman Bilstein.

CHAPTER SEVEN
ANOTHER FRIDAY

"It's almost nine, Judge."

Carmen never fails to remind me when it's time for me to take the bench, not because she particularly cares whether I'm on time but because she knows that I do. I pointed to my two judicial robes, hanging on adjacent pegs of the hat rack in my office.

"Which one would you say has better-pressed pleats?" I asked. She looked at me for a second to see if I was serious; then inspected the two robes carefully and made her choice. I entered the courtroom through my private entrance, took my seat, arranged my notes before me. Bailiff Bud Teachout, he of the railroad-conductor voice, bellowed for order in the court.

The lawyers' tables were, for the first time this week, almost bare: no boxes of files, no exhibits, no stuffed briefcases. The junior man of the Williams, Santos faction had a legal pad and pen, perhaps because he feared that he might be called upon to make notes of some kind or perhaps because he felt naked in a courtroom without a legal pad and pen. Before Raul was a single manila folder that appeared to contain very little. If I had to guess

I would have said it contained two statements to be issued to the press after my ruling: one in case of victory, and one in case of defeat. On the table at which Dr. Gumbiner and his lawyers sat was nothing at all.

The front row of the gallery, the press row, was packed as tight as a sardine can. Reporters elbowed one another for room to make notes on tiny pads. Behind them, the public gallery was, as it had been all week, filled to bursting. Press photographers and videographers are not allowed in the courtroom with their cameras, but Carmen had seen them jockeying for position in the hallway.

I began my remarks by thanking the lawyers for their outstanding work. There are some judges who do this as a matter of form in every case, or at least in every case covered in the press, but I did it in this case because I meant it. Bad lawyering makes good judging difficult and bad judging easy. The attorneys had done a superb job and they were entitled to hear it. They were even entitled to hear it on the evening news.

Then I spent a few minutes reviewing the facts of the case – its remarkable history, the unique and valuable art collection that was the object of the litigation, the nature of the legal proceeding themselves. The contract in question provides that a dispute arising in the discharge of obligations under the contract shall be submitted to arbitration. If what was meant by a dispute was simply a legal question, I was empowered and obliged to resolve it, the arbitration provision of the contract notwithstanding. If, however, there were material disputed issues of fact, those issues were to be referred to the designated arbitrators. I cited several cases from appellate courts that addressed the meaning of a factual dispute for the purposes of contract law, and I went over the rulings in those cases.

In light of those appellate opinions, I said, it is clear to me that there exist in this case material disputed issues of fact. The contract contemplates that such issues shall be submitted to arbitration. The next question for my consideration, therefore, is whether there is anything about the arbitration provisions of this particular contract that would cause me to find them to be unenforceable. I discussed another group of rulings from higher courts, these dealing with situations in which arbitration provisions in contracts were held to be unenforceable for one reason or another: for reasons of social policy, for example, or because arbitration in a particular context would frustrate the larger intent of the contract. I laid out the facts and holdings of these cases in detail.

None of these reasons, I concluded, is applicable here. True, the venue for arbitration identified in the contract is unusual in the extreme, but that without more is no grounds to depart from the written words of the contract. Perhaps the form of arbitration called for in the contract will be unsuccessful. But that is something we cannot know now, and is no reason not to try. The parties, advised at all times by highly competent legal counsel, had agreed to the arbitration provision appearing in the contract. No reason appears for the court not to enforce that provision.

"This matter shall proceed forthwith to arbitration as provided in the contract and related documents. The parties shall, sixty days hence, file status reports indicating whether the matters in dispute have been resolved.

"So ordered." I gave the bench a good smack with my gavel – I had become quite a gavel-swinger since coming to civil court – stood and headed back to chambers. Behind me the courtroom filled with the sound of voices and movement.

Carmen, without being told, came to my office, helped me off with my robe, asked if I wanted coffee. "Not just yet, thanks." I sat at my desk, loosened my necktie a little. "I saw Rabbi Stein in the courtroom. I just dumped this case in his lap. See if you can catch him before he leaves and invite him back here for a moment." She was gone for ten or 15 minutes, and I thought the rabbi might have left, or that Carmen had simply been unable to get to him in the crush of bodies in the hallway; but then I heard the outer chambers door open and close, and seconds later Rabbi Chaim Stein -- black hat, long black coat, white beard, and luminous blue eyes -- was standing in my private office. He was a little short of breath from having worked his way through the crowd, but he was smiling, still full of energy. I stood, offered him a seat, and he took it. I offered him coffee, and he took that too, although my feeling was that he accepted more as a matter of social grace than because he wanted the coffee.

I asked him if he was comfortable and he assured me that he was. Quite a case we have on our hands here, I said, and he nodded, still smiling. I doubt that there's ever been one quite like it, I said, just to have something to say.

"Van Meegeren."

"Pardon me?"

"You are familiar with the famous case of Van Meegeren?"

"Uh, no. No, I can't say that I am."

He seemed concerned that he might have given offense. "No, no, I did not mean to suggest that you should be."

But now I had to know. "Who was Van ... what was the name?"

He took a deep breath, let it out, paused. "Van Meegeren." He paused again. "He was a Dutch artist in the years between the wars. A good painter, not a great painter. He did a painting of one of Queen Juliana's deer, which I believe is still used on holiday greeting cards and calendars in Holland. Perhaps you know the one to which I am referring?" I shook my head.

He shrugged. "It does not matter. Van Meegeren was not a great artist, but he was a great collector of and dealer in the works of Vermeer." He paused again, waiting for a look of recognition on my part. I nodded; yes, I knew of -- well, I had heard of -- Vermeer, the great Dutch master of the 17th century. "During the war he sold Vermeers from his collection to top-ranking Nazis, perhaps even to Herman Goering himself. You can imagine that this was considered an outrage, a betrayal, by the Dutch people. Worse; it was a crime, a species of treason.

"Of course nothing could be done about it during the pendency of the Nazi occupation of Holland. But in the immediate aftermath of the war Van Meegeran was arrested, imprisoned, and prosecuted.

"The sale to the Nazis of Holland's artistic legacy had been a shock, but Van Meegeran's defense was a greater shock still. He asserted that the paintings in question were not Vermeers. They were forgeries. Van Meegeran knew that they were forgeries – because he himself had forged them. He had been dealing in forged Vermeers for years. He was not a traitor, claimed Van Meegeran; he was simply a forger.

"Can you imagine how the matter was resolved?"

I couldn't imagine. "I can't imagine."

"Van Meegeran was locked in prison, under round the clock observation. He was given paint, brushes, and so on. And he produced a Vermeer. He produced a Vermeer that Bredius, and the other great art critics and historians of the day, were completely persuaded was authentic."

"No. Really?"

"Yes, it's quite true. Not precisely the same as our present case, of course, but ... well, *'ayn kol chadash tachat ha-shemesh.'"* He shifted gears. "There is nothing new under the sun."

His discussion of Holland and historic events there brought my mind back to something that Lu Warneke had said at lunch yesterday. She had mentioned the excommunication of Baruch Spinoza, the brilliant Dutch-Jewish philosopher of the 17th century. "Rabbi, was Spinoza excommunicated?"

Now, how was that for a transition? But it didn't throw him. "Yes. He was."

"We have excommunication in Judaism?"

His face contracted in a very thoughtful look. There were, apparently, not many yes-or-no questions when it came to matters of Jewish religious law. "We have ... well, certainly we had, *niddui* and *cherem*. A *cherem* was pronounced on Spinoza, a very strict *cherem*. Of course that was three and a half centuries ago, in very troubled times."

"And he was excommunicated?"

"Yes."

"Because of his philosophy?"

Again the very thoughtful look. "I ... I think not. Spinoza was very young at the time that the *cherem* was pronounced against him. He had not yet published any philosophical papers. He had, as a boy, been considered the most brilliant of all *yeshiva* students in Amsterdam's Jewish community, a favorite pupil of the great Rabbi Mortera." He sighed. "Perhaps Spinoza had, as a young man, expressed heterodox views. But this is not uncommon. Many of the greatest rabbis expressed heterodox views in their youths. Great minds will consider, and in time reject, false ideas. Ibn Ezra himself said, '*Ha mavin yavin*.'" He paused to consider an appropriate translation. "'The one capable of understanding will come to understand.' We do not excommunicate every restless young mind."

"Then why did the rabbis excommunicate Spinoza?"

He shook his head slightly. "It was not Mortera, not the rabbis, who insisted on the *cherem*. It was the *parnassim*, the ... what today I suppose we would call the lay leadership, the ... the synagogue board of directors." He shifted slightly in his seat. "You must understand that the Jewish community of the Netherlands in those days lived entirely by trade and finance. There was no manufacturing, no farming ... everything was trade and finance. Trade and finance, of course, require good faith between man and man. Any suggestion that a member of the Jewish business community would dishonor his debts might have undermined that faith. It might have destroyed the economy of the Jewish community in Amsterdam, even brought about the expulsion of the Jewish community itself.

"Spinoza's father was a financier. Just before his death, he experienced serious financial reverses. Under the Jewish custom and practice at that time, Spinoza inherited his father's indebtedness, just as he would have inherited his father's estate if the father had died solvent. But Spinoza had no desire to be a financier, and certainly not to start a career in finance with a large indebtedness.

"He was, I believe, about 23 years old. Under Dutch law, he was still a minor. So Spinoza applied to the Dutch courts to be relieved of his inherited debts.

"The Jewish community was enraged. This was a terrible precedent. If debts could be dishonored simply by applying to the Gentile courts, what confidence would anyone have in doing business with Jewish traders and financiers? The leading businessmen of the Amsterdam Jewish community could not tolerate such a thing. It was they who brought about Spinoza's *cherem*." Another sigh. "That, I should say, is my belief. I cannot be certain, of course. But there is rabbinic authority for the pronouncing of a *cherem* on one who undermines the authority of the *bes din* by resorting to Gentile courts." I can't imagine what a look came across my face, but Rabbi Stein, seeing it, broke into a warm smile. "That does not apply here, Judge. You and the Holtzman Museum will not be the objects of a *cherem*, I can assure you." He chuckled.

"That's very good to know." I tried to chuckle too.

"When we read Spinoza today, his writing seems anything but radical and iconoclastic. He seems to me to have a great love of the Almighty, and to accept the oneness, the unity of the Almighty. In these respects at least he was a very good Jew. And yet he is thought of today as having been excommunicated by an intolerant Jewish community that could not accept his philosophical revelations." The twinkle had gone out of Rabbi Stein's eye. He seemed very sad at the thought of the 350-year-old injustice done to Baruch Spinoza.

I stood up and stretched my back, a little stiff from sitting. When I was a lawyer I never used to get stiff from sitting, but the longer I served as a judge, I noticed .... I walked over to the window and looked out. "Rabbi," I asked the man seated behind me, "may I ask you a question? One unrelated to the case?"

"Yes, of course," I heard.

"If I know that someone has committed a crime, and if no one knows but me, what ... what is my obligation? What ought I to do?"

I heard him sip the coffee, and then place the cup back on the saucer. "In *va-yikra*" -- he paused, shifted gears again -- "what is referred to in English as Leviticus, chapter 5, we are taught that one who has eyewitness testimony to give and who fails to give it is subject to punishment. But the passage probably refers only to one who has been formally called upon to testify. And the punishment for failure to testify may be left to the Almighty." He cited to a passage from Talmud, another from Maimonides's *Mishneh Torah*, and still another from *Shulchan Aruch*.

"And will God punish those who deserve it?"

"Certainly."

"And protect the innocent?"

"Yes, certainly."

"And yet we see injustice all around us, Rabbi."

"Because we do not see with the eyes of the Almighty, who sees all things, always."

I looked back at him. "The wheel of justice grinds slowly, but it grinds exceedingly fine?"

He cocked his head to the side and mulled it over for a moment. "This is a *mashal*, a ... a proverb of some kind?"

"Yes."

"How is it again?"

"The wheel of justice grinds slowly, but it grinds exceedingly fine."

"Yes." He smiled and nodded a little. "Yes, it is just so."

"Justice is of God, and the universe is just because God is just?"

"Certainly." Certainly. His face and voice were so full of expression. Certainly the universe is just, because God is just. For those whose faith is perfect it is a simple matter. But what about for the rest of us, Rabbi? What about poor judges armed with nothing but their human uncertainty, a statute book, and a gavel? How are we to find our way from falsehood to truth, from injustice to justice, from guilt to innocence?

He saw my thoughts and broke in on them. "In the *akedat Yitzchak*" – again the pause to shift linguistic gears – "the binding of Isaac, the Almighty gives Abraham a command that seems to Abraham very unjust: to kill the child Isaac. Abraham draws his knife to perform the divine command, but at the last moment the Almighty stays his hand. The great gentile philosopher Kierkegaard concludes that Abraham was the greatest moral hero of the Torah, because he was willing to set aside his own merely human notion of justice in deference to the Almighty, who is the source of justice."

"And is that what you believe?"

He took a deep breath, let it out slowly. "Most rabbinic interpretation holds that this was a test of Abraham's faith, and that Abraham passed. At the conclusion of the passage the Almighty tells Abraham *'ki ya'an'* you did not withhold your child from me, I will make a mighty nation of you. *"Ki ya'an'* they translate as 'because.' But there is another translation. Some rabbis teach that *'ki ya'an'* is an ancient idiomatic expression meaning 'even though.' If that is the interpretation, then Abraham failed the test. The Almighty was waiting for him to say that it would be wrong, it would be unjust to kill the child, even upon divine command. But *'ki ya'an,'* even though, Abraham failed the test, the Almighty would be with him and make a great nation of him."

"And what do you believe?"

"Would it be sufficient ...." He stopped in mid-question, then shook his head. "I do not know. I have never felt a conflict between my conscience and my faith."

"Never?"

"Never."

I turned to look out the window. The roof of the parking garage across the street was a couple of floors below me. Cars parked on the lower floors were sheltered from the sun, but not those parked on the roof.

I said nothing, and he said nothing. Then he asked, quietly: "Does it concern a friend?"

"Pardon?"

"The crime that you know of. The one about which you are unsure what to do. Does it concern a friend?"

"No. It concerns a stranger," I said. "It concerns the man who murdered Herman Bilstein."

I was still looking out the window. I heard no sound of movement, not the slightest sound of movement, so he was still sitting behind me, in the chair opposite my desk. "Herman Bilstein was lured, or followed, down the corridor and into the stairwell. The man who lured him, or followed him, picked up a large, heavy ashtray that was sitting on a hand-truck in the corridor. The ashtray was about seven inches on a side, with the design of the Lorillard Mill. On the stairwell landing he struck Bilstein with the ashtray, one blow forceful enough to kill him and send his body tumbling down half a flight of stairs to the landing below. Bootsie Weber happened to be walking up the stairs from the clerk's office at just that moment. Bilstein's body must have landed almost at her feet. For a second or two she must have been frozen and mute with terror – and that second or two was enough time for the murderer to kill her too, just to keep her from becoming a witness. Then the murderer left the stairwell and returned to the courtroom. When I adjourned court and ordered the area cleared, he left the courthouse with everyone else."

I paused. There was no hurry, no need to speak quickly. "The ashtray disappeared within the folds or pockets of the long, heavy, black coat worn by the murderer. I'm sure it has been disposed of and will never be seen again." Floyd Kroh Jr. would have to live with one piece missing from his father's ashtray collection.

Funny, isn't it? In a week full of questions, so many questions, questions that went unanswered; in a week of questions that were merely foolish, in a week of ever-changing questions, there was one constant. There was Floyd's collection of ashtrays and pipes, the collection about which he pestered me relentlessly throughout the week. I suppose he must have pestered the Administrative Office of the Court as well. I suppose he must have pestered anyone and everyone.

It was possible, of course, that every pipe and ashtray but one had been delivered to his chambers, and that one ashtray had been lost or broken. It was possible; but it wasn't very possible.

Every pipe and ashtray but one, and that one a big, hefty, heavy piece, seven inches on a side, a collector's item? It was barely possible, I suppose. But it seemed to me more likely, much more likely, that if that ashtray disappeared it disappeared on purpose and not by accident. It wasn't a pipe that had disappeared. It wasn't a small item, a light-weight item, a fragile item. It was a well-made, good-sized item, something sturdy, something sizeable, something a man could get a good grip on. Spend enough time as a judge in criminal court and you find yourself thinking: wouldn't that ashtray make a good murder weapon?

Then how had the murder weapon, and the murderer, disappeared? The murder weapon, the ashtray, hadn't been found; which meant that the murderer had taken it with him and disposed of it elsewhere. He could have walked up a flight of stairs, or down a flight of stairs, then taken the elevator to the ground floor and left the building. But not with a bloody ashtray in his hand. He couldn't take that chance. And he couldn't leave the ashtray somewhere in the building, either. That was another chance he couldn't take. If the murderer were a lawyer he might have a large briefcase, a briefcase large enough to conceal an ashtray seven inches on a side.

But I couldn't think of any connection between Herman Bilstein and any lawyer in the civil courthouse, or any lawyer in Miami, or any lawyer in Florida. I couldn't think of any reason for a lawyer to risk his safety, his reputation, his life, by beating Herman Bilstein and Boots Weber to death and then leaving the building with the murder weapon in a briefcase.

Of course it was possible that the murders weren't about Herman Bilstein at all. It was Bootsie Weber who lived here in Miami, had her family and friends here, knew so many people here. Everyone spoke of her cheerfulness, her positive outlook, her popularity. But what if she was unpopular with one person, just one person? What if just one person, for reasons none of the rest of us could even imagine, hated her enough to want her dead? And what if frail old Herman Bilstein had the misfortune to wander into the stairwell just as Bootsie was being murdered, and so had to be murdered too?

It was possible; barely possible. But if someone wanted Bootsie Weber dead, wanted her dead so much that he – or she – was willing to commit murder, wouldn't that murder have happened at another time, in another place? Would someone who seethed with blood-lust for Bootsie Weber have come to the civil courthouse in broad daylight to do his killing? Would he have known the exact moment when Bootsie would be hiking up and down the stairs? Would he have lurked in the stairs for hours, waiting for his opportunity, poised to strike, unconcerned who else might be present? And would he have counted on finding a heavy ashtray, seven inches on a side, just waiting for him in the courthouse hallway?

It was possible; but it wasn't believable. It was asking too much of coincidence. Ashtrays and other murder weapons can't be counted on to be at hand when you need them.

Apart from the fact that Floyd Kroh's ashtray collection had a piece missing, there was one other fact that I couldn't get away from. Herman Bilstein had been interned in Weeghman. And only one other person who had been imprisoned in Weeghman had been anywhere near the scene of Bilstein's death. Only one.

I turned and walked back to my desk. Rabbi Stein was still sitting there, sitting patient and still, but his breathing seemed slightly more labored than it had been.

I sat. "I can't imagine the horrors of a place such as Weeghman. No one who wasn't there can." He was avoiding my eyes, but I think he expected me to say more. Trouble was, I had no more to say. I had to wait for him.

He really couldn't just get up and walk out, and he knew it. He was looking away, far away, when he began to speak. "Once upon a time there was a boy, a big, strong Austrian farm boy. He could work all day on the farm, but he was so uneducated that he could barely scrawl his name. When the war came he was too young to serve, but he looked older than his age, so they gave him a uniform and sent him to be a camp guard. They sent him to be a camp guard . . . at Weeghman."

Now he looked at me. "You say that you cannot imagine the horrors of Weeghman. Everyone says that. What you cannot imagine are the joys of Weeghman". He nodded slowly. "Yes, joys. The inmates of Weeghman were the cream of eastern Europe's intellectual community, professors and scholars of every stripe. Their families, their friends, their communities were dead. They knew that they were going to die. They knew that their world was going to die. They had but one hope: to leave a legacy of their scholarship, the scholarship that had been their lives' labors and their lives' love. But how, how in such a horrible place, could they possibly leave any legacy at all?

"Then the Almighty in his wisdom and goodness provided for them. Miraculous as it seemed, the husky young farm boy who had been set as a guard over them was blessed with the most extraordinary intellect they had ever encountered. Ignorant as he was, he absorbed knowledge and learning like a sponge. He, he would be their living legacy. He would become the repository of their wisdom and scholarship. They would pour their knowledge into him, and then they could die in peace.

"Yes, Weeghman was a place of horror for the body. But it became a place of delight for the mind. Men dying of starvation, of scurvy, of every horrible disease, expended their last breaths to imbue knowledge into the young boy. First, he was taught in his native German, taught language and literature. He was taught French, even some Latin and some English. He learned history, he learned philosophy. And above all our beautiful Hebrew, and the holy books: Torah and *haftorah, mishneh* and *gemarrah.* All, all of it he absorbed eagerly, with a genius that brought a final moment of inspiration to the dying souls who tutored him."

He looked down and fell silent. He rocked back and forth slightly, as if in prayer. I waited, still and quiet, for him to resume his narrative.

"There was an infirmary in Weeghman. They called it an infirmary. It had three rooms: in the first were those sick but not dying; in the second, those dying but not dead; in the third, those on death's doorstep. There was no medical treatment in the infirmary – a patient was simply moved from one room to the next until he was dead, and then his body was disposed of. As the allies marched into Austria, a boy lay dying in the last of the three rooms. He was a frail boy; he had begun to die the moment he set foot in the camp. He was the son of many generations of rabbis. His name" – he stopped rocking – "his name was ... Chaim Stein."

He looked at me. His face, an old man's face, was young with uncertainty, with desperation. The light blue eyes were dark with tears, and the mouth trembled. "Could the young Austrian boy be expected to go back to the life he had known, a life among pigs and chickens, a life without books and knowledge and discourse? Could he?" I had no answer to offer, and I offered none. So he did. "No! No!" He shook his head angrily. "The frail young boy who was Chaim Stein lay dying, and the strong young guard took from him something he would never need: He took his identity. He took his name.

"The Almighty in his wisdom has seen fit to bless that name for almost sixty years. In the name of Chaim Stein *mitzvot* have been performed, good deeds have been done." He was rocking again, faster now; and he closed his eyes, and he cried.

Yes, I thought, good deeds have been done. Good deeds have been done and murder has been committed. Two murders. Committed by a holy man who stole the name of a boy who died more than half a century years ago. I thought of what Uncle Billy had said in the hospital: An old man's stories are his identity. Question his stories and you tell him he didn't exist.

"Did you know Adler?" The sobbing continued, but he nodded his head, yes. "And you saw his works, the paintings and drawings he was doing in Weeghman?" Yes, he saw them. "And Bilstein? You knew him, too?" Again he nodded.

But that still didn't explain it; not all of it. "But it's been almost six decades. In the time that he was in my courtroom, the few minutes that he was in my courtroom, Bilstein couldn't possibly have said or done anything to suggest that he knew who you were." The sobbing continued, but now the head shook from side to side. No. Bilstein hadn't said or done anything to suggest that he recognized the rabbi.

Then why? "Then why? My God, why?"

He struggled to gain control of himself, wiped his eyes and face with the sleeve of his heavy coat, then gripped the armrests of the chair. "Adler ... his work ... it was, like manna from heaven. It was a miracle upon which sick men fed and sustained themselves." He breathed deeply, twice, three times, and squeezed the armrests tighter. "But there were no materials. The scraps that he had, the bits of charcoal, pencils, pieces of fabric, they were used up in no time. Everyone was desperate that Adler continue, but how? With what, and upon what, would he paint and draw?

"Bilstein was a trustee in the infirmary. He obtained materials for Adler. He obtained" – his head dropped forward, and his body was again racked with sobs – "he obtained ... human remains. Human remains. Hair. Bone." For a moment he was unable to speak, he shook, he gasped for breath. "Skin. Human skin." He cried. I sat in silence, knowing that he would speak when he could. He wiped his eyes and face with his sleeve again, wiped his white beard, now damp with tears. "But Bilstein was a trustee. He could not hand these things to Adler himself."

Oh God. Oh my God. Now it was obvious. Obvious and horrible. So obvious and so horrible that he could not, would not, say it. So I leaned toward him and said in a whisper what he could not bring himself to say. "Bilstein gave the body parts, the human remains, to someone who could give them to Adler." He nodded. "And the person to whom Bilstein gave them was ... a camp guard. A strong, young Austrian boy who was a camp guard. An Austrian boy who had become the pet and protege of the scholars and academics interned in Weeghman."

I didn't expect him to answer, or even to nod. His eyes were shut tight, his face red with crying, and a keening noise, an animal wailing noise came from his open mouth as he rocked back and forth. My God. My God. Even I know enough of Jewish custom and ritual to know that the desecration of the remains of a fellow Jew, of any human being, is an unspeakable abomination. Would Bilstein have testified to what was done, implicating himself? Would he have attempted to justify it, to claim that the remains of dead Jews were converted by Adler's art into the last hope of living Jews? Would he have testified about the Austrian farm boy? And as a trustee in the infirmary, would he have known that the real Chaim Stein had died in Weeghman?

Questions that would remain unanswered. But the mere thought of their answers, the fear of their answers, had driven one old man to the murder of another. Men have been prompted to murder by lesser fears.

Gumbiner. My God, Gumbiner. He is a physician, a pre-eminent physician. Did he realize, or suspect, or guess? Had he come to know, or to fear, the truth? Was that why he had refused for decades to permit anyone to examine the Adler collection? The *Herald* said that it was Gumbiner who had insisted on the *bes din* as the arbitrating body. Had he learned, somehow, of Rabbi Stein's true identity? Was he playing a dangerous game, betting that Stein would arrange for the Adler collection to be authenticated without chemical or other scientific testing, knowing too that if the truth came out – if it came out that Adler's work included human remains – the *bes din* would demand that the entire Adler collection be buried, actually buried in the ground? Or was Gumbiner as much in the dark as the rest of us? Was he simply the pompous eccentric he appeared to be on the witness stand?

"Did Gumbiner know?"

The question seemed to surprise him, and it stopped his tears. "I do not know." He tried to breathe steadily. "I have never met Gumbiner. I have never spoken to him." And then the crying, the sobbing, began again.

I thought about asking him about Mordechai Braun, the young rabbi or rabbinical student who had disappeared. My guess was that Braun had seen Rabbi Stein secret the ashtray in his coat, or seen him taking it out, or seen him throw it away. He had realized that a man whom he venerated as next to God himself had done that which God has told us we shall not do. He had run away because he didn't know whether to speak out or to keep silent, didn't know whether he could trust the evidence of his own eyes, didn't know whether there was anything in this world he could still believe.

I thought about asking, but I didn't. It didn't matter.

There was nothing more for him to say, or for me to hear. I watched him cry, and then I didn't want to watch him cry anymore. I pushed back from my desk and stood. I walked out of chambers, past Carmen, down the hallway to the stairwell. Then I walked down the stairs to the ground floor and out of the building to the area where Bud Teachout and the other bailiffs gather to smoke and gossip. Bud wasn't there, but two or three bailiffs whom I vaguely recognized were. One of them must have recognized me, too, because he said, "Hiya, Judge."

He was smoking, of course. I pointed at his cigarette. He fished out his pack, jiggled it so that a couple of cigarettes protruded far enough to be pulled out, and held it toward me. I took one and put it between my lips.

"Didn't know you smoked, Judge," he said.

Neither did I, but I didn't say so. He thumbed his lighter for me.

I took a puff and expected to cough. Whenever you see someone take his first drag on a cigarette he coughs, a sickly cough from the belly up. But I felt no urge to cough. I felt the smoke burning in my throat, but I felt no urge to cough. I wandered away from the bailiffs, three or four steps to the wall of the building, puffing twice, three times. Still I didn't cough. I leaned against the building, facing away from the bailiffs, facing away from anyone. I felt a wave of nausea, felt it head and gut, and I dropped the cigarette and stepped on it.

I stood there, leaning against the wall, and I felt a hand on my shoulder. It was the bailiff who had given me the cigarette. He was an old guy, but big; probably an ex-cop from New York. "You don't want to smoke too fast like that, if you're not used to it," he said. "It'll make you feel sick. You feel sick?"

I took a couple of deep breaths. It seemed like the thing to do. I nodded.

"A little thing like that can make you feel good and sick," he said.

"Good and sick," I repeated. Good and sick.

• • •

Jack actually did show up for dinner that evening. He showed up late, but he showed up sober. He must have had fun at the Ace High Bar Association meeting, because while we ate dessert he told the kids about how back in 1876 Wild Bill Hickok was holding aces over eights in a poker game in the Dakota Territory when he was shot in the back by Crooked Nose McCall.

Miriam thought that we should call Billy, so we left the kids to clear the table under Jack's desultory supervision and went into the family room. I called the hospital, gave his room number.

"Hello?"

"Does this mean you're not coming to dinner tonight?"

That got me a laugh. Not much of a laugh, just a couple of chuckles, but it was enough. "Next week, I promise." I asked him about the hospital food to give him something to complain about, and we made small talk.

But there was something important he wanted to say. "Clark, I've thought it over and I've made up my mind. When I get out of here I'm going to close the store and move up to Boynton Beach. It'll be better for me there. Everyone I used to know here has moved up there." Everyone his age had moved to the retirement communities in Boynton Beach, to play gin rummy and shuffleboard, to talk about their surgery and their grandchildren. Billy had never wanted to retire. "What do you think?"

"I think it's a good idea, Billy."

"You'll ... come up to visit me there?"

"Of course I will."

"And Miriam. And the kids."

"Of course we will, Billy."

He sighed. "Then I'm going to do it. I think it's for the best. Because I'll tell you the truth," he said. "The *schmatte* business isn't what it used to be."

I told him to get some rest, and we hung up. Miriam hadn't said anything, but she had been sharing the phone with me, and Billy's words had saddened her. I touched her hair, left her seated on the couch, and wandered back into the dining room.

The table had been cleared and cleaned, and the room was empty. I heard voices coming from the kitchen, and I followed them there. Seated at the kitchen table Blackjack Sheridan was playing five card draw with my children, using toothpicks for chips.

Alicia's three of a kind took the pot. She looked up at me and asked, "Do you know how to play, Daddy?" Jack gathered up the cards and started to shuffle.

I picked up an empty chair, turned it around, and straddled it, cowboy-style. Jack handed me the deck. I took it, but he wouldn't let it go. He looked at me. "Are you dealing me in, Clark?"

I held the deck at one end, and he held it at the other. "Are you sure you want back in?"

"I'm sure." Now he let go.

I shuffled and started dealing. "You're in, then."

CHAPTER EIGHT

EPILOGUE

I was looking at an autopsy protocol. Two of them, actually: One for a man named Herman Bilstein, and one for a woman named Boots Weber. As far as the police can tell, Mr. Bilstein and Ms. Weber never knew each other in life. But their dead bodies had been found together, hers almost piled on top of his, in a courthouse stairwell.

Carmen spoke on the intercom. "It's Que Sera Sera on the phone for you, Judge."

I told Carmen thank you and picked up the phone. "Clark. Have you seen the headlines?"

Yes, I had seen the headlines.

"Such a tragedy. I thought of you, of course, because he testified in your courtroom in that remarkable case last week. Did he seem to be in ill health?"

No, he was in excellent health. Very strong, very vigorous.

"Of course he was well into his 80's, wasn't he?"

Yes, he was well into his 80's.

"What a life he led."

Yes, what a life he led. "Kay, look, I ... it's really not working out for me here in the civil division. I'd like to come back to criminal court."

She didn't miss a beat. "I expected that you would, although I didn't think it would be so soon."

"Is there a place for me?"

"Clark, I'll be taking retirement status in three years, three months, and two and a half weeks, not that I'm counting. Someone should take over as chief administrative judge for the criminal division before I retire, to insure a smooth transition." She sighed. "I always thought that you'd make a good chief administrative judge."

"I can't bake cookies."

"It's your principal failing. I don't know how you'll keep all the judges and lawyers and other crazy people in this building under control with store-bought cookies."

I wasn't sure what to say for several long seconds, and then I was: "Thank you, Kay. Thank you very much. For everything." She said I was welcome, and she hung up.

For half a week I had toyed with the idea of calling Lt. Cabrera, but I never did. I could have called and told him that a man who was thought of as a saint and an angel was a fraud and a murderer. If he asked me for proof I could have told him of a lost ashtray that would never be found. But somehow, I knew that I would never have to make that call.

There had been no autopsy performed on Rabbi Stein. Herman Bilstein had an autopsy, and poor, sweet, cheerful *gordita*

Bootsie Weber, but when an octogenarian dies in his bed there is no need for an autopsy and none is conducted; especially in this case, because the Orthodox do not like autopsies and Doc Riggs would have been under a lot of pressure not to conduct one.

So I, and I alone, know the real cause of Rabbi Chaim Stein's death. I know it just as surely as I know that if we watch for it, look hard enough for it, wait long enough for it, justice will come lurching at us like any force of nature. Rabbi Stein knew that too. So he went home and lay down in his bed and waited to be crushed to death.

To be crushed to death, and ground to dust, by the wheel of justice.

THE END